big skye littleton

ALSO BY ELISA LORELLO

Fiction

The Andi Cutrone Series

Faking It
Ordinary World
She Has Your Eyes

Why I Love Singlehood
Adulation
The Second First Time
Pasta Wars

Nonfiction

Friends of Mine: Thirty Years in the Life of a Duran Duran Fan
The Writer's Habit: Combining Knowledge, Skill, and Desire to Write the Best Novel You Can

big skye littleton

ELISA LORELLO

LAKE UNION
PUBLISHING

Published by Lake Union Publishing, Seattle

www.apub.com

Amazon, the Amazon logo, and Lake Union Publishing are trademarks of Amazon.com, Inc., or its affiliates.

ISBN-13: 9781542046756
ISBN-10: 1542046750

Cover design by Diane Luger

Printed in the United States of America

For Bob and Dina

CHAPTER ONE

April Fools' Day

Skye Littleton fumbled to pull open a stubborn bag of popcorn when it rebelled and sent its contents exploding out and raining down like confetti. Crammed in the middle seat of a row in the coach section, thirty thousand feet over God knew where, she apologized to her seatmates for the assault and quietly cursed herself. The bag was no longer a bag but a cellophane remnant with a logo; thus, she had no place to dispose the liberated kernels but in her purse.

Great. That was her last snack.

She'd bought two granola bars, a Snickers bar, and the popcorn from the convenience store on the way to the airport, figuring that would tide her over until her Minneapolis layover. She ate the Snickers on the way to the gate, after she was cleared by TSA. She gave one of the granola bars to a mom whose kid was complaining. She ate the other one while waiting to board.

It wasn't the flight that made her nervous, but who was waiting for her on the other end. Well, not nervous. More like excitedly anxious. The good kind. Like waiting for your favorite band to come onstage.

Chip, her blond tabby cat, lay in his carrier tucked under the seat; he was safely sedated yet still annoyed by his present incarceration, and communicated his dissatisfaction every few minutes. He sniffed at the stray popcorn but then snubbed it.

The college-aged boy (to Skye, any male under the age of twenty-five looked like a "boy") to her left was so engrossed with the game on his phone, one involving tanks and machine guns, that he barely noticed the popcorn fracas. His noise-canceling headphones likely muted her apology too. The older man (not much older than she, although she was pretty bad at guessing such things) to her right, not knowing what to do with the kernels that had landed on his lap, handed them to her and smiled in a forgiving way. Without staring too much, she thought he looked a little like a rugged Robert Downey Jr., with a pockmark on his cheek in place of a dimple, hair graying at the temples, and cracked hands. He was dressed in blue jeans and paint-speckled work boots and your basic faded black Hanes T-shirt.

One hour into the flight to Minneapolis following a layover in Detroit, originally departing from Warwick, Rhode Island. Final destination: Billings, Montana.

Next stop: *Happily ever after.*

When the flight attendant came to their row and served them drinks and snacks (Diet Coke for her, coffee and Baileys for Robert Downey Jr. guy, pretzels for both; the boy to her left begged off and chugged from one of those tall Mountain Dew Kickstart cans), Skye made eye contact with her window seatmate and smiled sheepishly. At least she didn't spill anything on him this time.

"Too bad there aren't any complimentary pet snacks," he said with a nod toward the cat.

"He's not been annoying you, has he?" she asked.

"Not at all," he replied. He flicked away a popcorn kernel wedged in his shirt collar, and she flushed with embarrassment. "Flying is pain-in-the-ass enough for adults. Must be pure torture for animals," he said.

"At least he doesn't have to take off his shoes."

The man chuckled. "I'm Harvey, by the way," he said, and he extended his hand.

She shook it. "Skye."

"So where are you headed?" he asked and tacked on, "Final destination, I mean."

"Billings," she replied.

He lit up. "Hey, me too," he said. She smiled. "What's taking you there? Business or pleasure?"

She paused for a moment to munch on a pretzel before replying. "You'll think I'm crazy."

"I just came back from a comics convention in Providence, where I dressed up as Captain America, so no, I won't."

For a split second, she pictured him in costume and stifled a giggle with a cough; it was like picturing someone in their underwear. Her eyes narrowed, as if determining whether to trust him. So far, he'd helped her load her carry-on into the overhead bin, made polite conversation with the flight attendant beyond please and thank you, and didn't seem at all bothered by Chip's protests.

Yes, she decided. He was trustworthy. Plus, it was just airplane talk, right? He didn't seem like the kind of guy who would live-tweet his entire flight (hashtag CrazyPassengers).

"I'm meeting someone," she said.

He stared at her blankly, as if waiting for more.

"I mean, we know each other already," she quickly added. "We've been talking for months now."

"Talking?"

"We met online about six months ago," she explained, "and we had this instant connection. It was like talking to a man who had known me my entire life. He just . . . *got* me."

Vance Sandler. The name reverberated within her heart, as did his words and inflections every time they talked or texted.

She continued. "Online chatting led to phone calls and FaceTime"—and pet names and sharing best and worst memories and cultivating inside jokes—"which led to him coming to visit me in February."

They'd spent a glorious three-day weekend together when he flew into Logan Airport in Boston seven weeks ago, and they toured the city and walked the Freedom Trail bundled up in forty-five-degree-but-sunny weather and stuffed themselves with seafood and made love in a hotel room overlooking the Charles River. She would have been just as happy holing up in her two-bedroom Warwick apartment, not far from the mall where she worked, but it had been so long since she'd been *out*, and she reveled in the romance of it all. Nonstop hand holding in Faneuil Hall and Quincy Market, stolen kisses on the T, and feeding each other forkfuls of Boston cream pie.

Being with Vance Sandler was like being in a storybook come to life.

Harvey nodded slowly. "So now it's your turn to visit him?"

She nodded as happy butterflies with heart-shaped wings fluttered inside her. "Not just visiting—*moving!*"

Chip howled in his carrier underneath the seat. Skye reached down and put her hand to the carrier's mesh window so the cat could touch her fingers with his nose.

Harvey recoiled as if she'd spat at him. "That's rather brave of you."

Her smile faded. "How so?"

"Moving across the country for a guy you only spent one weekend with? And after knowing each other for a few months? I'm not knocking you, I'm just saying. It's brave."

Says the grown man who wears superhero costumes in public.

"Well, it's about time I was adventurous," she said.

"So why not just put off moving until you visit Billings first?"

Who is this guy, the Life Police? "Why should I? It's not like there was anything holding me back in Rhode Island." Well, except for the promotion to district manager that she'd turned down right before she

4

quit her job at Top Drawer. Not that she'd ever wanted to devote her entire life to the retail lingerie chain.

"You might not like it," he suggested.

"How bad could it be if a hundred thousand people already live there? Plus, it's got a Target."

"I guess so," he said, clearly unconvinced.

"Well, what about you? You live there. What do you think?"

He considered her question. "I like it very much. In some ways, it's a scrappy little town. In other ways, it's an active, bustling city—not like New York or even Providence. But it has its appeal. Montana overall is incredible. But hey, now you know someone in Billings besides your boyfriend," he said with an amiable smile.

Something within her stirred, like a breeze lifting a plastic bag in a carefree swirl, and made her eyes linger on him for just a split second longer than she was comfortable looking at a stranger. Until it hit her that the moment he said those words, he no longer felt like a stranger to her.

"How long have you lived there?"

"Going on ten years now. I started working for a pharmaceutical company in California, and they moved."

"Hey, my boyfriend works for a pharmaceutical company too!" Her heart fluttered at *boyfriend*. Prior to being with Vance, it had been a long time since she'd used that word. "Maybe you know him!"

"Very likely. What's his name?"

"Vance Sandler."

Harvey's face first turned pale, then red as a hot plate. Skye became alarmed. "What is it?"

He turned as far as he could in his seat to face her. "OK. We don't know each other, so you can do whatever you want with what I have to say. It's your life and none of my business. But if it's at all possible, when we get to Minneapolis, turn around and get on a plane back to Rhode Island."

The pitter-patter in her chest turned into thumping timpani drums. The conversation had gone from friendly to foreboding so fast, the pretzels suddenly tasted like slivers of balsa wood.

"You're going to have to explain why you just scared the shit out of me," she said.

"Vance Sandler is bad news. Worse than bad news. He's a Venus flytrap."

Impossible. He sent her long-stem roses. He blew kisses to her from across the country. He texted her love notes at 2:00 a.m.

Skye glowered at him. "You're right," she snapped. "It's none of your business." She wished she could borrow her left seatmate's noise-canceling headphones so she could tune Harvey out. But it was too late. He'd gotten into her head.

"My apologies," he said, sounding somewhere between remorseful and irked. "I wish you all the best." He plugged his own headphones into a tablet and leaned back in his seat.

Skye sat upright, jarred by the submarine alarm that was sirening between her ears. She waited for it to quiet, but to no avail. Just as Harvey closed his eyes, Skye interrupted.

"Hang on. You can't just dump something like that on me. Why should I turn around? What's wrong with Vance?"

He opened his eyes and peered at her. "I told you. He's a bad guy. Villainous. He makes assholes look like angels." He said it matter-of-factly.

"How do you even know him?"

"We worked for the same company. I'm not there anymore."

"What, did he take your job or something?" She didn't mean for the question to sound as inconsiderate as it had come out, but she couldn't help her defensiveness. She paid for it too.

"No, thanks for asking." He shook his head in mild exasperation. Whether it was with himself for saying anything in the first place or with her for challenging him, she wasn't sure.

"Then what makes him so awful?"

He locked in on her so determinedly that she couldn't avoid his eyes even if she wanted to. A storm seemed to be brewing behind them, as if he were fighting whatever had compelled him to share his thoughts on the subject of Vance Sandler in the first place. And she realized she was bracing herself, as if a crash were imminent.

"Because he stole my wife," he said.

CHAPTER TWO

"What do you mean, exactly?" Skye asked Harvey as Chip meowed again. The guy wasn't as good-looking as she'd originally thought.

"I mean he systematically pursued my wife, wooed her, slept with her, and persuaded her that he was much better for her than I ever was."

She looked at him, incredulous. "You make it sound like it was premeditated," she said.

"It was. Want to know how I know?" He barreled ahead without waiting for her reply. "Because six months prior he looked me in the eye and said, 'I'm going to take your wife.' He'd say the same thing to rival sales reps. 'I'm going to take your clients.' No threat, no cursing, nothing. Just those six little words. Now that I think about it, his tone was downright friendly."

Skye was aghast. "What did *you* say?"

Harvey winced at the memory. "Nothing at first. I was too stunned. Business rivalry was one thing. But moving in on a guy's wife? Then I told him he didn't have the balls. That was my mistake. Never dare a sociopath."

Skye tried to imagine the man who was so sweet and gentle toward her being so cold and callous to a colleague or this guy with the rough hands and the dirty boots and the pockmarked face sitting beside her. "I don't believe you," she said. "I can't. It's just not him."

"You think I'm making it up?" he asked. "I've got the divorce papers to prove it."

"Divorce papers prove nothing."

"OK, how about depositions?"

Depositions? Holy shit.

The plane gave way to a momentary lurch. Or was that her stomach?

"When did this allegedly happen?" she asked.

"We've been legally divorced for about six months. Happened close to a year ago."

Six months. That was when she and Vance first met online. Could he have been with this woman while they chatted? Was it possible . . . ?

"Are they still together?" she asked as her insides rumbled and churned and collided like boulders.

"I haven't heard anything to the contrary," said Harvey. He finished the last of his beverage and looked into the bottom as if disappointed and surprised to see it gone. "We share custody of our two kids, so I figured one of them would have filled me in."

Oh God, oh God, oh God, get me off this effing plane.

As the flight attendant paraded down the aisle, Skye stopped her and asked for a ginger ale. Her face, undoubtedly the color of a green egg, apparently conveyed that the request was urgent rather than entitled. The flight attendant replied, "Right away," and returned in ten minutes with not only the ginger ale but a package of oyster crackers and a blanket and pillow set from first class. Skye thanked her. Her mind was spinning faster than she could process time lines and replay conversations.

"I just . . . I don't understand," she said. "Why would he keep something like that from me? Wouldn't it be obvious the moment I got to Billings? He gave me every indication that he wanted me there. He knew I was coming—heck, he helped me plan it. He was so excited when I told her I'd made up my mind."

"He's also a narcissist," said Harvey. He said it with such conviction. As if it were common knowledge. And yet there was agitation in every word. "It was all about the challenge."

Skye shook her head, shell-shocked. "No. No, no, no."

For the remaining hour of the flight, Harvey stared beyond the window at the clouds shielding the view beneath them. Skye didn't think he was ignoring her, but rather was lost in his own thoughts and giving her the space to process all that had transpired. Meanwhile, Skye searched for missing pieces. Signs she might have missed or brushed aside or excused away.

- The photo of the maroon Moroccan-print bedding Vance had selected and asked her opinion on before purchasing. She'd given him a thumbs-up and told him how thoughtful he was. He'd never specifically said he was buying it for her, but she'd assumed it.
- About a week before she left, he'd said to her, *You know, if you had a change of heart and wanted to stay where you are, I'd completely understand and support you.* When she asked if *he* was having a change of heart, he'd replied, *Never! I'm just thinking of you. You're giving up a lot.* Had he said that as a warning? Was it a pang of guilt? Or had he really been thoughtful and sincere, as she'd believed he was?
- Nothing was Vance's fault. His marriage ended because his wife left him. He lost the city council election because his opponent sabotaged his campaign. He got a speeding ticket because the cop singled him out for driving a fancy car. She'd accepted every excuse as fact because he'd said it so matter-of-factly.

She thought of the hours they'd spent texting and messaging—how did that work, if he had been with someone else all this time? Was Harvey's ex-wife somewhere else while Vance texted, or was she by his side?

She thought of all the little tidbits they'd shared about themselves: He was thirty-eight years old. She had recently turned thirty-six. Neither really knew their family ancestry. How they took their coffee (him: *bitter is better*; her: *sweet is neat*). How she loved the feeling of sand between her toes. How he loved the first snow of the season. How she loved the smell of pine needles. How he loved the smell of vanilla. How she loved rhythm and blues. How he loved country. And then, when they were together, and he'd covered just about every inch of her body with kisses and she'd run her fingers along just about every crevice of his . . . she thought they knew just about everything two people who were about to go all in needed to know. Most of all, she had thought for sure that they knew they were both going all in.

But as she sat there, next to this guy who had allegedly worked with Vance day by day, side by side, knew where Vance lived and the people he associated with (like his now ex-wife, for one), Skye still wondered if they were talking about the same man. Had she really been so blinded by the boredom of her own existence that she'd fallen for a charlatan? Was she that hungry?

Why had he wanted her? She'd asked Vance one late night.

Because I'm the one who sees the treasure you are, he'd replied. She'd melted at the time.

Besides, I like the challenge, he'd added. How had she forgotten that part?

What challenge? she'd asked. He'd never answered her.

Harvey had said, *It's all about the challenge.*

The nausea returned upon her recollection. How had she seen that as something sweet and loving rather than utterly insulting and condescending?

Skye gulped her ginger ale, wishing it would soothe more than her stomach. She took out her phone and clutched it, powerless in mid-flight, desperately wishing she could call Vance and ask him to explain himself; or better yet, to tell her that this guy sitting next to her was the liar and the sociopath and the narcissist. She could make use of the airline Wi-Fi and e-mail him. Or she could keep her wits about her, give him the benefit of the doubt, and wait until she got to Minneapolis before she contacted him, like she'd promised. Tapping on the photo app, she opened the album labeled "Vance" and scrolled through the countless selfies he'd sent her (she'd even saved the Weiner-esque poses, against her better judgment), and couldn't even look at the couple selfies they'd snapped in front of the Paul Revere statue and outside Fenway Park and eating the best New England clam chowder either of them had ever tasted. She raced through the photos he'd taken of *their* king-sized bedroom with en suite, *their* kitchen with stainless-steel appliances and quartz countertops and mosaic-tiled backsplash, the street *they* would be living on with its idyllic streetlamps and early twentieth-century restored homes, the downtown *they* would be frequenting together with its gridlike street system and art installations and up-and-coming shops and eateries. *Us. Our. He* had used those words, not she. She finally settled on a selfie of him standing next to a luxury SUV. His, he'd said. She couldn't believe she was even questioning something as simple as a car. She enlarged the photo to better see his salt-and-pepper hair. His neatly trimmed goatee. His striking blue eyes. She tried to look into those eyes now and see if they were shifty, eluding, fake.

Skye practically shoved the phone into Harvey's face. "Is this him?"

He squinted and peered at the photo. Then he frowned. "Yeah, that's him. Fuckface." He gently moved the phone away. "I'm sorry," he said. He was either apologizing for the positive identification or for the whole damn mess. Or maybe both.

Just because he recognizes Vance doesn't mean he's right, she thought. And yet: *Oh God, oh God, oh God, get me off this effing plane.*

CHAPTER THREE

Here was the truth: on October 10, six months prior to her departure from Rhode Island, Skye had not only turned thirty-six years old, but also freaked the fuck out.

She'd had to work that day, and the most she could hope for by way of celebration was a giant cookie with *Happy Birthday, Skye* scripted in frosting from the Mrs. Fields outlet in the mall's food court, which was exactly what her twentysomething-year-old coworkers presented her with. Her best friend, Julie, had taken her out for drinks after work, but refused to buy cake because "it's either alcohol calories or cake calories, and I don't know about you, but tequila trumps red velvet." Skye hated that women were forced to make such choices, that calories were equated with sins, and penance was the treadmill.

Earlier in the day, while Skye was working, her sister, Summer, had left her a text—a simple Happy birthday—and a voice mail: "Mom and Dad told me to tell you they're in Vermont leaf-peeping and will be out of phone range. They'll call you when they get back. Let me know if you want to come over or something, although Kayla's got cheering practice."

Summer, four years older than Skye, lived in Wakefield, was a professor of marketing at University of Rhode Island and a part-time consultant. She also wrote two textbooks, one of which was the most frequently assigned in marketing curricula and departments across New England colleges and universities. She was married to Brent Coster, a stay-at-home dad who ran a business via Etsy selling novelty items made from old vinyl records. Skye had first met Brent at a career expo she attended through her high school. He was clearly a college boy, looking positively adorable with his Red Sox cap on backward and his logoed T-shirt limply untucked and his Converse sneakers with holes in the canvas. So cutely disheveled and boyish. He handed out free samples of some energy drink. She handed him her name and phone number. *Skye Littleton—are you Summer's sister?* he'd asked. She had been asked that question so many times it was a wonder she didn't just tattoo the answer on her forehead. And every single time, she answered truthfully. She could have lied and said, no, she was an only child. But she never did. Either she had integrity or was a glutton for punishment. That had been her undoing with Brent. *She's in one of my classes at Harvard,* he'd said. *I should call her.* And that was that. They even toasted Skye at their wedding, to thank her for bringing them together.

One week before Skye's thirty-sixth birthday, Summer and Brent had announced the news of their daughter Kayla's winning some kind of national school art contest. "Hope we didn't steal your thunder," said Summer.

"What thunder?"

"Your birthday?"

"Oh. I appreciate that," was all Skye said in response. What else could she say? That there was no thunder to steal? That being upstaged by her niece was a suitable birthday gift? Besides, Summer had been stealing Skye's thunder since she was born. When Skye had graduated first grade, Summer won a junior track meet, which their parents attended in lieu of the graduation. *It's first grade,* they had reasoned. *What's the big deal about graduating the first grade?* When Skye won her tennis tournament in eighth grade, Summer won a full scholarship to Harvard Business School.

Skye was thirty-six and unmarried. Not even in a relationship. Thirty-six and childless.

Thirty-six and making less than fifty thousand dollars per year. At least she had benefits.

Thirty-six years old, and exceeding that number in pounds overweight.

Thirty-six and still renting an apartment.

Thirty-six and hadn't had sex in over five years. And even then it had been nothing to brag about. Her cat, Chip, named after the funny, hunky-in-a-geekish-way *Fixer Upper* star, was the only male she'd shared a bed with since. She'd always dreamed of being with a man like Chip Gaines. Easygoing. Handsome. Rich. Someone who would build her dream home with his bare hands, and then spend the rest of their lives together in it. Joanna Gaines was the luckiest woman on the planet.

Her other friends from high school and college—Pamela, Rory, Cam—all had kids and dogs and houses and careers that required sitters and travel and tutors, leaving very little time for Skye other than the occasional pop-in to Top Drawer at the mall on their way to Build-A-Bear. Sometimes she went out for drinks with her coworkers after work, but was a step behind when it came to things like Tinder or Snapchat or the latest in music. She was old enough to remember a time when phones were used only to make calls.

"What's the matter, Skyebaby?" asked Julie that night at the bar. "You look sad."

"I have no life anymore," lamented Skye. "This is not where I thought I'd be at thirty-six. I thought I'd be living in a high-rise apartment in a big city doing something really cool, like running a real estate agency or a design firm. I thought I'd be married. I thought I'd be *happy*. Instead, I sell bras for a living."

"You give women's breasts the gift of a bra that actually fits," said Julie, who, years ago, had dubbed Skye "the bra whisperer." "I'm serious, that's an important service."

Skye dropped her head. "You're not listening, Jules. I want more. You have a house and a good job. Something you're proud to tell people when you introduce yourself and hand them your business card."

"I also have an ulcer."

"I even want your ulcer."

She was tired of her meager little life. Tired of claustrophobic Rhode Island and mall food and being surrounded by 36B and C cups that she couldn't fit into. Tired of sharing a bed with Chip the cat instead of Chip the man.

She yearned for more than back-to-back Manager of the Month awards at Top Drawer, catching up on DVRed TV shows, watching Summer's and other people's glamorous lives play out on social media. She yearned to *be* someone.

She'd joined a Facebook fan group for the TV show *Chicago Fire* shortly after the new season began, and Vance Sandler had not only "liked" her critique of the previous season's finale, but also sent her a friend request. She liked his profile photo of a hand facing palm out, with a happy face drawn on it. When she saw he was from Montana, she was intrigued. To her, Montana was a different country rather than a state, one she'd never given much thought to or had much interest in. And that was how it began. Every day, Vance regaled her with stories about his travels to cities called Missoula and Butte and Bozeman and sent her photos of the Crazy Mountains (which didn't look crazy at all) and posited that small towns like Sidney or Livingston were larger than life in comparison to, say, Warwick, Rhode Island. Pretty soon he was beckoning her to join him in Big Sky Country. *I want to explore Big Skye Country too,* he'd teased. The remark had stung, but she'd told herself that he meant it in a flirtatious way.

He *wanted* her. That was more than she could say for anyone within a twenty-five-mile radius of her apartment or job. She'd once had a robust social life, going bowling and to the movies with Julie and Cam and Rory, and taking her niece on excursions to the Boston Museum of

Fine Arts or a Paw Sox game in Pawtucket. But as her friends dropped out of her social circle, so did she. To make matters worse, her online-dating inbox remained empty, and her prospects dimmed with every pound she gained. Her calendar was filled with her work schedule and a weekly board-game meetup that she'd started—the group was up to a dozen men and women, but she hadn't even shown up to that in several weeks. She'd been thinking of starting a *Fixer Upper* meetup, in which people gathered to watch and talk about the show and possibly even start their own fixer-upper business.

How had she let it come to this? Why? She didn't know, but there she was.

Vance Sandler looked nothing like Chip Gaines, but he was already making all of her dreams come true. He promised her a new home and a new life in Billings, Montana. He promised that big things would happen to her. *She* wanted a better life for herself. So why not go big?

And so, in March, when Dan the regional manager visited her store one week after her and Vance's weekend getaway, and praised her for the best sales numbers and lowest shrink figures in the east, the cleanest store, and the staff with the most retention, instead of feeling proud of herself and the work as she usually did, she thought, *Get me the hell out of here.* Because it suddenly occurred to Skye that nothing was going to change for her unless she changed it. When Dan offered Skye the district manager job, which meant more pay and more travel, she only saw more loneliness ahead. Besides, even though she'd always been good at her job and taken pride in her work, she'd never felt much passion for bras. Or retail. Or working Sundays.

So she'd not only declined the offer, but also put in her two weeks' notice on the spot. Then she called Vance and told him what she'd done. Told him it was official: she was moving to Billings, Montana.

He cheered. He said, "Welcome home, baby."

Vance Sandler: soul mate and . . . wife stealer?

CHAPTER FOUR

Almost an hour after her connecting flight to Billings had been scheduled to take off, Skye was stranded at the Minneapolis–Saint Paul airport at 8:37 p.m. Central Time, and she was hungry and exhausted. On the floor beside her foot, Chip lay in his carrier, safely sedated and just as exhausted from all the meowing he'd done all day. She knew he'd start up again soon. She'd just fed him a dinner of Meow Mix—less smelly than Fancy Feast—and an extra treat in an effort to appease him.

It was raining outside, although that wasn't the cause for the delay. A representative from the airline announced the cause as "mechanical problems."

She and Harvey had parted company on polite enough terms. He'd helped her pull her carry-on from the overhead bin; she'd thanked him. He bid her a good final flight; she bid him the same. But the tension between them was palpable—he'd handed her a grenade, and she was doing her damnedest not to pull the pin. Once in the terminal, they each headed for the restrooms. She didn't see him again until she arrived at the gate. He sat at the end of the same row of chairs, both of them pretending not to see each other.

Skye had never been in the Minneapolis–Saint Paul airport before. Or Minneapolis, for that matter. In fact, she'd never been west of

Warwick, Rhode Island. Before Vance, she'd never even heard of Billings and wouldn't have been able to locate it on a map.

With every passing minute, she watched people dragging suitcases, musical instruments, backpacks; hustling children along; talking on smartphones or glued to their screens to check messages, flight info, Facebook, who knows. She looked at all the convenience shops selling candy and gum and soft drinks and magazines and coloring books to keep you occupied either on the ground or on the plane. If you weren't in a rush, you were waiting. There seemed to be no in-between. She imagined the seating as sofas and recliners and chaise longues so one could take a power nap in the meantime. She imagined coffee tables and cup holders and phone chargers at every chair. She imagined artwork rather than ads on the walls.

And yet, the Minneapolis airport ran rings around TF Green in terms of offerings and size.

What's the mechanical problem? What if I have to spend the night in this huge airport? What if they think they've fixed it and then I get on the airplane and it breaks somewhere over the mountains? Are there any mountains between here and Billings?

Those were far more distracting worries than the one she was failing to avoid: *Just who is waiting for me on the other side of this trip?* She couldn't stop seeing the images that Harvey had planted in her mind: Vance systematically pursuing Harvey's wife and stealing her away. Vance making sweet love to her the entire time another woman was waiting for him at home. Vance lying about everything—about his wanting Skye to be with him, live with him, make a life together. Worse still, she'd been texting and calling him since the plane landed in Minneapolis, and he had yet to respond.

Skye called Julie and spoke to her in hushed tones. "I think I may have made a mistake."

"About what?" asked Julie.

"About Vance. I met a guy on the plane who knows him and, well, he told me some scary shit."

"Like what?"

"Like, he stole this guy's wife."

"That's crazy!" Julie yelled, so loud that Skye was sure Harvey, who was sitting three chairs away from her and scrolling through his phone, seemingly unfazed by the delay, had heard her.

"But what if it's true?" Skye said even softer. "What if he's been lying to me this entire time and has been cheating on me—or worse, been cheating *with* me?"

"Shit, I knew this was too good to be true," said Julie. The remark cut right through Skye, flooding her with foolishness.

"Then why didn't you say anything before, Jules? You were all like, 'Oh, he's your dream man,' and 'Go for it, girl.'"

"What else was I supposed to say? You had your mind set on going. There was no way I was going to talk you out of it."

Skye thought back to Julie's reaction when Skye had first told her about Vance: *Seriously, you couldn't get a man who lived a little closer, like in this time zone?* Skye had gotten angry at her for not being more supportive. And when Vance had whisked her away for the weekend and Julie thought it strange that he met her in Boston rather than Warwick, where he could meet her friends and see her home and work, Skye told her to quit being so suspicious. *You're just jealous,* Skye had said. She'd felt horrible the moment she blurted it and apologized. It was no wonder Julie had shut up and shared in her best friend's happiness.

"Well, now what should I do?" asked Skye.

"Get yourself a plane ticket home right this minute. I'll come pick you up; I don't care what time it is."

"I can't do that."

"Why not?" asked Julie.

"Because Vance is waiting for me. He expects me there. I've got a truck scheduled to meet me at a storage unit. What do I do about that? I should at least confront him, don't you think?"

"Skye, you just quit your job and sold almost everything you own, including your car, to move across the country for a man you spent one weekend with. What has he done for you?"

He made me feel loved and wanted and validated and sexy and special and . . .

"Jules, I have to confront him at the airport. If I see that he's lying, then I'll make arrangements to come home. But I have to see him first."

Julie sighed loudly, which needled Skye even more. "You haven't been able to tell he's lying so far."

Had Skye not been sitting among a bunch of already irked, impatient passengers, she would have gone off on Julie. Instead, she said coolly, "You know, it's possible that this passenger is some kind of nutcase who makes shit up. Didn't that ever occur to you? Maybe he's the creep and not Vance." Skye furtively eyed Harvey as she spoke.

"I hope to hell you're right," said Julie. "Just call me back as soon as you're safe in Montana. I love you."

"I love you," said Skye, and tapped her phone following their goodbyes.

That's it, she told herself. *Harvey's the creep. Not Vance. Good riddance, Harvey.*

Still no word from Vance. She checked Facebook to see if he'd posted anything there. He rarely posted anything personal. Just things like memes and quotes, or links related to *Chicago Fire* or any of the other TV dramas he watched. And suddenly that too was a red flag: *He never posts anything personal.* She'd never even questioned it. Why? How had she dropped the ball like that?

No, no, no. It's just Facebook. No one is who they pretend to be on Facebook.

That was supposed to be comforting. But the dreadful truth of it expanded in her chest, pressing down on her like an anvil.

◆ ◆ ◆

Skye glared at Harvey, still sitting in oblivion. She slid down the row of chairs, away from him, dragging along her carry-on and Chip's carrier and her purse, as another update on the flight delay was announced at the gate. "They're almost finished, and we'll just have to fill out some reports . . ." She settled into the hard chair and clutched her phone, obsessively checking for a sign of life from Vance.

"You OK?"

Skye, startled, looked up to find Harvey towering over her. He plunked into the empty seat beside her.

"I don't want to talk to you," said Skye. She had suddenly become afraid of him and began to grab her things to move when Harvey stood up again.

"Don't bother. I'll leave you alone."

"Really, where do you get off saying such stuff to someone you've just met? You're psycho. You probably don't know Vance Sandler or live in Billings or anything you told me."

"I understand," he said. "I'm really sorry to have upset you. Best of luck in Billings. I mean that." With a backpack over his shoulder, he sauntered to the other side of the gate and found an empty seat between an older man wearing a cowboy hat and boots and a young woman dressed in workout clothing. Skye suddenly, inexplicably wanted him to come back. She wanted to interrogate him, ask him just *how* he knew Vance, show her *proof* that Vance was a wife stealer and a liar and all the things Harvey had accused him of being. Or maybe she wanted company. Surrounded by swarms of people and not knowing a soul or recognizing a single inch of space was wearing on her. Like the saying: "Water, water everywhere and not a drop to drink."

At least she had Chip, even if he was still being a mouthy little asshole.

She couldn't really blame him.

◆　◆　◆

Another twenty-five minutes later, the airline was finally ready to board passengers. As Skye waited, impatiently shifting her weight from side to side, her phone buzzed, and she nearly burst into tears with relief when Vance texted her a simple message: I'm alive. See you soon, followed by a thumbs-up and a kissing emoji. And yet, her heart sank from the lack of enthusiasm—no *I can hardly wait to put my arms around you, baby,* or *My lips are missing your supple skin,* like he'd been saying all week and even this morning before her first plane took off from TF Green. But he'd contacted her. He was safe. He was waiting for her. He blew her a kiss. All was well.

The final section was called, drawing a swarm of irritated, hungry, exhausted passengers to the jet bridge. Skye boarded with them and lumbered down the narrow aisle toward the back of the plane, trying not to bump Chip's carrier against the seats, and hoping to snag an overhead bin with room to stow her carry-on. Just as she was about to stash it, an oaf in a faded Denver Broncos cap elbowed her out of the way and shoved two carry-ons into the bin. Skye shot him a dirty look, but the oaf was impervious.

"Way to be a dick," Harvey said at full volume behind him.

The oaf turned around—he had a good four inches on Harvey in both height and width. "You got something to say to me?"

"I'm saying you owe your fellow passenger an apology as well as the storage space that was rightfully hers."

"Fuck off," said the oaf, and looked at Skye and then Harvey. "Both of you."

As Skye sheepishly turned to find another place to stow her bag, Harvey opened the bin, removed one of the oaf's suitcases, and grabbed Skye's bag to replace it. The oaf, in return, socked Harvey in the jaw—or rather, he tried. Harvey ducked and the oaf wound up clocking a fiftysomething woman in the side of her head. Skye frantically gripped the cat carrier so as not to drop it as she was jostled and pushed into a passenger's lap while two other passengers subdued the oaf.

If she hadn't been completely mortified, not to mention aching from the shoulder muscle she pulled trying to save Chip, she would have been furious enough to deck Harvey too.

Amid shouts and obscenities and pushing, she apologized profusely, to both the passenger she fell on as well as Chip, as the flight attendants called security, who removed the oaf from the plane while he screamed more obscenities and pled his case to no avail. The scuffle resulted in yet another hour's delay as the woman received medical attention and the crew sorted out the mess and filed reports.

Skye sank in her seat and fought off tears, feeling the angry stares of surrounding passengers, the smallness of her being bullied by the oaf in the first place, and the powerlessness of Harvey's unsolicited chivalry. She ached to take Chip out of the carrier and stroke him on her lap, soothing the both of them. She did the best she could to pet him through the mesh window and console him.

She thought perhaps that was the end of Harvey, that they would kick him off the plane too. But then she saw him charge down the aisle after giving his statement, none the worse for wear, not even sporting the slightest hint of self-consciousness, moments before the captain came on speaker and apologized for the delay. As bad luck would have it, Harvey sat in the row right in front of hers; his seat was the aisle, hers was the middle again. As the plane taxied down the runway prior to takeoff, Skye leaned to the slit of space between the seats and asked with clenched teeth, "Did you really have to play Superman?"

He turned to address her, unable to see her scowl. "Not Superman. Captain America."

"Whatever," she said. "Did you?"

"I have a low tolerance for assholes," he replied.

"You're lucky *you* didn't get kicked off the plane," she said. "Not to mention you narrowly escaped a broken jaw, and made a fool out of me."

Skye caught Harvey's glower before he shook his head and turned back around, muttering, "You're welcome."

Well, shit. Now she felt bad.

Once the plane was off the ground and had reached the proper altitude, Harvey asked the passenger sitting to her right to switch seats with him, and next thing she knew, he was beside her. She leaned as far over as she could without sitting on the left passenger's lap. "Look," he said, "maybe that was a dick move on my part, but I was trying to help. You're clearly upset about your boyfriend and you've not had a pleasant day. That bin was yours."

"My day was perfectly fine until you unleashed all your crazy lies on me."

He looked stung. And yet, he refused to relent. "Didn't it occur to you to visit Billings before overturning your life?" he asked. "Meet some of this guy's friends, check out his story?"

Skye gave him a dirty look. "I am not *overturning* my life. I'm making a change. And what kind of dunce do you think I am? I Googled him. No mugshots. No orders of protection. He even ran for city council."

This time, Harvey laughed. The kind that reeks of skepticism and condescension. "Well, if he ran for city council, he must be OK, because those guys are never corrupt."

"Look, just shut up, OK? Don't talk to me anymore."

"You engaged me first, but OK."

While Harvey closed his eyes and seemingly slept (how come it was so easy for him?), Skye spent the duration of the turbulent flight in silence, appeasing Chip, closing her eyes, and concentrating on positive thoughts. *Vance and I are meant to be together. I'm doing the right thing. Never talk to fellow passengers on airplanes about your life because they're likely to be whack jobs.* But it was no use. Every shimmy and jolt of the plane sent her stomach whirling like clothes in a dryer. *It will be better when the plane lands,* she assured herself. *I'll see Vance, and then I'll know.*

◆ ◆ ◆

When the plane finally landed at Billings Logan Airport (it was going on two in the morning Rhode Island time), Harvey waited for Skye as she collected Chip and her carry-on and purse, barely having the strength to move her legs, much less lug a ten-pound cat and pull a suitcase. She couldn't even admit that she was secretly grateful Harvey was waiting, but she hoped to ditch him the moment she saw Vance at the bottom of the stairs. She walked two paces behind Harvey through the jet bridge, past the waiting area, and down the escalator to the baggage carousel, the background Muzak making her jumpy rather than calm. Her stomach was one giant knot, pulled so tightly she could hardly speak as she descended the stairs, searching for Vance's patient, smiling blue eyes. As people welcomed their loved ones with open arms and bouquets and tears and squeals of joy, she longed for the crowds to part and to find Vance waiting off to the side for her, a bouquet of roses in hand. He would then smile ever so softly and utter a simple, *I've been waiting for you, baby.*

But by the time she reached the bottom, she knew what she would find. Or wouldn't find.

No sign of Vance.

He wasn't stranded. Wasn't lying in a ditch. She just *knew*. He wasn't coming.

And then, at the baggage carousel, when all the luggage except hers had been paraded and claimed, she broke into a full-out ugly cry.

"Oh my God, *oh my God*, what have I done?" she wailed. "How could I have been so stupid?" She saw it so clearly now. The challenge was over. She was there. She was sure Vance knew it, even though he wasn't physically there to see with his own eyes. He knew it, and now he could move on to the next challenge.

Harvey, who she didn't realize was still in the airport, sidled beside her. "I'm really sorry," he said quietly.

"I have nothing—*nothing* now. No job. No apartment. I have three thousand dollars. That's it. Even if I go back to Warwick, it won't cover a first, last, and security."

"Listen," said Harvey. "It's bleak and overwhelming right now. I get that. But what you need is a good night's sleep. I'm betting your luggage will be here first thing in the morning. Then you can make a plan."

Skye looked at Harvey as if he were a consolation prize, and a disappointing one at that, especially in comparison to Vance or, say, Chip Gaines.

All the bile of the last six months rushed up—turning thirty-six, her pathetic life, the months of Vance making her feel as if she were beautiful and special, enough to make her take the leap that was in actuality jumping off a cliff. She'd fallen for a con man. Willingly gave everything up because she let herself believe in his promise to take care of her, and she was just so tired of going it alone. And yet, she was now more alone than she'd ever been in Rhode Island. The dread and loneliness and hurt and deception filled her throat, and Skye set Chip's carrier on the floor, released the handle of her carry-on, and ran to the restroom.

After washing out her mouth and splashing water on her face, she looked in the mirror, hoping to find some clue that would tell her she'd dreamed the entire thing. That she'd wake up any second and get ready for work like any other day. She suddenly craved the sight of bra-and-panty sets.

No such luck. All she saw was Skye Littleton, major chump.

She emerged from the restroom. Harvey was still there, keeping guard of Chip and her carry-on. She was actually relieved to see him.

"I'm sorry about that," she said. "Thank you for watching my cat and my bags. I just couldn't hold it down any longer."

"Is there anybody in Billings that you know besides Vance? Someone you can spend the night with?" he asked.

She shook her head. "No. I'm going to either call a cab or use Uber and find a hotel that takes pets." She took out her phone and began to make inquiries.

"There's a Best Western not far from here. They take pets. I can drive you, if you want."

"Thanks, but no. I'll be fine."

"How about I just stay here with you until a cab shows up? And you'll probably get a cab quicker than an Uber driver. Or you could just rent a car over there." He pointed to the far end of the airport, past the baggage claim area, to a sign noting car rentals. Was it even open?

Her head swam. Which would be cheaper? And what was she going to do tomorrow?

"Harvey, I really appreciate your concern, but frankly, I don't trust you." It was the first time she'd called him by name. And just as she'd felt guilty the moment she'd accused Julie of being jealous, she felt the same for what she'd just said to Harvey. But wasn't she justified in her distrust? She didn't know him, really. Sure, she knew his first name and that he'd been to a comic convention in Providence and liked Captain America and he was recently divorced with kids and had worked for a pharmaceutical company . . .

Then again, it was possible she knew more about Harvey than about Vance.

Now you know someone in Billings. She could hear the way Harvey had said it, with such warmth and honesty and invitation. Tears surfaced again.

"I'm sorry," she said. "I just—"

"I get it," he said. "No worries."

"I'll just call a cab and go to that Best Western you suggested. Tomorrow I'll deal with my luggage and everything else." She longed to be somewhere safe and familiar.

"OK," said Harvey. He stood there, as if unable to move, deliberating. He then extracted his wallet from the pocket of his jeans, pulled out a business card, and handed it to her. "Here's my number. Call me if you need assistance with anything tomorrow."

She took the card without reading it and rammed it into the front pocket of her purse before zipping it closed. "Thank you," she said, her voice distant, shot, spent.

"OK, so I'm going to go now."

"OK," she echoed.

He remained in place, as did she.

"OK," he said once more. And then, finally, he picked up his backpack and slung one strap over his shoulder as he gripped his retrieved suitcase handle with his opposite hand. "I really hope everything works out for you, Skye. I'm so sorry this happened. You seem like a really nice person."

He was the only friend she had at the moment. For a split second, she contemplated hugging him. Why didn't she trust him? Because of the things he'd said about Vance?

"Thank you," she said above a whisper.

He then looked down at the carrier and waved to Chip through the mesh window. "Take care, cat."

"Chip," she said.

"Chip," he repeated.

Chip meowed in reply.

And just as he turned around to exit through the revolving door, Skye realized she'd be completely alone, in a near-empty airport, late at night, in a city and state she'd never been to before.

She called out. "Wait!"

Harvey turned around.

"Will you stay here with me until the cab gets here?"

He smiled softly. "Sure."

As she called the cab, Harvey took hold of Skye's carry-on with his free hand and walked it over to a row of seats near the revolving doors. Skye followed him, carrying Chip and her purse. The two sat together for an eternity, barely saying more than a few words in broken sentences. When the cab arrived, Harvey instructed the driver where to take her, helped him load her luggage into the trunk, and extended his hand.

"Goodbye, Skye," he said.

"Goodbye, Harvey."

"I really am sorry."

"Me too."

"Call me at any hour."

"Thank you."

She closed the cab door and the driver pulled away from the curb, leaving Harvey behind.

She should have bought a one-way ticket back to Rhode Island. Or rather, she never should have left in the first place.

CHAPTER FIVE

Skye awoke close to nine the following morning, the room dark save for a ray of sun streaming through the slot between the curtains. Chip was sitting on her chest, patting her nose with his paw, his way of informing her that he needed to eat. He'd not left her side all night.

It took Skye a good five seconds to process where she was until it all came crashing down on her. Best Western. Billings, Montana. Vance Sandler. Her stupidity. Her gullibility. Her unemployment and homelessness. Twenty-four hours ago, she'd expected to wake up in Vance's arms, naked, taking in the scents of his cologne and the new surroundings and the hideous morning breath that would smell like the end of sleeping alone or with pets. She'd expected to wake up to certainty that the rest of her life was about to begin, and it was going to be big and glorious. Her joints ached with disappointment. She was groggy, disoriented, wrecked.

It was eleven o'clock in Rhode Island. She would have been at Top Drawer for two hours already had she been working the day shift. Just two days ago, she couldn't wait to get out of the minuscule state with its *paak the caaar* accents and bad drivers and we're-not-Massachusetts inferiority complex. Now she was aching for even just a hint of familiarity. An Ocean State license plate. A Paw Sox cap. A frozen custard. She longed to nestle into Rhode Island's crawl space and never leave it again.

Skye pushed Chip off and wrangled herself out of bed. She padded to her carry-on, where she found just one more ration of food for the cat and, thankfully, one change of clothes and toiletries in the event that her luggage disappeared, as well as her laptop. She appreciated her preparedness. She took one of the hand towels from the bathroom and laid it on the floor like a mat, filled a coffee cup with the food, and set it on the towel. Chip practically pounced on it and tipped it over, pulling out its contents with his paw and licking it. He seemed content, like he was playing a game. She envied his lack of want for anything more than what was in front of him at the moment.

Time to make a mental to-do list: *Shower. Eat breakfast. Call baggage claim. Check in with movers. Rent car for at least a couple of days.* She'd have to wait until the movers arrived before she could make a decision about going back to Rhode Island. She didn't see any other option, really. She would have to face the embarrassment of telling all her friends and Summer and now former coworkers that her new adventure of moving across the country to be with the love of her life was cut short by . . . well, the love of her life turning out to be with someone else's love of their life. Or just that he was a lying SOB who never gave a damn about her.

She would call Julie and ask to crash on her couch until she got back on her feet. And she would call Top Drawer and ask for her job back, or even start over as a full-time associate if she couldn't have her managerial position. She was willing to beg.

Her head spun. *Who to call first?* They all required her immediate attention.

Her stomach growled. *OK, breakfast first.*

The complimentary breakfast in the hotel lobby would end in ten minutes, so she slid into her shoes and pulled on the previous day's clothes (which smelled like airplane), and rushed downstairs in time to snag a stale corn muffin, a banana, and a cup of strawberry yogurt while the staff cleaned tables and packed up the spread. She poured a cup of coffee and doctored it with vanilla hazelnut creamer and three packets of sweetener. The only guest in the room, she sat at a table, feeling grubby and smelly and repulsive as she stared at the local news channel on TV, reporting on the day's forecast. Partly cloudy. Sixty degrees. No rain for the rest of the week. It was jarring not to see the satellite map of southern New England, which probably fit in half the state of Montana.

Montana—what was she doing here? How had she let herself so easily be talked into it? Or had she talked herself into it? She knew the answers, of course. Had dismissed and denied the constant stirring inside her as "the frenzy of love" rather than calling it what it really was: *crazy.*

When she finished eating, she bused her table and thanked the staff and returned to the room. Chip was back on the bed, his body leaning against the pillow she'd slept on. He wore an expression of bewilderment, as if he were just as puzzled by the point of all this upheaval and questioning when it was going to end.

"I know," she said to the cat. "Your momma went and fucked it all up."

Using hotel stationary, she made a list of everyone she needed to call, assigned numbers to them for order, and undressed again to take a shower. The warm, soothing spray was the first thing she'd been grateful for since arriving. And as she stood in the tub, with the bristly stickers under her feet to prevent slipping, her skin absorbing the steam, the answer became clear to her: *Yes, of course! Find Vance Sandler.* If she could just track him down, knock on his door, and stay there until she got some answers—if she could just figure out *why* he'd played with her emotions so callously, why he'd pretended all that time to love her, why he'd encouraged her to move right up to the day she got on the plane, then she could change it. She could show him what she'd just given up for him, could show him how good she really was for him so that he'd be overcome with remorse.

What about Harvey's wife? Well, she'd need to find out if she and Vance were still together, if any of it was even true. Then she could figure out what to do about it. But first she needed to talk to Vance. She wasn't going to let him have the last word by leaving her there at the airport, stranded.

Now with purpose, she vigorously washed her body and shampooed and conditioned her hair—oh, how good it felt to be clean!—and changed into the fresh clothes. Foregoing the list, she opened her phone and found Vance's home address—she had intended to forward her mail there, but Vance had talked her into getting a PO box first. *Just in case you don't like it in Billings,* he'd said.

That's silly, Skye had replied. *Why wouldn't I like it there? Especially if we're together?*

The red flag had been waving in her face the entire time, and she'd been color blind.

She'd gone ahead and forwarded it to his address anyway. She'd have to add an item to her list: *go to the post office to rescind the change.*

Next, she called the cab company.

◆ ◆ ◆

Skye instantly recognized the surroundings when the car pulled up to Vance's home off Poly Road, one of the restored models with new garage and second-floor additions, a professionally manicured lawn and flowerbeds and perfectly even trimmed shrubs, and pristine white door set against navy-blue siding. She had viewed it many times via Google Earth in addition to the photos Vance had texted her early in their relationship. (Ha. *Relationship.* The word echoed so falsely now, like a sham.) *That door wants to be aqua-colored,* she'd thought the very first time she'd seen it. She'd planned to paint it when she moved, with Vance's permission, of course. He'd said he loved the idea. Told her she could redecorate the entire house if she wanted. She'd practically squealed with delight and immediately started clipping pictures from her HGTV magazines for ideas.

The moment the cab pulled away, Skye's heartbeat increased both in speed and volume. Her insides churned and swirled with that same hornet's nest of fury she'd once attributed to love. *This is crazy.* Or was it just nerves? Either way, she was here. Vance had to be home. It was Sunday. He was usually home on Sundays, either watching baseball or tending to his lawn or washing his car—or so he'd told her.

She knocked on the door and waited.

Her heart felt ready to sputter out of her chest and fly away like a drone.

What are you doing here?

Just as she took a step back, the door opened.

Vance. Standing right in front of her. Dressed in Dockers and a button-down and shoes, as if he either had just been out or was about to go out for brunch. Clean shaven. Hair combed. No sign of remorse or even awareness that he'd spent months telling her how much he loved her, helped plan her move to Billings, and then stood her up at the airport. No sign of shock that she was standing at his doorstep.

"Oh," he said. "Hi."

Hi? That's it? Hi?

And then the full force of yet another example of her poor decision-making smacked her. *You've made a big mistake, and now you're making an even bigger one.*

Skye opened her mouth, and her voice stuck in her throat. She coughed to make it work again.

"Hi," she said. "Remember me?"

"Skye," he said, taking her literally.

"Remember what yesterday was?"

"Yes," he said. "I changed my mind."

She looked at him, flabbergasted. "What do you mean, you changed your mind?"

"I don't think it's going to work out between us."

She wanted to hit him with something. Alas, nothing heavier than a daisy was within reach.

"When were you going to tell me this?"

"Frankly, I didn't think you were going to go through with it," said Vance.

"I was on the *plane*," she said, enunciating every word. "You knew this. I gave up my job and my apartment. I gave up my *car*."

His eyes shifted side to side, on the lookout for nosy neighbors. And yet, he didn't invite her in. He spoke in hushed tones, as if she'd follow along. "Well, yes. That's unfortunate. You probably shouldn't have done that. I'm sorry you came all this way, but you should really go home."

Skye had never been physically beaten before, but she posited that this was the emotional equivalent. Every sentence Vance uttered was a blow to her head, a whack at the knees, a sucker punch to the gut.

She drew in a breath, as if gasping for air. "That's it? That's all you have to say?"

"I have an appointment," he said. "You need to go."

"I came here in a cab. Cab's gone."

"I can't help you," said Vance.

This man was a stranger. He no longer looked like the handsome blue-eyed, soft-spoken gentleman who'd sent her good-night texts in the form of lullabies and sweet serenades and kisses galore, who'd told her she was worth any man's time and attention. Her mistake was that she'd needed *him* to tell her that rather than believe it herself. No, this monster standing before her had ice for irises, a forehead with a formidable frown. Dried lips that spewed venom with every bite. A snake, that's what he looked like. Scaly and venomous and preying.

Skye didn't say goodbye, didn't curse him out, didn't smack him hard across the cheek, although he most certainly deserved it. Instead, she just turned around and walked away, powerless, beaten. She trotted down the sidewalk, toward the street corner, and turned around. Vance had closed the door on her. On them. She bent over to catch her breath the way runners do, and squeezed her eyes shut to keep the tears at bay. She took another breath. Her heart wrenched.

Now what?

Should she call the cab again to be picked up? Should she try to walk back to the hotel? She thought of poor Chip alone and waiting, fearful that she might not come back. She knew the feeling and was desperate to get to him.

More than anything in the world, she needed a friend.

She remembered the business card Harvey had handed her last night. Unzipped the front pocket of her purse and reached in, almost surprised when her fingers touched it and pulled it out, as if she'd expected it to have disappeared overnight. She flipped it and read, one line underneath the other: *Harvey Wright. Painting Services. Interiors and Exteriors. Furniture Refinishing.*

She dialed the number on the card and prayed not to be transferred to voice mail.

"Harvey Wright," said the voice. Skye exhaled a sigh of relief.

"Harvey, this is Skye Littleton, from the plane yesterday."

"Good morning," he said, his voice bold. "How are you feeling today?"

"Well, I know this is a lot to ask, but I need your help with something."

"Shoot," he said.

"I'm . . . I'm at Vance's house. On his street." She burned with humiliation. "I just did a stupid thing, and, well, now I'm stranded here and was wondering if you could pick me up. I know I should just call a cab again, but—" She sobbed. Of all the times to start blubbering again.

He cut her off. "You don't have to do that. There's a coffee shop several blocks away." He gave her the name of the place and the street.

"If you go there, I'll meet you. I'm just finishing up a job, so it may take an hour, but I promise I'll be there."

She exhaled again, grateful for his offering. Like the spark needed to reignite a fire. "Thank you so much," she said. "I know I've got no right to bother you, especially after telling you I distrusted you."

"It's the least I could do," he said. "I feel bad about my role in everything that happened."

"I was the fool not to believe you," Skye said, her voice mousy. Small. Weak.

"Not at all," said Harvey. "See you soon."

Skye tapped the screen and entered the coffee shop name into her GPS system. About twenty minutes later, she was there.

Harvey arrived in under an hour.

CHAPTER SIX

Aside from her first day of college in New Hampshire, Skye had never felt so alone in a strange place. At least in college, she took comfort knowing scores of fellow freshmen were likely feeling the same way. Skye watched customers come in and go out with their orders, sit contentedly with their laptops or phones, chatting knowingly with their friends and significant others, all oblivious to the stranger sitting by the window in the back of the café who hadn't been in town for more than twenty-four hours and whose life had turned to shambles. So when the familiar figure entered the coffee shop, she stood up and waved him over, tempted to hug him. He was dressed in a white T-shirt, blue jeans, and work boots speckled with paint. What she'd thought was even more gray in his hair since she'd last seen him also turned out to be paint. She tried to picture him in a suit and tie, hair slicked back, suave, and failed. He was attractive in a preppie-meets-scruffy kind of way. Like what Jake Ryan from *Sixteen Candles* might look like when he hit middle age. Which made Skye wonder what Harvey looked like younger, which then made her wonder who would want to see Jake Ryan all grown up. Preserve that teen dream at all costs.

Not that she ever wanted to look at another man again. Maybe she could join a convent. Or buy one of those tiny houses that you could hitch up on wheels and take with you wherever you went. Or a used

Winnebago to drive back to Warwick. And then live in it on someone's property.

No. Chip would never stand for it.

He reached her table. "You OK?" he asked.

She nodded, overcome with emotion just at the sight of someone familiar. "I can't thank you enough for picking me up," she said.

"You're welcome. Mind if I order something and sit down first? Are you in a hurry?"

"No, it's OK," she said, thinking about Chip.

"Want anything?" She shook her head and thanked him and watched him order coffee and a danish at the counter before joining her again.

"I'm really, really sorry to take you away from your work," she said.

"It's OK. Luckily, I only had a minor job today, and was just about finished with it when you called."

"Do you like it? Painting, I mean." Odd for her to engage in such casual conversation at that moment, but she needed the normalcy; otherwise she would break down on the spot. It grounded her.

He nodded. "I find it relaxing, believe it or not." He took a bite of danish followed by a sip of coffee, and tossed the chitchat aside. "So what's up, Skye? How can I help you, aside from giving you a ride back to your hotel?"

"I feel foolish. I had another bout of temporary insanity and thought facing Vance would make everything better."

At first, she thought he might grill her, like Julie would, or even scold her, like Summer would. Instead, he nodded. "Yeah, that's understandable, albeit futile."

"He just stood there, completely nonchalant, and told me he changed his mind. Just like that. Told me to go home."

Harvey shook his head in disbelief. "Fucking coward."

She winced. Twenty-four hours ago, he wasn't a fucking coward. Or rather, she didn't know him as such. Twenty-four hours ago, he was the man she was about to spend her life with. The severity of the change was dizzying.

"Anyway, I should have just called a cab or an Uber driver, but . . . I don't know, I was just feeling so devastated and abandoned and alone and . . ." She dropped her head in shame.

He sat and listened and looked at her compassionately. "I'm glad you called, Skye. I told you you could. I'll take you back to your hotel whenever you want."

"Thank you," she said. "I left Chip there, and he's probably freaking out. I also need to start making a plan to get back to Rhode Island."

"You're going back, huh?" said Harvey. His tone had changed. Not that he had become harsh or judgmental, just . . . different.

"What else is there for me here? I didn't secure employment. Vance said there was no rush for me to find work, that the job market was good and he'd support me for the first couple of weeks. He made it sound like a vacation. And while I've always been able to pay my bills, I've mostly lived paycheck to paycheck, putting away a lot of money into retirement."

"That's smart."

"Maybe, but it leaves me with next to nothing in the meantime. I sold or gave away most of my furniture and kitchen stuff, and it still cost me a grand to move boxes of books, keepsakes, winter clothes, stereo, things like that. Plus, I had to put money down on the storage unit, buy my airline ticket . . . I even sold my car." She grimaced as she recalled telling Vance how exciting it would be to drive across country, and Vance in turn telling her that she wouldn't need it because he lived close to downtown and thus she could walk to "everything."

What about work, though? I'm going to need a car to get to and from a job, she'd said.

So, you take the money you made from selling your car, and use it as a down payment on a new one here, he'd replied. *It's a new chapter to your life, after all.*

41

She'd been so naive to think he was encouraging her rather than setting her up for disaster. She should have known she wouldn't get much for a 2004 Honda Civic that she'd bought used ten years ago.

Harvey leaned forward and looked directly at Skye. His brown eyes were less almond- and more oval-shaped. Sad, even. Puppyish.

"Skye, I know he took everything, but make him pay for it. Don't give him the satisfaction of having beat you."

Skye straightened her posture. "And how do I do that?"

"Did you ever watch *The Six Million Dollar Man*?"

She eyed him quizzically.

He tried again. "Lee Majors? The bionic man?"

She remained stupefied. He seemed irked for a second, as if to say, *How could you not know something so vitally important?* but quickly resigned to her lapse of knowledge.

"Before your time, I guess. Well, here's what I'm getting at. It was a TV show in the seventies. Steve Austin was an astronaut whose spacecraft wiped out, leaving him all but dead. And this guy named Oscar Goldman says: 'Gentlemen, we can rebuild him. We have the technology. We have the capability to make the world's first bionic man. Steve Austin will be that man. Better than he was before. Better. Stronger. Faster.' They spent six million dollars to make it happen. Hence the title of the show."

He was passionate and resolute. She, on the other hand, stared at him as if he were a foreign object, speaking gibberish.

"Honest to God, Harvey, I have no idea what you're trying to tell me."

Harvey smiled amiably, mischievously, knowingly. "I'm telling you that we're going to rebuild you, and your life. And for a hell of a lot less than six million bucks."

Something flickered in her chest. "We?"

"Well, figuratively, we. Actually, it's all on you. But you can do it. And you'll beat the shit out of that frogface fuckmonger Vance Sandler when you do."

She considered her alternatives yet again: Go back to Warwick and Top Drawer if they'd have her back (Dan the regional manager did say they were sorry to see her go, asked if there was anything they could say or do to convince her to stay), and forget all about Vance Sandler. Pretend none of this ever happened, like it was all a bad dream. She could do that, and eventually things would go back to normal.

But "normal" was what sent her off the deep end in the first place, wasn't it? She had been thoroughly dissatisfied with "normal."

And she didn't want her job back. She'd never wanted it in the first place. At least not for as long as she'd had it. She had attended a job fair at her college prior to graduation, stopped at the Top Drawer booth, and filled out an application, figuring it would be good for something to do until she decided what she was going to do with her degree in marketing and management. Almost the same degree as Summer's, which her parents had said would be far more useful (*Look at what it's done for your sister*) after they'd practically bullied her into going to college rather than get a real estate license straight out of high school, which was what she'd wanted to do. She'd even lined up an internship at a real estate office for the summer. *You may think selling houses is all glamour and makes you rich, but it's not and it won't.* Trying to explain that her motive for getting into real estate had little to do with money or glamour fell on deaf ears. She'd wanted to be around the houses themselves. So she gave up and did what she was told to do.

The Top Drawer booth representatives had told her about "promising career opportunities" for people with marketing and management degrees such as hers. Enticed her with phrases like "corporate benefits," "upward mobility," and "free product." Punch lines, she eventually came to see them as. *Of course, you'll need to begin at the store level and learn the ins and outs,* they'd said. She'd been OK with that condition, was eager to learn. And she was, indeed, promoted to assistant manager within her first year at the Providence Place location and, two years later, elevated to manager of the store in the Warwick Mall. For twelve years. She'd occasionally hear about a job opening at corporate head-quarters, located in San Antonio, Texas, for something like a marketing analyst or operations director or a position in human resources. But the positions either required a master's degree, which she'd never gotten; extensive travel, which she didn't want because she thought it would hamper her social life (Ha!); relocation, which she didn't want to do, especially not to someplace like Texas that only had two seasons—hot and hotter; or qualifications beyond her scope and experience. The "free product" part was an occasional bra-and-panty set for whatever new line had launched; however, neither ever fit her, and she wound up giving them to her sister or Julie.

She'd dreamed big and gone nowhere. And her latest dream—living happily ever after with Vance—shattered her heart and soul.

She had to walk among the shards of her life and figure out a way to keep it going.

She had to start over and use every ounce of strength to fight from being suffocated by her regrets.

But what if starting over wasn't a punishment, but an opportunity? What if it was a chance to do what *she* wanted to do, on her own terms and in her own way?

And wouldn't staying in Billings be a better way to "make Vance pay" rather than crawling back to Rhode Island with her tail between her legs?

Yes. Yes to all of it. She just needed to figure out what she wanted and how to make it happen. Above all, she needed to prove to Vance—no, to herself—that he might have beaten her down, but she could get back up.

She looked at Harvey, who finished the last of his coffee and danish.

"So what happened to the Steve Austin guy?" she asked.

Harvey stood up. "He went after Bigfoot, hooked up with a bionic woman, and did everything in slow motion."

She was totally fucked.

"C'mon, Skye," he said, gathering his trash. "Let's get you back."

CHAPTER SEVEN

Harvey and Skye walked down to the end of the street, where a boxy, ocean-blue Toyota FJ Cruiser was parked. He opened the passenger door for her, brushed the seat off, and she climbed in, meeting the smell of paint fumes. Harvey started the car, turned off the classic rock that assaulted their ears, and drove Skye back to the airport to check on her missing luggage first. The airport wasn't far—"just on top of the rim-rocks," according to him—and they made conversation along the way.

"So why did you get into painting, aside from the relaxation part of it?" she asked. The small talk was paying off in that she'd calmed down quite a bit. She needed a level head to figure out what to do next.

"I was burned out in my other job."

"Pharmaceutical sales, right?" she asked, recalling their conversation on the plane.

"Yes," he said. "That's how I know Vance. He tried to steal my clients, undermine me at meetings, one-up me every chance he could get. At least half my misery was caused by him. And then, after he stole my wife, all of it."

"I'm sorry," she said, as if she'd been partly responsible. As if she were the one who had brought Vance into his life. Or, at the very least, brought Vance back. She was still raw from her morning confrontation—his complete lack of empathy, the ice in his eyes—and shivered.

"I had a lot socked away in savings and investments, however, and despite paying alimony and divorce lawyers, I was able to walk away and take the risk of starting a business that was a little more personal."

"Do you get a lot of work?" she asked.

"Enough. Sometimes I go from house to house and do a room here, a room there, or something like a piece of furniture. Other days I'm doing entire levels, basements, garages, you name it. I've only been at it for about a year. I'll probably be closer to thirty this year. Maybe even more."

"Thirty *thousand?*" Skye blurted. How did one live on thirty thousand dollars per year?

"You sound like my ex-wife." He said the words with a half-smile, but Skye could still feel a nip. "Sure, the six-figure salary from pharmaceuticals was great. But the ulcers the job gave me weren't, nor were the hours, the soul-selling, the blatant politics, and the fights I got into with my ex on a weekly basis because I was so miserable."

"I just . . . I don't know, for that kind of money, I would have put up with it," said Skye.

"Easy to say when you're on the outside."

She frowned. "I'd say it no matter what. I've never made more than forty-eight thousand a year."

"That's a good salary," he argued.

"For here, maybe, but not in Rhode Island. Not when you're on your feet all day and putting up with customers' nonsense and part-time staff earning minimum wage calling in sick or quitting on you with no notice. Not when decent two-bedroom apartments go for twelve to fifteen hundred dollars a month, and that's after a first, last, and security. Not to mention gas and car insurance and taxes and all that stuff. A *six-figure* salary? I'd put up with abusive coworkers, marathon hours, whatever it took, as long as I could come home to a beautiful house in a nice neighborhood in a car I didn't buy off someone from Craigslist after scraping the last of my savings."

"I get that," said Harvey. "But I'm telling you, more money means more headaches. I've got college funds, the kids' expenses, and insurance up the yin-yang, and that's on my current salary. When I was still married, sure, we had a nice house, but we also had a mortgage, property taxes, maintenance fees, utility bills, repairs—and with a house, you're always repairing or replacing something. My job required a lot of travel, so I needed a good car, not to mention something high class since we're in sales and need to impress, good business suits, a top-of-the-line laptop and tablet, and first class if we flew anywhere. The company refused to let us fly coach. Crazy. We at least got travel expenses reimbursed, but still. Total waste."

"Sure," she said, "first class must be *awful.*" She rolled her eyes. "I can see why you quit."

She'd gone too far with that last remark, she realized, when Harvey clamped his lips and rolled his eyes. He said nothing until they reached the top of the hill and circled a roundabout.

"We're here," he said.

"I appreciate your picking me up and giving me a ride here," she said. "Really, I do. And I'm sorry for what I said."

"It's fine," he said, although she wasn't convinced of his sincerity. "Are you going to rent a car too?" he asked.

"I guess I should," she said. "At least until I can make a new plan of action. I think I'm going to try to make a go of it here. I mean, I came all this way, didn't I? Seems like a complete waste to turn around and go home. Besides, what would be better revenge against Vance than my staying here?"

"That's the spirit," said Harvey. He seemed friendly again. "Well, in that case, I'll get going, unless there's a reason you need me to stay."

"No, I'm good," she said. "Thank you, again. I really needed a friend this morning."

"Well, you've got one in Billings now," he said. She took in the words like hot chocolate, could actually feel them coating her insides, soothing and warming them. Vance's sweet nothings had always felt like firecrackers shooting off inside her. She'd gotten high off the intensity. Had he ever comforted her, though, the way Harvey just had—with a simple act of hospitality? At the moment, she couldn't recall any instance in which he had. But why compare the two? Vance had been her lover, or so she'd thought. Harvey was just . . . well, a friend, she guessed.

Skye entered the airport—it was a fraction of the size of TF Green and especially Minneapolis—where her two suitcases were waiting for her as if she'd left them behind rather than their being misrouted. They contained what she'd saved of her spring and summer wardrobe, shoes, cosmetics, blow dryer, and other such sundries. She was suddenly grateful that the luggage hadn't arrived on time, imagining herself trying to lug two large suitcases, a carry-on, her purse, and Chip in his carrier, all by herself. The rest of her life was en route via moving truck and was scheduled to arrive the day after tomorrow. She rented a car for one week—groaned when she saw the total dollar amount, but figured it would be easier to have a car for her employment search rather than rely on public transportation or Uber drivers or cabs, which was also costly. She hoped she'd find something soon; staying at the Best Western long-term wasn't feasible either.

Next, she found a supermarket—Albertsons—and stocked up on food and pet bowls and a disposable litter box for Chip and microwavable meals and soft drinks for herself. When she came back to the hotel, Chip practically howled, as if to say, *How could you leave me here?!* Skye scooped him up and carried him to the bed, apologizing profusely. She knew the feeling. She wanted to howl the same question to Vance. Cradling the tabby, she rocked him and pet him under his chin and spoke softly to him until he was content and wriggled out of her arms to the plastic sack of food. She took out one of the snack pouches and dumped a few of the nibbles on the bed. And while he occupied himself, Skye leaned back and fought tears. She wished someone would do the same for her—cradle her in his arms, stroke her hair, and tell her everything was going to be OK.

Maybe she was crazy to stay in Billings. She'd certainly been crazy to leave Warwick. She realized that now. Or maybe, just maybe, it would have been crazier to stay in a job that didn't please her and in the shadow of a sister who could do no wrong. Maybe it was time to stake her claim.

She had to start somewhere.

CHAPTER EIGHT

Skye spent the following day at the Rimrock Mall, going from store to store asking for job applications. Some sales associates told her she needed to fill out an application online. Others handed her the forms, and she sat at one of the food court tables and filled out each one, leaving the address section blank and explaining that she was "between apartments" at the moment. If that didn't jeopardize her chances, her overqualification as a store manager did, since many of the positions she was applying for were part-time sales or stock. Skye figured she'd be able to work her way up to assistant manager or keyholder quickly.

Even the plus-sized clothing stores eyed her warily.

Never mind that she'd won Manager of the Month three months in a row. Never mind that her store maintained its figures, financially speaking. She was a thirty-six-year-old, graying-haired, overweight, practically homeless woman. She wasn't projecting *asset*. She was projecting *desperation*. She was projecting *loser*. She was projecting *I need you way more than you need me*. Which was probably what had made it so easy for Vance to lure her in six months ago. That, and Vance had promised her that eventually she wouldn't have to work at all unless she wanted to, because he was "well-off."

Stupid, stupid Skye for believing him.

Why didn't she ever learn her lesson? Skye Littleton had always let her fantasies get the best of her, only to be let down. She'd been doing it since she was nine years old, when she erected a lemonade stand, complete with a yellow patio umbrella and pretty, flowered Dixie cups, with ambitions of netting one hundred dollars by the end of her first business day. After three days, she'd counted nine dollars in quarters. When she was twelve, she'd entered a magazine-selling contest, thinking that if she sold enough subscriptions, the grand prize would be something like a trip to New York for a tour of the publishing company, where she would be named Junior Executive for a day, and in ten years, when she graduated college, there would be a job waiting for her. She came in third and won a large candy bar, which she ate alone, in her room, in one sitting, already full with disappointment. The grand prize turned out to be nothing more than a giant teddy bear.

At age seventeen, when Donnie DiMarco said hello to her for the first time after class and walked with her to her next one, she had proceeded to send him secret-admirer notes and carnations for the following six days, although her identity was far from concealed. After thoroughly planning the wedding in detail, her hopes were shot after her future husband let her down in no uncertain terms and wouldn't so much as look in her direction in the hallways.

And when Professor Schumacher wrote an encouraging note on her term paper in college, she dreamed about making commencement speeches at graduation rather than explaining the actual Bs and Cs to her parents, who demanded honor roll. (Her sister Summer was a straight-A student, of course.)

And let's not rehash her current situation, thanks to Vance Sandler responding to her comment on a group Facebook page. And freaking the fuck out on her birthday.

Back in her hotel room, exhausted, she watched reruns of *Fixer Upper* on the HGTV channel and considered moving to Waco, Texas, to ask Chip and Joanna Gaines to find her a house. She'd seen couples snag a cottage on *Fixer Upper* for as little as ten grand. She didn't need much more than a two-bed, one-bath with a screened-in porch. Maybe, if she moved to Waco instead, she could even work at their Magnolia store.

Stop it, Skye, she chided herself. *You don't need any more fantasies.*

She called Julie to update her on her disastrous confrontation with Vance and her decision to remain in Billings.

"Are you crazy?" Julie practically yelled.

"Probably," said Skye, eating a dinner consisting of a burger, fries, and Coke from Sonic. *So healthy.* "But why should I give Vance the satisfaction of knowing he played me?"

"You shouldn't," said Julie. "But you don't have to stay in Billings-fucking-Montana to do that. You can get a new job and a new place and have a fabulous life right here in Rhode Island. Maybe move closer to the water or live in Providence or something."

"Doing what? More retail? More staring at an empty online-dating inbox? I can do that anywhere. Jules, I have to do this. I have to start from scratch. If it doesn't work out here, then I'll leave. But I have to try. I have to figure out what I really want. I haven't asked myself that in so long. At least not realistically."

Julie sighed. "OK, Skyebaby. You know I'll always support you. I just miss you, you know?"

"I miss you too, Jules. Thank you for caring. And understanding."

"You talk to your sister yet?"

Skye huffed. "No. Not in the mood for the I-told-you-so speech."

"She might surprise you."

"I doubt it."

"You should do a Facebook update too."

"Why?"

"So people don't think you were eaten by a bear or something."

Skye snorted. "I don't think there are bears in Billings. Anyway, let them think whatever they want. I'm not in the mood to fill people in on my pathetic life."

"You're not pathetic!" yelled Jules. "You're doing something very courageous. Crazy, but courageous."

"Or just plain stupid. We'll find out soon enough."

When Skye ended the call, she extracted her laptop from her carry-on and flopped back on the bed. She filled out the online applications and went to an employment website looking for matches to her skill sets and qualifications, temp jobs, anything that could give her momentum. Two hours later she turned up the volume on the TV, which she'd kept on but muted since her phone call with Julie. *Beachfront Bargain Hunters* was on. She flicked the TV off at first sight of the gulf view from a high-rise condo in Galveston, Texas, threw the remote on the floor, and turned to her side, crossing her arms and folding herself into a fetal position. This was reality. She was never going to be more. She was never going to have more. It was time, once and for all, to stop dreaming of more. To stop wanting more. To stop wanting anything.

No. No, no, no.

She sat up. "No pity parties allowed," she said to Chip, who was curled up on the edge of the bed. He picked his head up, looked at her apathetically, and lowered it back on top of his paws. Retrieving her laptop, she opened a Word document and started at the blank page. Then she typed:

IF MONEY WASN'T AN OBJECT, WHAT WOULD
YOU WANT TO DO OR BE?

She stared at the screen. Then she stared at the black screen of the television. Then she stared at Chip. Then she started at the curtains hiding the darkness outside.

She turned the TV on again. A commercial for *Property Brothers* was on.

And then she typed:

I want to be Drew and Jonathan in one. And Chip and Joanna. And Dave and Kortney.

I want to be a fixer-upper.

She wasn't even entirely sure what she meant by that second sentence, why she'd worded it that way instead of something like, *I want to buy and renovate and sell homes.* She didn't even know how one got into such a business. Where was she supposed to start?

And then she had an idea.

She texted Harvey: Is there a class I could take on learning how to paint?

Minutes later, Harvey replied: I'll do you one better. Come work for me.

CHAPTER NINE

Work for Harvey?

Skye began to text a reply but opted instead to call him directly. "Work for you? You're barely making enough to support yourself."

"Don't worry about that," he said. "You can be my assistant. Fetch supplies, clean stuff, maybe even help me get some promotion going, since you're so good with sales."

"I thought you were good with sales too."

"Doesn't mean I like doing it."

Skye conceded the point. "I was thinking more along the lines of working at Home Depot or a paint store or something like that."

"Why not work for me instead? It's easy to learn. Flexible hours. Plus, if it doesn't work out for you here in Billings, you could walk away with no strings attached."

An uneasiness settled into Skye's stomach, and not from the junk food she'd consumed hours earlier. "Why?" she asked.

"Why what?"

"Why are you going out of your way to help me? You barely know me."

"I know who hurt you. That makes me want to help you."

Tears began to brim yet again as her cheeks heated upon the reference to Vance. She missed him. Rather, she missed who she thought he was.

"He blocked me, by the way. From Facebook, his phone, everything. Completely ghosted me." She had made that discovery earlier, when, against her better judgment, she'd attempted to Facebook-stalk him.

"That bastard," said Harvey. "I'm sorry. But maybe it's for the best. Anyway, do you want the job? I can't pay you more than minimum wage, but you'll learn a lot."

A painter. Washing paint out of her hair and her fingernails and anywhere else it landed. Climbing ladders. Working in other people's homes and seeing how much better they had it than she did. Working for pennies. Working for Harvey. This is what she moved across the country and gave up her life for.

"When can I start?" she asked.

CHAPTER TEN

Harvey met Skye outside the Best Western lobby at seven forty-five on Monday morning. She had spent the weekend watching YouTube videos on everything ranging from how to paint a wall to doors to furniture. She still didn't know the difference between paint that would be used for indoors as opposed to outdoors, or the different wall types—she didn't even know there was more than one type of wall until she watched a video—or types of brushes, rollers, even drop cloths. The day before, she'd bought an oversized T-shirt, leggings, socks, and the cheapest tennis shoes she could find at Walmart. She hoped this "uniform" would suffice, given that the last thing she wanted to be seen in was a pair of coveralls. Next to jumpsuits and pajama onesies, coveralls were a large woman's nightmare outfit, turning her into the shape of a watermelon. Or at least, that's how Skye saw herself.

She emerged from the hotel in her new work clothes and climbed into Harvey's FJ Cruiser, where he handed her a tall travel cup of coffee.

"I don't know how you take it, so I brought some stuff for you to doctor it up," he said, pointing to a bag shoved in one of the cup holders between them. Her first thought was of Vance messaging her a list of getting-to-know-you questions: favorite color, band, TV show, movie, ice cream flavor, and how do you take your coffee. He'd proven that he'd memorized it during their Boston jaunt, when they stopped into a coffee bar and he ordered it extra sweet for her. (*Because that's what she is,* he'd told the barista, which, of course, turned Skye into a pool of melted butter.) She'd been so pleased, having once seen a chick flick in which the guy remembered how the girl took her coffee, indicating that he was Mr. Right. Plus, she'd believed it was a romantic gesture. She wondered if Harvey would remember if she told him. From everything she'd seen so far, Harvey was polite, thoughtful, helpful, even gallant. She'd thought all those things about Vance too, so maybe there was something hiding in plain sight. Or perhaps something right smack in front of her that she was oblivious to. Could any man be that good?

She opened the bag and peeked inside, spying a to-go-sized creamer and various brands of sugar packets. Taking the creamer and three of packets of Equal—and how stupid was it to use a sugar substitute when you supersized and fatted everything else up; alas, it eased her self-consciousness—she dumped each into the coffee and stirred it with one of the wooden stirring sticks.

"Thank you," she said. "That was very nice of you." She took a sip following her preparations. *Not bad.* "I've been craving coffee milk ever since I left Rhode Island."

"What's that?" he asked.

She went slack-jawed and stared at him, incredulous. "You were just in Providence. How is it possible that you've never heard of coffee milk?"

"Because I'm an idiot," he said, and she couldn't help but giggle. "What is it, some kind of latte?"

"It's only the greatest thing in the history of everything. Like chocolate milk, only it's made with coffee syrup instead."

"I didn't even know there was such a thing as coffee syrup," said Harvey.

"Oh man, have you been missing out."

"I guess it's a Rhode Island thing."

"You bet your sweet ass it's a Rhode Island thing," she said, and the utterance of the tiny state's name instantly filled her with pangs of homesickness. She missed coffee milk. She missed I-95. She missed WaterFire nights in Providence. She even missed the stupid Warwick Mall. She missed Julie and everything else she'd left behind.

What on earth was she doing in a car with some guy she'd only known for one week in *Billings-fucking-Montana*? About to go to a job *painting*.

Harvey displayed a crooked smile upon the words "sweet ass." "The coffee shop where I bought these has really good huckleberry-flavored Italian cream sodas. Maybe you'd like them."

"Huckleberry? I thought that was a Mark Twain character."

He chided her. "And you think I've been missing out."

Skye gave him a dubious look and sipped her coffee again. Now all she could taste was not-coffee-milk.

"So where is today's job?" she asked.

"In the Heights," he said. "The Bench, to be precise. That's what it's known as. On the other side of the rimrocks. Very pretty over there. Newer neighborhood."

"What are we doing?"

"Two rooms in the basement. A couple of authors want to convert them into offices."

"They live together?"

He nodded. "I guess so."

"You don't know them?"

"I know friends of theirs."

"What do they write?"

"Books." He winked.

Skye huffed in mock exasperation. "Well, *duh*. What kind of books do they write?"

"What am I, Google?" said Harvey. "I just said I don't know them personally."

"They can't be very good authors if they live here," she said.

"What is that supposed to mean?"

"Billings, Montana? What famous author lives in Billings, Montana?" She uttered the city name with more than condescension. Downright resentment.

Harvey glared at her. "You'd be surprised, Skye. This city is teeming with authors, artists, poets, musicians, actors, chefs—you name the medium, and Billings will give you its makers. And they're well supported too. People show up for living room concerts, library readings, theater performances, and film screenings. Of course, you have to willingly look for it."

Skye couldn't remember the last time she even heard of a play being performed in Warwick, much less attending one in Providence. The last concert she'd attended was Blake Shelton, whom Julie was crazy about, thanks to that singing talent show *The Voice* (which Skye didn't watch because it usually interfered with her work schedule, and she kept forgetting to DVR it), but whose music Julie was thoroughly unfamiliar with. At the end of the night, Julie had said, *Well, that was underwhelming, wasn't it? I wish we'd had a little more sangria.* As for Skye, she had been hoping for a reunion of 'N Sync.

"Like it or not, this is where you live now," said Harvey. "You made your choice. And before you go dumping on it, maybe you should give it a chance. You've barely seen it."

"I freaking drove all over it while job hunting," she said.

"But you've not *seen* it," he said.

"Fine," she gave in. She looked out the passenger window. "So far I don't see anything I haven't seen in Warwick. Starbucks. Wendy's. Walmart . . ." After a beat, she added, "Although we don't have Albertsons supermarkets. We have Stop and Shops."

Harvey pointed at the giant wall of rock they seemed to be headed straight into. "Does Warwick have that?"

"It's a cliff," said Skye. "Big deal."

Harvey shook his head in exasperation.

"What," said Skye.

"The rimrocks aren't 'a cliff'—they're a geological wonder. They're formations of sandstone that overlook the entire city. Millions and millions of years of compression formed them and the bowl the city sits in—all this was underwater in prehistoric times. Think about it. That's how old the rimrocks are. And they're unique to this part of Montana. So is Sacrifice Cliff out by the Yellowstone River."

Skye stared at them and tried to be impressed, but she could see only what *wasn't* there—the Narragansett Bay. The Providence skyline—minuscule as it was in comparison to, say, Manhattan, but more impressive than what she'd seen of downtown Billings.

"I'm sorry. I guess I miss home."

She was afraid Harvey was going to come back at her again, but instead he responded with a docile, "I understand. Like I said, give it a chance. You'd be surprised at how many people have come to Montana for a visit and, twenty years later, can't see themselves living anywhere else."

Skye? In Montana for twenty years? She had never even seen herself here that long with Vance, and she'd believed that she was going to be with him forever. She'd give Billings a try because it was that or death by humiliation back in Rhode Island. But so far, she wasn't impressed. Maybe she should just stay until she could make enough money to get back home without having to rely on anyone else.

A year. That was a good marker. She could pretend everything was peachy with Vance, then start "vaguebooking" about possible disruptions in the relationship, then announce that she and Vance were over and she was moving back on her terms. Maybe she'd opt for someplace like Boston or even Cape Cod. She'd been so close to the coastline and had taken it for granted her entire life.

Yes, she'd give herself one year in Billings. One year to pick up the pieces of her life. One year to get to the next thing. Whatever it was, all it had to be was better. More. Or was even that little bit asking for too much?

CHAPTER

ELEVEN

First, the tedious part. The clients wanted only the walls painted, so Skye and Harvey needed to seal the edges of the doors, windows, floors, light switches, electrical outlets, and ceiling with painter's tape. In the time it took her to lay tape along the baseboards, Harvey taped off three-quarters of the room. Next, Harvey showed her how to "cut in" using a special brush and a minibucket of paint. She had to practice avoiding splatters, evidenced by the Pollock-esque drop cloth wherever she had stepped, as well as her clothes, arms, and the ends of her hair. Finally, they used the rollers on the walls—a hue she begrudgingly described as "New York Yankee blue" for the male author's room, and tangerine for the female's room. *Odd color choices for offices,* she thought, especially the orange. However, when they finished the second coats for both, she was struck by how vibrant they were, and perhaps a creative type of person needed that.

Harvey worked without uttering a word; Skye figured he was neither shy nor ignoring her but rather was used to working alone, being inside his own head. It was a far cry from the anything-but-silent atmosphere she lived in day in and day out at Top Drawer—pop music blaring through the store's sound system, constantly greeting and conversing with customers as part of their sales skills, chatting with her staff during the slow periods of the day, the vacuum running at night. She had no time to sit with her thoughts. Perhaps that was why she'd gone so long without really thinking about the things that she had wanted from life; all the outside noise successfully drowned it out. She hadn't wanted to think about it.

She wasn't used to the silence, however, and so she made conversation.

"You had mentioned something about kids?" she asked Harvey. "How many do you have?"

"Two. Boy and a girl. Kelly just turned thirteen, and Scott is sixteen going on I-hate-your-freaking-guts."

Skye chortled, even though a kid hating his dad was no laughing matter. Harvey had a knack for being funny and serious at the same time.

"Why does he hate you?"

"Divorce. Adolescence. I'm hoping he grows out of it." He paused for a beat. "I suppose this is obvious, but no kids for you?"

She shook her head. She'd never envisioned kids for herself. She could envision marrying Mr. Perfect, along with the perfect wedding and honeymoon and house, but the picture of perfect kids, or any kids, never quite formed in her mind's eye. The more her parents and Summer had nagged her about it over the years, told her what a gift children were, how a mother's love was the greatest form of love, the more Skye resisted. In the end, she'd been grateful to have dodged that bullet. Cats were more manageable, she'd decided. And didn't require student loans. Besides, with her biological clock relentlessly ticking away, what hope was there for her even if she did want them? She certainly couldn't take care of a child all by herself. At the moment, she wasn't even sure what her next decision was going to be in regards to taking care of herself.

She'd learned more about Harvey—and Vance—during that hour. How Harvey had grown up all over the country, thanks to being "an army brat," went to San Diego during his college years, and began his sales career in Denver before relocating to Billings with the company and meeting his now ex-wife, Deborah, shortly thereafter at a coffee shop on a blind date. How Billings was the longest Harvey ever stayed in one place, and how he liked the stability of it. How skillful Vance was at mixing lies with truths—hanging out backstage with Paul McCartney in Seattle (it was later discovered that although he'd gotten his hands on a backstage pass, he'd never gotten past security); turning down a contestantship on *The Apprentice* (he'd applied online and never got a callback); and the most laughable lie because it was so easy to fact-check: being valedictorian of his high school class. Skye turned crimson as Harvey explained how each myth had been debunked. She'd believed the valedictorian one when Vance had told her—why wouldn't she?—as well as one about playing golf with some famous football player she'd never heard of, but it sounded impressive. The only consequence of Vance's canards was Vance getting revenge by either spreading a vicious rumor about the whistle-blower, or some other form of psychological abuse.

"Vance will never use his fists to hurt someone," said Harvey. "Mostly because he knows he'd get the shit kicked out of him. But also because he's seen the instant effects of psychological warfare."

"How has karma never caught up to him?" Skye wondered aloud.

"Beats me," said Harvey. "But I don't believe in karma. Some people just get away with murder. Plain and simple."

Skye suddenly wondered if Vance was capable of actual murder. Or, worse than capable, experienced.

"You must think I was a complete idiot to fall in love with him."

"Not at all," he said. "Vance is charming. That's what makes him good at his job. Hell, even I liked the guy when I first met him—thought he was a good guy to have a beer with at the end of the day.

But when he's threatened by you, that's when he shows his true colors and destroys you."

Skye put down her roller. "Do you think *I* threatened him?" she asked, desperate for understanding.

He didn't break his stride, didn't even look in her direction. "I don't know. Maybe you did."

"How? All I did was love him."

"Maybe that's enough of a threat."

"But you said he's still with your wife."

"My *ex*-wife," he corrected.

"She must love him. Why is he not threatened by her?"

"I really don't know," said Harvey. "That's why I paint and don't do marital advice or therapy." He finally stopped and surveyed her work. "Looking good," he said. She smiled in self-satisfaction and appreciation for the encouragement.

◆　◆　◆

For as long as she could remember, Skye Littleton had what she called "vibes" about certain rooms. When she slept over at her friend Vicki Marcowitz's house in third grade, Skye moved her Crayola box sleeping bag three times before she found the "right" sleeping space. In junior year of high school, when her sister Summer moved away to college and Skye moved into her bedroom, she completely rearranged the furniture and insisted on a new paint color. *This room wants to be blue,* Skye had said. But not just any ol' blue. No, it needed to be *azure*. She couldn't sleep in the room, or even stand in it for more than a minute, until it was painted. And she replaced the square end table with a round one. And in college, when she shared a dorm room, the first thing she did when she moved in was burn an incense stick. She'd read in a magazine about "smudging" a room to "cleanse the energy." Afterward, the room seemed brighter to her. And whereas her roommate, Sabrina Collins, had been aloof upon their first meeting, she opened up way more after the incense, and she and Skye had become practically inseparable throughout college. Sabrina had moved to Vermont, but they still kept in touch via e-mails and visits.

Even at Top Drawer, if she was having a bad day or if customers were difficult to deal with, Skye would buy a Yankee Candle, light it, and carry it throughout the store prior to opening or after closing. Which scent she chose depended on the vibe she felt either she or the store needed. Coincidentally, when she did, fewer returns came in, customers were friendlier, and staff performances improved. The last candle she had burned before leaving was "Bahama Breeze." That same day, she and her staff doubled the previous year's gross sales, opened two new charge accounts, and the store didn't have a single return for the remainder of her employment.

Skye didn't know if these vibes were a quirk or normal, if they were a sign of intelligence or stupidity, or if they even mattered. She didn't know if the consequences were coincidental or something she assigned significance to. But it was happening yet again. Every time she walked through the authors' den to use the restroom, she couldn't help but feel something was off about the room. It was your basic den—TV mounted to the wall, leather sectional, all in various shades of taupe and mocha. Bookcases and artwork. So what was giving her the willies?

She felt boxed in, she realized.

When they finished the job, Harvey loaded the last of the supplies into his truck and checked the rooms to make sure there were no traces of paint spills or smudges; Skye stood in the entrance to the den, staring.

"What is it?" he asked.

"That coffee table needs to go," she said, pointing at the low table framed by the sectional.

Harvey looked at the rectangular glass top with wrought iron legs. "Looks fine to me," he said. "Goes with the rest of the furniture."

"I think that's the problem," she replied. "The TV, the bookcases . . . it's all too boxy. The table needs to be round."

"Maybe they like the boxy look."

"They may like it, but it doesn't *feel* right in here," she said. "It's confining."

He raised his arms in a *can-we-get-a-move-on* gesture. "Skye, we just paint. We don't give decorating tips. Let's go."

All the validation she'd felt from Harvey's encouragement disappeared with his curt dismissal. As he passed her, she followed behind him, squinching her face and mouthing, *We don't give decorating tips* in a silent mimic behind his back. On her way out, she passed a photo of the author couple, standing in front of the New York Public Library, her showing off an engagement ring. He must have proposed there. Why there and not in Billings? *Would you want to get engaged in Billings?* she asked herself.

They didn't look glamorous by any means—neither of them were slim; both were gray-haired and bespectacled, and the woman wore no makeup—nor did they have an air of rich or famous, despite being published authors. Their house didn't reflect this either. Accessory furniture that probably came from Target. A well-used recliner. Sparse decorations. But the house looked lived in and loved in. Photographs of smiling faces, young and old alike, adorned every room. Books, books, and more books everywhere Skye turned. A kitchen that smelled of baked goods. The engagement photo said it all. Here was a couple who loved more than each other. They loved the life they made. They resided in Billings, but they lived wherever they went, be it a town, city, hotel room, you name it.

She envied them fiercely.

◆　◆　◆

"So what do you think after your first day?" Harvey asked Skye as he drove her back to the Best Western.

"I think I need to soak in a warm bath," she replied. "For two months."

Harvey chuckled. "It's a good workout, that's for sure," he said. "You'll get used to it. How'd you like the job, though?"

"OK, I guess. A little boring." She instantly regretted that last bit of honesty. "I'm sorry," she said. "I didn't mean to be offensive or ungrateful. I just—"

"It's OK, Skye," said Harvey. "It's OK if it's just a job to you. There's not much room for creativity unless you get a say in choosing colors or painting furniture. Then you can have a little fun."

"I wouldn't know," she said. "My apartment had all white walls. Landlord wouldn't let me paint." She'd tried hanging swaths of colored fabric on the walls in lieu of paint but never liked the look. Also tried to compensate with accents of color on her furniture and accessories—she bought a purple couch cover, for example, and sunny orange and yellow throw pillows for contrast. Bought deep-blue bar stools for her kitchen nook, and even found cups and plates to match. Surprised herself by contrasting hot-pink towels in the bathroom with a black bath mat and a shower curtain with accents of both.

"I really appreciated the company and the help, Skye," he said. "You did well for someone with no previous training."

"Thank you," she said. "Especially for your patience."

"I'm sorry I can't pay you more than minimum wage right now."

She knew he was genuinely remorseful. And she liked that about him. She liked that he was equally sensitive and pragmatic.

"Considering that it's cutting into your own salary, I appreciate your giving me anything."

"I hope circumstances change where we'll both be able to get more work."

She never recalled a time when she viewed "more work" as a positive thing. Now she welcomed it. Funny how perspectives changed when circumstances changed. In that regard, maybe her life at Top Drawer really hadn't been as miserable as she'd made it out to be.

◆ ◆ ◆

Ugh.

The job had taken only four hours; and yet, Skye felt as if she'd worked a twelve-hour shift at Top Drawer during one of their semiannual sale days, or Black Friday.

Every muscle ached. Muscles she hadn't used since gym class in high school, when she took archery and golf.

In her hotel room, Skye lay diagonally across the bed, on her back, motionless, arms and legs splayed out. Chip lay beside her, content. Everything in the room felt balanced to her, although she hated the pine-green carpeting. *Too sad,* she thought. Or was she projecting her own state of being onto the carpet? She thought again about the coffee table in the authors' den. Should she tell the clients about it? No, that would be stupid. After all, who was she to give decorating advice? And what was she basing it on—a "feeling"? She wanted to see what the offices would look like once they moved in their desks and other stuff, though. Imagined them vigorously typing away on laptops or typewriters. Thought it would be neat to know that they were using and enjoying these rooms thanks in part to her, even though Harvey did the bulk of the work, simply because he was faster and more efficient. Maybe this wouldn't be such a bad job if she could make a difference. She'd rarely, if ever, felt as if she impacted her customers' lives. She'd sold underwear. Big deal. What did that do, other than turn on their boyfriends or girlfriends? Only once, when a customer came in following a mastectomy and reconstruction surgery and asked for the sexiest bra-and-panty sets in the store. Skye sent her home with her favorite lacy demi-bras and matching bikinis, one in elegant black and the other in seductive red, and the woman hugged her as she left the store, both of them in tears.

Skye had been in a deep sleep when her phone, resting just above her head, jolted her into a sitting position, annoying Chip, who let out a hiss.

It was Julie.

Skye looked at the clock—she'd been asleep for almost as many hours as she'd worked. It was about eight o'clock in Rhode Island.

"Hey," said Skye, groggy.

"Hey, girl!" said Julie, oblivious. "How's life in cowboy country?"

"OK, I guess." It occurred to her that she had yet to see someone in a cowboy hat or boots, although she saw pickup trucks everywhere she went.

"How did it go with the painting job?" Skye had told Julie all about Harvey and her new employment.

"Fine. I mean, it's a job. It's painting. Hopefully it'll lead to bigger and better things." She knew she was sounding nonchalant, ungrateful, dismissive. But for some reason she needed to keep quiet about her bigger plans, even her best friend. Like if she said anything, it might not happen. She remembered her former college roommate, Sabrina, who spent her downtime knitting. Skye once asked her what she was making, and Sabrina was quite evasive. *If you keep opening the oven door, the cookies never get baked,* she'd said. *You'll see it when it's ready to be born. Or baked.* Maybe this was what she had meant.

"OK. So tell me all about Mr. Marvelous!"

"Who?"

"This Harvey guy. Is he cute? Rugged? He's certainly been good to you."

"Oh." Odd that Skye hadn't immediately made the connection. A wad of tension balled up in her abdomen. "Yes, he's been a really good friend so far. He's nice, I guess."

"What does he look like?"

"Imagine Tony Stark wearing flannel. And no goatee."

Julie squealed, "Oooooo, lucky you!"

"Jules, don't."

"What?"

"Don't go there. I'm still missing Vance. I can't even look at another guy that way, much less think about one."

"Skye, you have to move on. How do you know some cosmic force didn't bring this guy into your life on purpose?"

"Because I have no such luck."

She huffed. "OK, fine. Tell me about Billings."

Skye fought off a yawn. "Billings is very different from Warwick."

"How so?"

"Well . . . you should see the sky, for one thing. It just goes on and on. And the rimrocks," she added after a beat.

"The what?"

"This big wall of—never mind. It's just different."

"How are the people?" asked Julie.

She realized that aside from Harvey and cashiers and customer service people at the car rental, she barely interacted with anyone, and that depressed her even more. She liked to be around people, generally speaking. One reason she'd been able to stay at Top Drawer for so long. "They're nice enough, I guess. I haven't met many." She changed the subject. "I'm so dying for a coffee milk, though."

"No sir," said Julie. *No sir* (pronounced *suhhh*) was Rhode Island slang for *no kidding* or *no way!* and Skye lapped it up. "I'll have to send you a care package. Hey, everyone here misses you. Your sister asked me if I'd heard from you. How come you haven't checked in with her or your parents?"

Skye's heart panged with longing. She didn't think anyone would even notice she was gone. She swallowed hard, shoving tears into her throat. Felt like she was exiled, imprisoned, sent to live on another planet with no way home. She repeatedly stroked Chip, happy she hadn't left him behind too.

"I just can't face them yet," she said.

"You're your own worst enemy, you know that?" said Julie.

The comment took Skye aback. It wasn't her fault her parents made her feel less-than with every comparison to Summer. Nor was it her fault that Summer soaked every bit of it up and acted like she was better than Skye and everyone else—not even acted. She *was* better, dammit. Damn well near perfect.

"Gee, thanks, Jules." Julie started to apologize, but Skye cut her off. "I have to go scrounge for dinner. Talk to you tomorrow."

She knew she'd just hurt Julie by blowing her off so quickly. But Julie had hurt her too.

Then again, maybe Skye was so hurt because Julie was right. She knew all Julie's secrets. Julie knew just about all of Skye's. But Julie, despite her own love-life struggles, at least had a bit of job security as an insurance agent. Julie had had more boyfriends than Skye. She also had a house. And a newer car. And a trimmer figure. Maybe Skye was afraid that, like Summer, Julie had bested her at life, or that Skye had lost a long time ago. And that was no one's fault but her own.

CHAPTER
TWELVE

Another week went by, and Skye did three more jobs with Harvey. Two were small—sanding and finishing a table and chairs the clients had picked up at a garage sale, and a kitchen in the midst of renovation— and the third was a two-day job of painting the walls and ceiling of a commercial space to be used as a co-operative bookstore downtown. That one, however, was a volunteer project. There, she finally met other Billings residents, all of whom welcomed her and treated her as if she'd been living there for years rather than days. When they found out she was new to Billings, they almost always replied by asking her how she liked Montana so far. Or rather, they asked things like, "Don't you love it here?" "Isn't it the best place on earth?" She politely nodded and said, "Yes, it's lovely," but she never did have a good poker face. And even though Harvey introduced her to everyone as his new assistant, Skye couldn't help but wonder if all those people thought he and Skye were a couple. And if so, did she like that? Or maybe they would judge Harvey for his poor taste. She further wondered what kind of boyfriend Harvey was. Did he open doors for the women he dated? Was he comfortable with public displays of affection? Was he a dinner-and-a-movie kind of guy, or a long-walks-on-the-beach kind of guy? (Not that there were any beaches in landlocked Montana.) Was he a good kisser? Was he good in bed? How had he wooed his wife? What had made him attractive to her? And what had made it so easy for her to leave him for Vance?

And what about Vance? What if one of these people knew him? What if they happened to mention her to him (not that she was significant enough to remember, except to say, *Hey, I met this weird woman who looked like a watermelon in coveralls*—she'd broken down and bought them after seeing the toll painting was taking on her clothes). Was it a matter of time before *she* ran into him herself? What would she say if or when she did? What would he say to her? Would he look the other way, pretend he didn't know her, act as if they had never spent a glorious weekend together in Boston two months ago?

This was a stupid and futile line of thinking, she decided.

Don, the bookstore manager, asked her outright: "What brought you here?"

"Just wanted a change, I guess," she said, hoping her vague answer was sufficient without being standoffish.

"Well, I imagine that coming from Rhode Island, you got change and more."

Hell, yes. More heartbreak, more stress, more adversity. But less money.

She nodded and raised her eyebrows, as if to say, *I certainly did.*

"You're in good hands with Harvey, though," said Don, pointing to Harvey, who was helping one of the other volunteers paint around a tricky nook in the far corner. "That there is one of the most selfless men you'll ever meet in Billings. You're lucky to have found each other."

"Oh, we're not—I mean, we just work together. We met on the plane, and—" She decided not to babble out another word. Fortunately, Don needed to handle a shipment of books that had just come in, and she was spared any further self-explanation.

Skye mostly tried to be as efficient as possible with cleaning and removing the supplies, anticipating what Harvey needed done, taping off and cutting in, and so on. Don was right. So far, Harvey had been selfless, patient, generous, you name it. But the nicer Harvey was to her, the more she wanted to retreat. She knew this was an irrational reaction, but every gesture of friendship and kindness from Harvey reminded her how horrible Vance had been. How he'd lured her in with sweetness and praise and tenderness, only to yank it from under her feet. How he'd been so full of charm until the moment she set foot on Montana soil. How he'd gone from saying all the right things to not saying a word.

She tried so hard to reciprocate Harvey's generosity, but every return felt so lacking.

In addition to meeting new people, Skye was also introduced to downtown Billings during those two days as she and Harvey bought breakfast and midday coffees at the café around the corner; when the job was finished, they went to the pub down the street for drinks and appetizers. No one seemed to mind that they were both covered in paint splatters.

"Hey, sweetie," said the pretty server who greeted them. Harvey kissed her on the cheek and spoke to her as if she were his sister.

After they were seated, the server asked, "The usual for you?" He nodded.

After Skye placed her order, she asked him, "So do you know, like, everyone in this city?"

Just as he was about to answer, the pretty server returned with a drink for each of them, courtesy of a buddy at the bar.

"I guess that's my answer," she said.

"My success as a salesman relied on networking," said Harvey. "So I did. It's come in handy for painting as well. Plus, I like being part of a community. I like being civilly engaged. I go to town meetings, support small businesses, especially now that I own one. Not that I want to run for mayor or anything like that."

The more time she spent with Harvey, the more intrigued she was by him. She noticed that he extended his friendliness and good nature to everyone, not just her, which she liked. He was easy to talk to, even though they shared few interests. He loved talking about comics and superhero characters, many of whom she'd never heard, like Nightwing and Animal Man. But she liked how animated he was when he talked, like a little kid. She wished she had something for which she was just as passionate, other than HGTV shows.

For all her progress, she had her dumbass moments, like when she unwittingly stepped in a tray full of primer and ruined her ten-dollar Walmart sneakers, or when she accidentally dipped the honey-wheat-paint-soaked mixing stick into the can of snow-white paint, and thus turned it into what looked like a milkshake with caramel swirls. Moreover, she practically bought out the CVS supply of Advil due to all her aches and pains and pulled muscles from leaning, reaching, bending, and stretching. Harvey assured her that she was doing fine, that he pretty much started the same way, and that month after month he was getting jobs done faster, which satisfied the clients.

At the end of the week, Harvey took Skye to his condo to unload some new supplies they'd just purchased. They turned onto a side street and into an underground parking garage. Harvey parked in a numbered space, killed the ignition, and opened the back of the SUV to retrieve the stuff. Together they walked to an elevator, rode it up three floors, and emerged into a hallway with four side-by-side doors. He approached the first door in two steps, found the key and inserted it, and flicked on a light as they entered. They were immediately greeted by a golden retriever, who jumped up to meet Harvey in a hug, and then did the same to Skye as if he'd known her for years, practically knocking her, and the supplies she was carrying, to the floor.

Harvey laughed. "Hang on, buddy!" To Skye, he said, "You can just leave it all here by the door for now. I'll take care of it later."

"You sure?" she asked.

"Sure." They each placed their armload on the floor while the dog circled them panting, practically smiling. Harvey finally was able to give him attention, and talked to him in a voice she'd never heard from him before, one that oozed love and sweetness. "How you doing, good boy?" He nuzzled the dog and roughhoused him, and the dog delightfully responded.

"Don't worry, he's a mush," said Harvey. To the dog, he said, "Bucky Barnes, meet Skye Littleton. Skye, this is Bucky. Shake hands." The dog sat and lifted a paw. Skye smiled and took it.

"Bucky Barnes?" she asked, raising an eyebrow.

"Captain America's sidekick."

"I didn't know he had a sidekick."

"Every superhero needs a sidekick, don't you think?"

"I guess so," she replied.

With the supplies unloaded and Bucky the dog making up for lost time with Harvey, Skye turned her attention to her surroundings. She was met with an open-concept layout containing sparse furniture and decor, white walls (*A painter with white walls—is that similar to my never wanting to go to the mall on my day off?*), and a chef's kitchen with blue subway tiles and stainless-steel appliances and white cabinets. The place smelled like paint and paper. It was a nice apartment—twelve hundred square feet, Harvey said. High ceilings. Open concept. Lots of natural light. Comfortable, yet cold. Not in a temperature or even a temperament sort of way. Something felt *off*, just like in the authors' den.

She scanned the great room again. "Where's your comic-book collection?" she asked.

"In storage for now," he said. "I have an action-figure and card collection too. I was going to use the guest room, but I need that space for my kids. Not that they share the room. My daughter uses the guest room, and my son prefers the sofa bed if they're here together."

"How long have you lived here?"

"Since the divorce. I bought it shortly after I moved here, then sublet it the entire time I was married. I eventually want to get a bigger place, but I'm keeping my costs low for now while I get the business going."

"Seems nice," she said. "Hope I can find a rental just as good." With her mounting hotel and rental-car bills, she knew the sooner she could find an apartment, the better. But with one-bedroom apartments going for about seven hundred fifty dollars downtown and on the south side of Billings, she feared she wouldn't be making enough to sustain a lease. Which meant that she needed to find a second job. And what about things like health insurance? Top Drawer had just begun offering their managers benefits packages. She would have gotten a really sweet one had she taken the district manager position. Which made her reconsider calling the company and asking, if not for her old job back, then a position in the Rimrock Mall store (she'd checked; there was a Top Drawer there, although the place looked deserted when she passed the opening the day she went job hunting).

No.

Fresh start.

You can do this.

Harvey paused, as if deliberating whether to give voice to his thoughts.

"You could stay here, if you want."

Skye's neck practically snapped as she whipped her head around to look at him, completely taken off guard.

"What?"

"Why not?" he said. "You need a place to live. I have a guest room."

"For *your kids*," she pointed out, as if he'd forgotten.

"They're staying with their grandparents in Seattle for a few months," he said. *Why did he withhold that information until now?* All the time they'd been spending together, and he never even hinted that they weren't close by? *Were they attending school there? Did their grandparents homeschool them?* If he wasn't comfortable mentioning that they weren't even living in Billings, then how could she probe him about his kids' education?

"Harvey, I . . . *I can't.*"

"Why not? Is it a co-ed thing?"

"No, it's . . . I don't know, it's *weird.*"

He frowned and pressed her. "What's weird? We could ride to and from work together, which means you can give up your car rental and save some dough. And you can save more dough by paying half your share here instead of the full load."

He made a good point.

It had been almost twenty years since she lived with a roommate. Last time had been in college. She had enjoyed the camaraderie of her suitemates in her dorm, but hated sharing a bathroom and girls borrowing her things either without asking or without returning them. She hated coming to the door and finding a ribbon tied to the doorknob, which informed her that her roommate had snuck a boy in and they were, er . . . "studying" each other, leaving her to find someplace to keep herself occupied for the next hour. Most of all, she hated that *she* wasn't on the other side of that door with a boy.

Could she live with a roommate again? It was a viable option. But where would she find someone her age? She didn't want to live with just any random stranger. Sure, Harvey knew a lot of people, but would he know someone willing to take her in, if not as a roommate then as a boarder?

Could she really live with *Harvey?*

Harvey caught her staring at him, lost inside her head. He waved his hand in front of her face. "Hello . . . Earth to Skye . . ."

Skye snapped out of it and blinked several times. "Oh. Sorry. I was just . . . do you know anyone I could move in with or rent a room from? I've mooched off you enough already."

Harvey was taken aback by the question. "How have you mooched? You're working for me, and you're a good worker. As I said before, you'd be paying your share of rent and expenses."

"I just mean that you've done so much for me already. You've been so generous. Especially after I . . . well, I wasn't very nice to you in the beginning."

"You'd just been hurt badly by someone you'd trusted."

Had any friend ever been this good to her? Aside from Julie in eighth-grade gym class, had she ever become so friendly with someone so quickly? She had Julie over for a sleepover the first Friday after they met.

"I've never lived with a roommate of the opposite sex," she said.

Harvey laughed, which made Skye flush with foolishness. "It's not much different from living with someone of the same sex," he said. "Just no parading around naked or in underwear." When she didn't react, he said, "That's a joke, Skye. Although true. Look, this makes sense, don't you think? And I like your company."

He likes my company. She liked *his* company, she realized. And maybe that was what scared her more than anything else.

She anticipated one glitch. "What about Chip?"

"What about him?"

She pointed to Bucky Barnes, who was slurping from his water bowl.

"Bucky loves cats. He loves all animals. He's quite special." Harvey glanced at the dog lovingly, who looked up long enough to reciprocate before returning to his drink.

"Yes, but Chip doesn't know that."

"He will, I promise. It'll be fine, Skye."

She stood and peered at him, looking for something to indicate that maybe he had doubts, or some ulterior motive. "You're really OK with it?" she asked.

"I'm OK with it," said Harvey. "You can move in tomorrow, if you want. We don't have any jobs."

Something about *we* stirred in her, but she pushed it aside and breathed a sigh of relief. "Thank you. I mean it. I can't thank you enough, Harvey. You're like a saint."

"Saint Harvey," he said, as if trying out the name. "Patron saint of goofballs."

"You are *not* a goofball," she said. "You're a prince."

"Who said *I* was the goofball?" He winked. She rolled her eyes in mock offense.

Harvey smiled and extended his hand. "It's a deal, then."

Skye shook it—was it the first time they were touching each other, or the first time she'd taken notice? His skin was rough and dry, but warm. His fingertips were calloused, but his grasp was firm. And then, as if seeing it for the first time, she took notice of his smile. His teeth were straight, but off white. His lips were almost as dry as his hands, but full. Not Steven Tyler or Mick Jagger full, but not thin to the point of barely being there. Her eyes then traced the contours of his face, starting with his squared-off chin, and moving up around his highly defined cheekbones, along his graying sideburns, to the wrinkles in his forehead and the slightly receding hairline. It wasn't as pronounced as she originally thought. His hair was neither too fine nor too coarse. Neither too long nor too short. Styleless, and in need of a good conditioning, but inviting.

No.

No, no, no.

Don't go there, Skye.

She admonished herself. Hard. *All he is doing is being nice to you. He is not asking you to marry him, he doesn't have any interest in you beyond that of an employee, and you are never, ever, going to get hurt again. You are nothing to him. He is nothing to you but a landlord and a boss. Don't look at him. Don't think about him. Don't even talk to him unless you need something from him. Just mind your own business and get the hell out of here as soon as possible.*

One year in Billings was a decent goal. But the sooner she was out of Harvey's condo, and his life, the better.

A thought struck her: *I'm moving in with Mr. Wright.*

Ha, ha, ha, an inner voice sarcastically retorted. *You wish.* Which, of course, was always her downfall.

Wishes were a sham.

CHAPTER
THIRTEEN

Skye didn't have much to move in to Harvey's condo—just the belongings that came with her on the plane and Chip's belongings. Her other cartons that had arrived—books, CDs and DVDs, photos, keepsakes, winter clothes, and small pieces of furniture that she didn't want to part with—remained in storage. She took stock of the room she slept in: Bare white walls. Cement floors with a faded and frayed area rug framing the full-sized bed. A pink children's chest of drawers and end tables with white trim. The closet had previously contained paint supplies of all kinds stacked in plastic bins, and hanging sets of paint-splattered coveralls, but she and Harvey moved them to the storage area of the condo building's basement. She stuffed her clothes into both the dresser and the closet and put her toiletries and other essentials in the bathroom on a shelf Harvey cleared for her.

When she let Chip out of his carrier and Bucky Barnes made a beeline for him, every hair of the cat's coat stood at attention; he raised his back and hissed in self-defense.

The dog licked him.

Chip looked downright confused. As if he were thinking, *Seriously?*

Skye was ready to scoop Chip into her arms lest Bucky unintentionally frighten Chip or be too overbearing in his playfulness, but instead she stood still, amazed.

Chip scooted away and began scoping out the place, sniffing every corner and crevice, while Bucky followed in an *I'm-here-if-you-have-any-questions* manner.

Harvey grinned proudly. "What did I tell you?"

Skye took it as a good omen.

Not only had Skye never had a male roommate, but she had never thought she would live with a man who wasn't her lover or husband. Especially one she hadn't known for more than a couple of weeks after moving to a new state and city and not knowing a soul. They were going to have to learn things about each other, like who took longer to get ready in the morning, or if one was doing laundry, did that mean they had to combine it with the other's laundry, or how loud to make the TV. Were they going to fight over which shows to watch? Was he going to object to the way she loaded the dishwasher? Was he going to leave the toilet seat up? What if his kids came back and wanted to stay over or move in?

Just how much of her presence should she assert? Could she buy a Yankee Candle?

That night, Harvey made a simple spaghetti and meatball dinner. Conversation consisted of little more than his informing her about the condo's quirks (the living room windows stick; the dryer squeaks when you run it on high; not all pots and pans go in the dishwasher). The meal could hardly be construed as datelike, but she couldn't escape the intimacy of it. Not in a candlelight-and-soft-music kind of way—neither of those were present—but in the exclusivity. Just her and Harvey, with Bucky lingering nearby in hopes that one of them might be clumsy enough to lose a spaghetti strand or drop a piece of meatball.

Skye set and cleared the table as well as did the dishes while Harvey turned on the TV and channel surfed. When she finished wiping down the table and countertops, Skye thanked Harvey for cooking, and he thanked her for cleaning. Exhausted from the day's moving and unpacking and getting settled, she excused herself and retreated to the guest room. Chip followed her. Bucky did as well until Harvey called him back.

"You can watch TV if you want," he said as she left. "I mean, you don't have to leave on my account. We can find something we both like."

"I appreciate that," she said. "I'm just tired. Going to hit the hay early."

"Sleep well," he said.

Of course, once she was alone in the room with Chip, she wanted to rejoin Harvey. Because when she was alone, she had to once again think about how ridiculously awry the plan had gone. How she went from loving Vance to living in a condo with a guy she'd met on a plane. It was a bad *Twilight Zone* episode. No point. No moral. Just . . . insane.

She stayed where she was, though. She'd invaded enough of his space already.

◆ ◆ ◆

The following morning, the sunlight streamed into the bedroom and onto her face, forcing her to sit up. Chip had slept with her again. Once again, it took her a second to situate herself and her new surroundings. *Oh right. Harvey's condo.* She lived here now. Temporarily.

When she opened the bedroom door, Chip sauntered outside, and Bucky greeted him again with more kisses. At best, Chip tolerated the affection, which made Skye laugh.

Harvey sat at the dining nook, thumbing through a catalog full of sports memorabilia and superhero posters and autographed graphic novels and Pokémon trading cards. He really didn't look like the comic-book-boy type. Getting a glimpse of him in the natural light, she thought he looked like more a banker or a corporate guy. He wore jeans and a T-shirt, but they were both high-end brands. His hair was slicked back like the character from that classic *Wall Street* movie. Just wet following a shower.

She'd been resisting what had become increasingly obvious to her. He was handsome. And he looked . . . at home. What's more, and what simultaneously comforted and scared her, was that she felt as if she were in the right place as well.

He looked up when Skye entered, and smiled widely. And then she realized she was wearing purple cotton pajamas with cartoon sheep in sleeping caps all over them. And her hair was sticking in different directions.

"Morning, roomie," he said. Bucky Barnes greeted her just as warmly, approaching her for some pats on the head.

"Good morning," she replied, self-consciously smoothing out her hair.

"Sleep OK?"

Did he not see what she was wearing? Was he just being polite? Maybe he slept in Captain America pajamas.

She nodded, uncertain of where to go or what to do or say next, until Chip blocked her path, howling.

"Someone wants breakfast," said Skye to Chip. The mere utterance of the word *breakfast* made Skye ravenous.

"What about you?" he asked. "Hungry?"

"Starving," she said.

"Bacon and eggs?"

Her stomach growled. "That would be great."

"Buttered toast?"

"Please."

"Coffee?"

"By the gallon."

He smiled and went to the refrigerator, where he extracted the ingredients. The kitchen was big enough for two, but cozy, and she felt something not unlike pinpricks on her skin due to invading Harvey's personal space. While she fed Chip, Harvey opened one of the upper cabinet doors and extracted a tall mug a with a Wonder Woman logo and placed it on the counter. "I'm more a Marvel guy than a DC Comics guy, but they were a gift, and I figured you'd like this one."

Skye never knew how to respond to such statements.

Next, he placed a K-Cup into the Keurig machine—vanilla hazelnut, he informed her—and placed two bottles of flavored creamer and a handful of assorted sugar and artificial sweetener packets on the table, inviting her to sit, which she accepted. Within minutes, he set the mug in front of her. She first inhaled, then ingested, and could already feel the kick.

The smell of bacon was as pleasurably intoxicating as the coffee. Hard to think of anything pleasurable when your life has gone to shit, but she would take whatever scrap she could. Five minutes later, Harvey brought the plate to her.

"Geez, Harvey. A girl could get used to this really fast."

Again he grinned. "I like to cook."

"Well, as you can tell, I like to eat."

His forehead wrinkled.

"What?" she said.

"You shouldn't say such things about yourself."

She flashed back to the weekend in Boston with Vance. They'd just finished breakfast, and she'd remarked how full she was.

I love a woman who's not afraid to eat, he'd said. She'd been hurt by the statement, and he had assured her that he'd meant it as a compliment, but she'd never been convinced. For the remainder of the weekend, every time they had been intimate, he'd made mention of her luscious curves, her voluptuous breasts (and if one more person substituted *big* with *voluptuous*, she was going to give them thirty lashes with an F-cup underwire bra), her fleshy arms as a way to flatter her, but she felt the exact opposite, like he was making backhanded compliments. She chalked it up to her skewed body-consciousness, because Vance was so tender in his touch. He never once shied away from her nakedness, never once recoiled in revulsion. Quite the contrary.

Skye noticed Harvey's lack of place setting on his side of the table. "You're not having anything?" she asked.

"I've been up since seven," he said. "I already ate."

Skye frowned.

"What?" he asked.

"I feel funny with you watching me eat," she said.

Harvey went back to the pantry, pulled out a package of Oreos, and brought a handful to the table along with a quart of milk from the fridge. He quickly popped one in his mouth before pouring a glass of milk for himself. "How's this?"

"Thank you," she said, feeling awkward that he'd made the concession for her, and ashamed of herself. "I'm sorry. That was rude of me."

"No worries," he said. "Oreos are the perfect midmorning snack."

She managed to smile and took a bite of the perfectly scrambled eggs, followed by a piece of applewood-smoked bacon, followed by buttered toast on artisan whole-grain bread. *Heavenly.*

She'd always wanted a man who could cook. Found it downright sexy. Although a man in Montana with superhero mugs and costumes wasn't what she'd had in mind. Then again, so far her expectations of mornings in Montana had defied her in every way.

"Good?" he asked before dunking a second Oreo and popping it whole.

She nodded, still chewing. "You make this bread yourself?"

He shook his head. "Haven't attempted that one yet. But I will soon. Eventually, I'd like to start a garden somewhere too. Grow and make as much of my own food as possible."

He didn't look the earthy-crunchy type any more than he looked the comic-book-boy type.

Skye practically inhaled the rest of her breakfast. She pointed to the catalog. "See anything good?"

"Yes," he said.

"You know, you're so into this stuff. I'm surprised you're not a dealer or something."

"I've considered it, although I fear that would take the fun out of it for me. There was a time I wanted to open my own comic-book store."

Skye widened her eyes. "Why didn't you?"

He shrugged. "I started working for Birch-McHale pharmaceuticals as a way to raise the capital. Next thing you know, I'm ten years in, married with two kids, and my wife thinks comic-book stores are for losers."

Skye felt a tug on her heart. He'd let his dream go. She knew something about that. She knew something about complacency setting in, and giving in to other people's judgments, struck down by their discouragement.

She had no right, Skye wanted to tell him. But she wasn't sure if she was talking about his ex-wife or Summer or even her parents.

"So why did you go into painting instead after you quit your job?"

He shrugged again. "This city needs a painter more than they need a comic-book store."

She didn't believe him, but she didn't press him further. He must not have wanted to pursue the conversation either, because he changed the subject. "So the guest room was OK?"

"It was great," she said as she took another sip of coffee. "Thanks."

Harvey peered at her. "You sure?"

She deliberated on answering truthfully, but decided to go for it. "I want to say something, but I'm afraid it's going to come out like I'm ungrateful or stuck-up."

"OK," Harvey replied tentatively. "Shoot."

"That bedroom wants to be yellow."

He stared at her blankly. "Excuse me?"

"The guest room. Where I'm sleeping. The walls. Painted yellow."

He scratched his head and aimed his eyes in the direction of the room, as if he had X-ray vision. *"Yellow?"* he asked. "Seems awful bright for a bedroom. And I think my daughter is at the age where she doesn't want anything too childish. She's even outgrown the pink dresser."

"I don't mean to criticize your home or decor," said Skye. "It just . . . I don't know, the room just wants to be yellow."

"The room wants it? Not you?" he asked her in a slight mocking tone. She couldn't tell if he was being sarcastic or good-natured.

"I know that sounds stupid, but yes."

"Well, OK," said Harvey. "Next time we make a supply run, we'll pick up some yellow samples and test them out. Then you can paint it."

"OK," she replied. Although she didn't need any samples. If she closed her eyes, she could see the shade. In fact, she'd remembered it the last time they went through swatches at the paint supply store: *lemon zest.*

"Anything else?"

"That's all," she said, and then smiled. "I think I'm going to like living here." As she looked around the open room for Chip, she found him—on Bucky Barnes's bed. With Bucky. Purring contently.

A very, very good omen.

There were no painting jobs for three days. Skye continued to pore through employment websites like Monster.com and Craigslist, looking for additional work, although she wasn't sure what she wanted or was qualified for other than retail. She thought about what Harvey had said about taking a high-paying job in pharmaceuticals to pay for his comic-book store, and then giving up on the store altogether. If she got a job unrelated to her interests to finance what she eventually wanted to do—something having to do with the home—then would she fall into the same trap? Wasn't that, in a way, what had happened with Top Drawer? Hadn't she had enough deferred dreams?

Nevertheless, she kept hitting dead end after dead end. She fiercely envied people who found work that not only matched their talents, but also their joy. Harvey said he never dreaded getting up in the morning and loved his work, even though he wished there was more of it. The upside, he said, was that he could pursue other interests on his days off, like cooking or his comic-book and card and action-figure collecting. He was even putting together a sort of collector's guide that was meant to be humorous as well as informative, to publish and sell at the conventions.

"Do you ever miss your former sales job?" she asked him.

"Never." He paused as if he read her mind. "You think I'm crazy," he said.

"Not *crazy*, just . . . I can't see myself giving up a job like that if it brought so much security."

"You wouldn't be the only one. I think my therapist is the only one who agreed that I did the right thing."

Skye raised her eyebrows. "You see a therapist?"

"Not anymore," he said. "Only when I feel I need it now. Used to go weekly. Just counseling. Not a psychiatrist with meds and all that."

Skye was struck that he had been to therapy and that he trusted her enough to disclose such a thing. "Why did you go in the first place?"

she asked, but quickly followed with, "I'm sorry, that's none of my business."

"No, it's OK," said Harvey. "Counseling is nothing to hide or be ashamed of. My world fell apart when my wife left me. It was already on the skids with me quitting my job, but the crash was especially brutal."

Skye again thought about Vance giving Harvey advance notice of stealing his wife, and then following through. How could one be so callous, so calculated in hurting another human being? And why didn't Harvey take him seriously if he knew Vance was the scorpion he'd shown himself to be time and again?

"I'm sorry," she said.

"For what?"

"That you had to go through that."

The color of his irises darkened, as if a cloud had covered them. He stared at the catalog in front of him, seeing nothing. Her hand moved, caught in a magnetic pull, wanting to reach over and take his hand, but she resisted by sitting on it. He was vulnerable. It suddenly occurred to her that she had never seen Vance vulnerable. That was probably something he made no room for in his life. Rather, he derived his power from exploiting other people's vulnerability.

"It's OK," said Harvey, his voice wistful. "I learned a lot. About myself, my marriage . . . it was in trouble before fuckface came along. I just didn't see it at the time. Or rather, I didn't want to."

She could say the same about her life. She'd been lost, floundering, perhaps even heartbroken before Vance took his coldness to it like a sledgehammer. She'd ghosted herself long before he did.

What, specifically, had made Harvey's marriage so miserable? Had the marriage been unfulfilled, or had he? Had he regretted being a dad? Had he regretted quashing his plan to open the comic-book store? What had made it so easy for Deborah to leave him for Vance? For anyone? What role had Harvey played in her leaving, other than complacency?

"If you could go back in time and change one thing about your marriage, what would you change?" she asked.

Harvey stared into nothingness, his mind transporting himself back in time, perhaps to one crucial moment.

"I wouldn't have played right into fuckface's script. And I would have paid more attention."

"To what?"

"To everything."

How would she have answered her own question, or some form of it—what moment of her life would she go back and change if she could? What was the exact pivot point where if she'd just made a different choice—a left turn instead of a right, Door Number Two instead of Door Number One—her life would have become something bigger and better, more meaningful?

Skye let her eyes linger on Harvey. Visually traced the contours of his face and along his shoulders. The more she got to know Harvey, the more she wanted to know.

"So how did you meet?" asked Skye. "I remember you saying it was a blind date, but who set you up? What made you go out with her a second time?"

"Slow down, slow down," Harvey said with a laugh. "One at a time. OK, so yes, we met on a blind date. One of my coworkers knew Deb and thought we would hit it off. We had similar tastes in music and movies and—"

"Comic books?" interrupted Skye.

"No, she hates all that stuff."

Of course. She was the one who'd put down his store. Skye felt stupid for having said it. She also didn't want to tell him that she didn't understand most of that world either. But not getting it was different from hating it, right? She would never have discouraged him from opening his store. Would have supported him one hundred percent.

"Anyway," continued Harvey, "we met for coffee at Rock Creek Café and did indeed hit it off."

"What did you like about her?" It was as if she was trying to home in on some secret, like figuring out his type.

"She was witty. Smart. Attractive. Cared about her work."

"What does she do?"

He gave her a look, as if bewildered by her curiosity, especially regarding his love life or some faction of it. "She's an insurance agent."

Skye tried to imagine Harvey and Deb meeting, falling in love, what she looked like, what made her attractive to him, and vice versa. She wondered why it had always been so hard for her to meet someone as nice as he was. Why weren't any of the men on dating sites as good as what they advertised? Or had her expectations been too high? Again she thought about Vance. She remembered describing him to Julie as "too good to be true." Maybe that should have been the first and only red flag.

She pressed on with her questions. "What made you go on a second date?" she asked.

"The fact that I wanted to keep talking to her even after the first one was over." His eyes lit and the lilt in his voice returned. "We both lost track of time, we talked so much. That's always a good sign."

Had it been that way with Vance? Had two hours ever passed like two minutes with him? She suddenly couldn't remember. But oh, how she ached for it to happen for her now. She was desperate to keep going, a marathon runner coaxing every muscle to go another mile. Not just to continue the conversation, but to add more pieces, each one seemingly closer to the full picture of not only Harvey's life, but also her own.

"At what point did you know you wanted to marry her?"

He shifted in his seat, and his expression went dark yet again, if not out of a reluctance to relive the past, then from an awkwardness about discussing something so intimate with someone who was a colleague and a roommate, not to mention a woman who was fucked over by the same man who had fucked him over. She was pushing too hard. She should have dropped the conversation. Apologized for being so intrusive. And yet, he still answered, if not out of willingness, then politeness. "Somewhere around the fourth or fifth date, I think. We just kind of looked at each other and smiled and knew what we were thinking. So we married shortly after that, and a year later Deb was pregnant with Scott." His smile was soft, but sad. The impact of those last words practically knocked her over. As if she'd learned for the first time: He was *a father*. One who loved his son despite his son not reciprocating.

She tried to imagine Harvey deeply in love. Tried to imagine him on his wedding day, clad in a tuxedo and hair slicked back and nails manicured. Was curious to know what Deb looked like, what kind of gown she wore, and how her hair was styled.

"Wow," said Skye. "Talk about a whirlwind romance."

"Indeed," said Harvey. His posture had become stiff and foreboding. But in the same way she had pushed the conversation, so did he. "We were both young. I don't mean in age. I mean in life. We didn't have time to grow together. I was career-driven and she was restless. Those two things weren't compatible, and we kept sweeping it under the rug, thinking it would sort itself out. It never did."

Bucky came over and nudged himself under Harvey's hand, and Harvey took him into a half-hug. Skye found herself jealous of the dog for rushing to comfort him before she did, for so instinctively knowing that he needed it.

"I'm sorry," she said. He didn't answer her, now fully engaged with his dog, showering him with love and praise and affection. Meanwhile, Skye sat there, on the periphery, so utterly disappointed. Why did couples begin so happy together and end up so miserable? How had Skye been so convinced that Vance was *the one*?

Because she hadn't dreamed of a marriage. She'd dreamed of a wedding. When she was a teenager, she bought bridal magazines and dog-eared pages of her favorite gowns; in her twenties, she mentally assembled her bridal party—Julie as maid of honor, Sabrina and Summer as bridesmaids, and her niece, Kayla, as flower girl. In her thirties, she and Julie had joked that Chip could be the ring bearer, the wedding bands attached to his collar, although they'd have to lure him up the aisle with a can of tuna.

She'd fantasized about photographs in Newport, perhaps even getting married on the lawn of one of the historic mansions, if such things were permitted, with the sun shining and the sky bright blue and her gown a perfect size six, because of course she would lose weight for that—what better motivator?

Of course, this entire fantasy had always taken place in Rhode Island, despite her being desperate to leave it. And then, a honeymoon someplace exotic, like a beach on the Caribbean, followed by happily ever after.

That bubble had burst long ago, however, when, based on what she'd observed of her married friends and family, it seemed that everything *except* happy came after the wedding. For a long time, she didn't understand. Every time one of her married friends or her sister said marriage is work, she silently insisted that they'd married the wrong man. How could life with your soul mate be *work*?

Love wasn't in the gown or the rings. Love wasn't in the flowers or the hearts. Love wasn't even in the first or second dates.

If only she'd known where it actually was, then perhaps it wouldn't have eluded her.

When his bromance session with Bucky was finished, Harvey turned his attention back to Skye. "Anything else you want to know?" He asked the question with impatience, even a tinge of annoyance.

She shook her head. "I'm going to get back to the job sites," she said, excused herself, and shut herself away in her room.

CHAPTER
FOURTEEN

Another two weeks passed, and Skye's painting skills were increasingly improving. She wasn't hurting as much by the end of a job, she was quicker and more efficient, and she liked seeing hard-core results instead of sales numbers at the end of the day that either praised or punished her. She was also beginning to understand the calming effect painting had on Harvey. If she got into a groove with the roller or the brush, her mind could easily take a break from worrying about paying credit card bills and saving enough to move back to Rhode Island and recovering from a lacerated heart, and she could let herself glide right along.

She liked the groove she and Harvey were in too. They had settled into a roommate dynamic in which she took over almost all the cleaning chores and he kept the cooking chores, and they carpooled to and from a job together. She was grateful to give up the expenses of the rental car and hotel, and she split living expenses fifty-fifty with Harvey right down to gas. She liked their banter while they painted—she doubted whether either of them could recall any conversation at the end of the day, but it was light and easy and passed the time. After dinner, she and Harvey usually retreated to their own spaces, where she'd keep looking for jobs and lurking on social media and resisting the urge to Google-stalk Vance.

She also finally called Summer, knowing the longer she put it off, the harder it would be.

"Hey, stranger," said her sister. "How's life in Big Sky Country?"

She instantly flashed to Vance saying, *I want to explore Big Skye Country too . . .*

"Not bad," she replied. "Weather's nice. Cool scenery. The sunsets are incredible."

"How's everything working out with you and Vance?"

Her muscles seized on her, and she sucked in a breath. "That, it turns out, is not so good."

"How so?"

"Let's just say it's not going to work out and keep it at that. And I'd rather you not tell anyone about it either."

"Well, that was predictable," said Summer. "We all thought it was a little weird that you ran off with this guy after knowing him for a weekend."

Skye's ears smoldered and her fists clenched. "Who is *we*?" she asked, hoping Summer heard the tension.

"Mom, Dad, Brent . . . we tried to tell you, but you wouldn't listen. You never do."

"Hey, Summer?"

"Yes?"

"Get bent," said Skye, and she ended the call and tossed the phone on the bed.

◆ ◆ ◆

Skye finally painted the guest room because she couldn't stand sleeping another night with those *blah* white walls, and because she wanted to do something nice for Harvey and the home he'd so generously opened to her. She also wanted to test herself, see how well and fast she could work on her own. Took her less than three hours, including three five-minute breaks. Skye stood in the doorway when she finished, taking in the results and smiling in satisfaction. The hue looked radiant. Invigorating. Inviting. She had chosen well. Had she additional money to spend, she'd select a bedding set of royal blue or plum to replace the pastel green that was already there. She wasn't sure about curtains, however. Maybe a deep red? The pink dresser was going to have to go as well. Maybe the following weekend she could repaint it herself with Harvey's permission, and maybe even his daughter's too. Maybe it could be something the three of them could undertake when his kids returned from Seattle. Or was that too much of a family project? The last thing Skye wanted to do was further insert herself in Harvey's personal life. Despite no change in their demeanor or interaction since the intense conversation she'd initiated regarding his marriage, he'd since clammed up when it came to any mention of his kids. Not that he didn't talk about them at all; but when Skye asked a follow-up question, he'd answer curtly and either change the subject or stop talking altogether. She knew it wasn't because he didn't love them—the anguish on his face from missing them was obvious, as was the pride in his voice when he spoke of them. She figured he simply didn't want to share his feelings with her. But she also worried that maybe she'd struck a nerve by being so nosy, although she didn't mean to be.

Harvey returned from the grocery store and inspected Skye's handiwork. "Looks good," he said. "You have so much more control now. No smudges."

Skye beamed. "What do you think of the color?"

He paused for a second survey. "I don't know how you'll sleep in here, it's so bright," he said, and her face dimmed with disappointment. "It's a great color—just not something I ever envisioned for a bedroom."

"Well, it's not always going to be a bedroom," she said.

"What do you mean?"

"You can turn this into your showroom. Display all your action figures and store your comic-book archives. Move in a sofa bed. A rich red one. Not candy apple. More like brick red."

Harvey looked at her, taken aback, as if he'd never thought of this idea himself. And maybe he hadn't. Maybe when you were a parent, you didn't put yourself and your desires first.

"You said your daughter is outgrowing the pink, yes?" asked Skye.

"Yes," said Harvey.

"And they're getting older, right? I mean, they'll be going to college soon, and they don't seem to spend that much time here anyway."

Harvey became crestfallen. "Yeah."

She hadn't meant to stir up any sadness, and attempted to compensate for it. "Well, this will be a nice room for your kids to come to. All around them, they'll see things that make their dad happy. I think that's what this room wants to be."

He scowled as if she'd just said something offensive rather than encouraging. "And what about them?" he asked. "Kids need their own space. It's especially important when their parents are divorced."

She looked around the condo, in search of a solution that would benefit everyone, but saw no little nook to carve out, no wall to remove or put up, no compromise on furniture or art or fabrics that would honor Harvey's kids' needs, as well as his own.

"I don't know," she finally said. "Maybe you can just get a bigger place. Or ask them outright what kind of space they want here, if they even want it. Make them part of the process."

Again with the eye daggers. "Just make sure you clean everything up and didn't spill paint anywhere," he barked and left the room to put the groceries away.

Stung, she followed him into the kitchen. "Harvey," she started. He didn't answer her. "What was that all about?"

"Nothing," he said, stacking cans on the pantry shelves and opening and closing cabinet doors with additional force.

"I was just trying to—"

"I know what you were trying to do. So butt out."

She stood and stared at him for a moment while the pain of the emotional door-slam moved through her. "No, I don't think you do," she said, and returned to the painted room, collected brushes and rollers and trays, and took them to the bathtub, where she washed them according to Harvey's instructions and took extra care not to make a mess. She stored the paint cans on a shelf in the basement of the condo building, where they awaited proper disposal once a week. Next, she folded the drop cloth and put it away, refastened the light switch and electrical outlet plates, and removed the tape from the baseboards, window frames, and ceiling. She cracked the windows open to let fresh air in and allow the fumes to fade so she could sleep comfortably that night.

Harvey had helped her move the mattress and furniture pieces out of the room before she painted, and now she needed his help to move it all back in. She tried to do it herself, but the pieces were just too heavy. Harvey had taken Bucky Barnes to the park for some exercise and, she presumed, to get away from her. He returned just before dinnertime. She was sitting in the living room, watching *House Hunters* on HGTV, Chip perched on the armrest of the couch and letting his legs hang over the edge. She hated how picky the couples were and had read that the show was completely staged—the houses featured on the show weren't actually for sale, and the couple was "choosing" a house they'd already bought. But she loved seeing the rooms and envisioning how she would paint and decorate each one. She loved the potential of each.

"Hey," he said, as if nothing had happened.

"Hey," she replied, completely devoid of emotion. Bucky, who had never known anger a day in his life, it seemed, trotted to her, licked her hands, and stuck his head in her lap, and she smiled and pet his head and greeted him warmly, temporarily forgetting that she was hurt and had spent the last couple of hours stewing in it. She had never been a dog person, but it was impossible not to adore Bucky Barnes. He moved on to Chip, who jutted out his head, seemingly for a kiss, which Bucky granted. Talk about a bromance.

Bucky's unconditional love was contagious. She decided to extend an olive branch. "Need help prepping dinner?" she asked.

"Nah," he replied.

The spacious condo suddenly felt the size of a closet.

"What are you watching?" he asked.

"*House Hunters.*"

He sat on the chair to the right of the couch and watched as a woman complained about all the ceiling fans she would have to remove were she and her husband to buy this ranch-style home somewhere in New Mexico.

"I hate these couples," he said. Skye whipped her head in his direction, asking telepathically, *You watch this show?*

"I know," she said. "I'll bet half of them are divorced now."

"Or should be."

They both chuckled.

Bucky sat on the floor perfectly equidistant between the two of them and panted, almost smiling, as if to say, *Isn't it so much better when everyone gets along?*

When the show neared the end, Harvey predicted the couple were going to choose the ceiling-fan house. Skye, having already seen the episode, abstained from confirming or denying his guess.

They went with a split-level that was under budget and needed work in almost every room. When they showed the follow-up two months later, the couple bragged about how they removed the fireplace.

"Are you shitting me?" yelled Harvey. You'd think he'd just seen a bad referee call in a football game. "That fireplace was the best feature in the house." He then muttered, "Assholes," under his breath, which prompted Skye to laugh outright. He was delighted by her reaction.

They turned to each other, eyes locked, and Skye knew the moment was there.

"I'm sorry about before," he said, almost sounding childlike.

"It's OK," said Skye. "I'm sorry too."

"You didn't do anything wrong. I—I just miss my kids, I guess. It was Deb's idea to send them to Seattle. Said she needed uninterrupted time to 'grow' with fuckface."

How could anyone just ship off their kids like that? Skye wondered. Then again, she knew Vance had a way of persuading women to do things they never thought themselves capable of doing and making it seem like the most normal, logical decision in the world.

"You couldn't take them?" Skye asked, hoping she wasn't being too invasive.

"I begged to take them," he said. "She said they didn't want to stay with me. Scott pretty much confirmed it. Told me he hates both of us and fuckface."

"Even knowing how much you wanted them?"

"He blames me for letting this all happen. He's justified."

Before Skye could say another word or offer a gesture of comfort, Harvey rose from his seat and went to the kitchen to start dinner. Pork tenderloin rubbed with fresh herbs, roasted asparagus, and cranberry-apple sauce.

If this was his contrition, then he was forgiven ten times over.

Harvey helped Skye move the furniture back into the bedroom. However, she asked him to return the bed to a new position, one where the headboard would be opposite the doorway as opposed to next to it. Harvey obliged, and together they set it up. Afterward, she placed the computer desk against the window, and they moved the chest of drawers against the wall at the foot of the bed. *Yes,* she thought. *Yes, this*

feels better. Harvey appraised the new layout and nodded in approval. His gaze lingered, however, and Skye was certain he was visualizing the memorabilia room she had proposed. Seeing what would go where. Watching people sit on the couch, talking Spider-Man or whatever comic-book collectors talked about.

He quietly left the room, and she didn't follow him this time. She thought he might be missing his kids again, missing tucking them into their beds in his former house, now Deb's. Or had Deb moved in with Vance? Given that he was at his house when she showed up that first full day in Billings, he obviously hadn't gone anywhere.

So what did become of the Wright family house? What would become of it? Was that maybe also on Harvey's mind? Did he miss it? Did he miss his old life?

Which got her thinking about Warwick, Rhode Island. What would she be doing were she there right now? Not in her old life at Top Drawer, but in the present moment?

She wouldn't take it for granted, that's for sure. She would savor every sip of coffee milk and try more restaurants in Providence and attend WaterFire nights with her friends. Maybe she would take a day trip out to Cape Cod or up to New Hampshire in the fall, and carve pumpkins and make cider donuts. Maybe she would live not in Warwick but rather in a town like Newport or Narragansett, closer to the water. Maybe she could afford a studio apartment or post an ad for a roommate. Maybe she could get a job at the paint department at a Home Depot or a Sherwin-Williams store. In a year's time, she'd have enough experience.

Will I ever miss Billings? she wondered.

No. Never. Sure, she was making a life here to prove that she could, but three weeks in, she still felt no attachment, no sense of pride or connection other than the jobs she completed with Harvey. She could paint in any town or city she wanted. It didn't mean she was home. She couldn't foresee a time when she wouldn't be on guard against Vance appearing at a café or bookstore, as if he may jump out from behind a door and scare the shit out of her as he clutched her throat and rammed his fist into her chest, ripping out her heart and tossing it into a trash can. No matter how successful she was here, the facts were still the same: She willingly overturned her entire life to be with a man who dumped her before her plane touched ground. Billings would always remind her of that.

Then again, what little of Montana she had seen had lived up to its nickname. She had yet to see a Billings skyscape that wasn't postcard-perfect, a newly painted mural every hour. Even from the guest room window of the condo, she could see past the streetlights and the downtown buildings to a horizon that stretched as far back as the edge of the world.

She would miss Harvey, though. A shiver shot up her spine, more like a striking match, actually, upon that realization.

She would miss Harvey more than she missed what she thought she'd wanted with Vance.

◆　◆　◆

Despite Harvey's concern that the room would be too bright, and the lingering new-paint smell, Skye had no trouble sleeping that night. In fact, it was one of the best night's sleep she'd had since coming to Billings. Moving the bed and the furniture around had to be the difference. Or maybe it was the color.

Something else had changed. She woke up feeling as bright and sunny as the walls. Energized, even. It wasn't just the room that felt different. *She* did. The world did. As if a seismic shift had taken place.

Could it really be all because of the lemon zest–colored walls and a new positioning for the bed? She took an invigorating shower, and when she emerged, she found a voice mail on her phone.

A request for a job interview.

CHAPTER

FIFTEEN

The voice message was from a furniture company on the west end of town called Devlin's. Skye had filled out an online application the previous week and attached her résumé, figuring it was a long shot. They were looking for a part-time sales associate and asked Skye if she could come in for an interview the following afternoon. She and Harvey had a painting job that same day, but when she told Harvey about the call, he told her to take the interview.

"But what about you?" she asked.

"I'll manage," he said. "You need to do this. You'd be really good at that job. Plus, you'd make more money than you're making with me, and you could potentially move into full-time and maybe even a promotion. It's also commission, I think."

"If I miss working with you, then I lose a day's pay."

"You could lose more than a day's pay if you don't do this. Skye, you absolutely have to take this interview and do everything you can to get this gig."

"You're right," she said. "I'll call a cab."

"Why not take the FJ?"

"The FJ?"

"My car."

She knew what he meant. She was just shocked by the offer.

"Drop me off at the site, and either pick me up or I'll get a ride home," he said.

Never in her life had she known anyone as magnanimous as Harvey. She found it formidable sometimes—how did one live up to that example? She wanted so badly to reciprocate, but other than doing extra chores around the condo, she didn't know how.

"You sure? I don't even know if I can *drive* that thing."

"It's a piece of cake."

Famous last words.

"Well, thanks," she said. She then cocked her head to the side. "You're a pretty wonderful guy, you know that?"

He blushed and excused himself.

◆ ◆ ◆

That night, Skye prepared by compiling as much information about Devlin's Furniture as she could. They were a family-owned company, in business since 1950. They originated in Bozeman and had four other store locations in Billings, Helena (the capital of Montana), Missoula, and Sidney. And yet, they were still hailed as a small business; they manufactured their own brand and hired specialized craftspeople in their factory.

During halftime of an NBA basketball game (Skye had never been one for sports, but she was beginning to enjoy the ritual of watching the games with Harvey at night and learning the different teams and players and terms like *pick-and-roll*), Skye and Harvey sat at opposite ends of the couch, face-to-face, and conducted a mock interview. Given that this was the first interview she was attending since college, she was grateful for the rehearsal. She had conducted dozens of them in her own store as the person in charge. But to be sitting on the other side of the desk was akin to taking an exam. She was a good student, but a lousy test-taker. She hoped and prayed that the interviewer at Devlin's Furniture would be able to see this. In fact, she hoped she would have a chance to prove it, even though she knew next to nothing about furniture other than its function. She had tried to learn more, but there was too much information to absorb in too short a time. Perhaps having owned furniture would be a good start. She'd taken that approach at Top Drawer, in which she would boast her own firsthand experience when selling a bra, despite none of the store's bras fitting her. She had boobs. That was enough.

Harvey started by asking her some basic questions—describe a situation where you put your managerial skills to work; what is your sales philosophy; what are your favorite and least favorite things about working in retail—and moved to some silly ones: which is better, Coke or Pepsi; if you were stranded on a desert island, which four books would you take; what's the all-time best flavor of Ben & Jerry's.

She had the most fun answering those questions, and Harvey joined her:

They both agreed on Coke.

Skye's books were *Gone With the Wind*, *Pride and Prejudice* (she'd always wanted to read it and figured she'd have plenty of time to do so on a desert island), *Bridget Jones's Diary* (her favorite), and *How to Get Off a Desert Island*. Harvey laughed at the last one and said, "No shit."

Harvey's books were *Neverwhere*, *Hitchhiker's Guide to the Galaxy*, the first issue of Captain America ("Although, knowing me, I'd want to keep it in pristine condition and protect it from the elements, so I'd never read it," he said. "Either that or I'd need a used copy as long as my mint edition was safe"), and *Harry Potter and the Prisoner of Azkaban* ("Because that's the best of the series").

As far as Ben & Jerry's went, Skye confessed that she preferred the standard classic Chocolate Chip Cookie Dough, "Although I'm more of a frozen-custard fan," she said.

"It's positively wrong that you've been in Billings all this time and you haven't been to Big Dipper yet," said Harvey. "In fact . . ." He stood up. "Get your jacket. We're going right now."

"What about my interview prep?"

"We can prep over ice cream. Call it multitasking. C'mon."

She concealed the childlike excitement that bubbled just underneath the surface of her skin. "OK, but this is my treat," said Skye.

"Deal."

They exited the condo onto the side street and walked to the corner of Broadway and First Avenue North. (An ice cream shop within walking distance. This could be glorious.) The shop was partway filled with parents and children, twentysomethings behind the counter, and an older couple. Two of the tables lining the sidewalks on First Avenue were also occupied. Skye turned her attention to the menu that extended the width of the wall to the right of the Broadway entrance. So many flavors to choose from—salted caramel, huckleberry (again with the huckleberry!), mint chocolate chip, yellow cake . . . the server behind the counter invited her to sample anything she wanted. Skye first chose Nutella, followed by yellow cake (she could fill up on samples at this rate), and stopped at huckleberry—*divine*.

"One huckleberry waffle cone, please," she said.

Harvey went with a mint-chocolate-chip banana split.

There was a nip to the night air; thus, they sat at the table against the picture window and enjoyed their treats.

"You like?" said Harvey.

She nodded, letting a spoonful of ice cream melt on her tongue before swallowing. "I've never tasted anything like it. It's like a blueberry and a raspberry had a baby. No, not even raspberry. I can't put my finger on it. It's just . . . I never thought I'd like any kind of berry flavor for an ice cream. I'm more of your basic vanilla and load it up with brownie or cookie dough or caramel and whatnot."

"I hear ya."

She and Harvey locked into a gaze—he had long lashes, she noticed—and a grin escaped her.

"What," said Harvey, mirroring her grin.

"This is fun," said Skye. "I haven't done anything like this in a while. Not since—" *Not since Vance and I bought gelato at a tiny shop in the north end of Boston.* She had thought it was the next best thing to being in Italy. "It's just been a while, that's all."

"For me too," he said.

"You come here with your kids a lot?"

He broke the gaze and redirected it to the window, watching cars at the intersection. "Yeah, all the time," he said.

"I'm sorry, I shouldn't bring it up."

"It's OK," he said. He didn't sound convinced. Neither was she.

He looked down at his dwindling sundae. "We should head back." He stood up and waited for Skye as they left Big Dipper with their remaining treats and extra napkins in hand. Goose bumps covered her arms as she zipped her jacket. Harvey wore nothing over his long-sleeved T-shirt and jeans.

They walked the three blocks back to the condo in silence, and never resumed her practice interview.

The following morning, Skye awoke before her alarm did; she'd tossed and turned most of the night, anticipating what she would be asked and how she would answer, doing several mental wardrobe changes, and replaying last night's ice cream date with Harvey—not that it was an actual date; no hand holding or good-night kisses had taken place. But they were undoubtedly becoming closer. It was a closeness she'd never quite experienced before, not even with Vance. It was organic and spontaneous. It was also the first time she took notice of the boundary lines, and how important they were to navigate. If only he would open up to her about his kids. She needed to stop pushing him, stop bringing them up and making him sad. She needed to trust their friendship.

She turned her head toward the window and could tell even through the shades that the weather was gray, possibly even raining. Temperatures had been unseasonably warm this spring, according to Harvey, but the weather app on her smartphone promised today to be cold and dreary.

At the moment, Skye was neither nervous nor confident. She also didn't have much in the form of professional attire, other than the black slacks and jackets and camisoles she'd worn to Top Drawer day in and day out. She remembered thinking it was stupid to keep them, even though her favorite blazer was tailored for a plus-sized curvy figure as opposed to a straight-stitched, extra-large blazer that you'd find in a department store that called negative attention to her figure rather than flatter it. And her favorite slacks were boot-cut, cotton, low-rise, and also from a designer that knew how to make plus-sized women feel sexy in clothes. For the first time since arriving in Billings, she wore makeup and jewelry and styled her hair and stepped into the clunky Naturalizer pumps that enabled her to get through eight-hour shifts without crushing her toes or making her ankles swell. The condo didn't come equipped with a full-length mirror, so Skye emerged from the bathroom and approached Harvey, who was already sitting at the table with a coffee mug and another catalog in front of him. As if he were waiting for her.

"Does this look OK?" she asked.

Harvey did a double take. *A double take!* His eyes widened and brightened—no, *twinkled*—as he took in her presence. Not an up-and-down look or a homing-in-on-her-rack look or the undress-her-with-his-eyes look. That was the way Vance had looked at her, she now realized. She had tried to convince herself there was nothing wrong with a man looking at her that way as long as she wanted him to. And she did want to be looked at. But this—this was something she'd never seen in a man's eyes before. It wasn't just that Harvey was looking at Skye all dressed up. It was as if he were seeing her for the first time, and instantly liking what he saw. Not because of what she wore, but because she radiated something from inside herself.

"I think you've got this job in the bag," Harvey said in a breathy voice.

She broke out in goose bumps again, as if she'd just had another sampling of Big Dipper ice cream.

"Knock wood," she said. "I'm never getting my hopes up again. Ever."

"Hope is a good thing, Skye. The best. And no good thing ever dies."

Either he is the most romantic man on the planet, or I am still in Rhode Island, and this is some long, weird-ass dream that I am going to wake up from.

She couldn't even respond. Just stood there.

Harvey seemed to have missed the cause of her being struck dumb. "You don't know where that's from?" he asked.

"Where what's from?" she asked, still floating somewhere in the clouds.

"What I just said," said Harvey. "It's from *The Shawshank Redemption*, the best film ever."

Skye hadn't watched the movie in a long time, but she recalled the scene with Red in the field, reading Andy Dufresne's letter.

"Oh," she said. "Right."

Harvey looked like he wanted to say more, like he wanted to challenge her on the subject, either on films in general or just *The Shawshank Redemption*, but he gave up and returned to his coffee cup. Not knowing what else to do, Skye went to fetch her purse from the bedroom, when she stopped and said, "It's not the best movie ever, by the way."

Harvey swallowed his coffee. "No?"

"No."

"What is?" he asked, seeming to brace himself.

"*Titanic*," she replied.

Had he taken another drink of coffee, he would've done a spit-take. He squinched his face, as if having just smelled something foul, and vigorously shook his head.

"No," he said. "No, no, no. Not even close."

"It won the Oscar," she argued.

"Good CGI," he countered.

"You don't think Kate and Leo gave good performances?"

"They were fine. But not best-movie-ever good." He squinched and shook again. "Ugh. Seriously? *Titanic*?"

"It's such a good love story!" she argued.

"Oh please. What, because he *died* for her? Rescued her from an asshole and a life of entitlement? That is a love story, and *Shawshank* isn't? Please. Andy and Red are a true love story. Just because they weren't hot for one another or neither of them was stunningly pretty . . . who says love stories have to be kissing and passion and you-are-my-entire-world and my-heart-will-go-on? That's not real life, Skye. It's certainly not real love."

She felt the sliver of his admonishment cut into her. She felt stupid. Like a teenager stuck in the throes of puppy love. She breathed hard in order to stanch the tears from staining her face and ruining her makeup. For once, she was successful. But it was obvious that Harvey knew he'd gone too far. His eyes became full and round and dark, like Bucky's when Harvey scolded him for snatching a piece of chicken off the counter. His lips were pressed together, as if glued, albeit too late.

◆ ◆ ◆

Harvey drove Skye to his job site before they would switch places and she would take the FJ Cruiser to the job interview. They sat side by side, not even exchanging a peripheral glance, much less a syllable. When he arrived at the client's house, he turned to face her.

"Well, she's all yours," he said as he patted the dashboard. "Good luck on the interview." He tried hard to sound upbeat, but every word was a strain.

"Thank you," she said quietly. He opened the door. As he was about to step out, she put her hand on his arm. "Harvey . . . I need it to be real. I need to believe in love stories."

For the first time that morning, he looked into her eyes with tenderness and sincerity. "Why?" he asked just as tenderly.

Please don't cry, please don't cry, please don't cry . . .

"Because without them, I have nothing. As long as I have Rose and Jack, and Romeo and Juliet, and Ross and Rachel, then I have something to look at. Something to believe in. Something to crave and aspire to."

He leaned in slightly. She could smell his aftershave, something musky and manufactured, but it set her on fire. She remembered the movie *While You Were Sleeping*, when Lucy, who'd had a major crush on Peter, discovered that she had feelings for Peter's brother within weeks of meeting him. Vance and Harvey were as far apart from brothers as could be, but she was startled by the revelation, by how quickly it had happened.

Screw Titanic. While You Were Sleeping *is way better.*

"Forget those stories. Live your own," he said.

She was even more crushed now.

"Skye, do you know who you need to fall in love with?"

She practically inhaled his voice, he was so close. And not in a tactile, physical way—although she certainly wanted to extend her hand, put it to his lips, and feel the pucker against them—but in the molecules that danced between them and ricocheted like jumping beans throughout her body.

"Who?" she whispered, so desperate to know, her heart ached.

"Yourself," he said delicately, and stepped out of the car.

CHAPTER

SIXTEEN

The moment Skye buckled herself into the driver's seat of the FJ Cruiser, she knew it was a bad idea. First, she pulled the seat *all the way up* to the steering wheel. Heck, she could barely see over it. She'd never driven a semi, but she imagined it probably felt like this. Being this high up from the ground in a passenger's seat was no big deal. Being this high up in the driver's seat felt like she was about to careen off the edge of a cliff, only she had no idea where the cliff's edge was. She'd owned a 2004 Honda Civic in Rhode Island, and before that a 1992 Prelude. She liked Hondas. She liked their size and shape and dependability. Toyotas, of course, possessed all these same qualities, but favoring Hondas to Toyotas was like favoring the Giants to the Jets or the Dodgers to the Angels. You just chose your team and stuck with it.

The windshield of the FJ Cruiser was straight, not slanted, and had three, not two, windshield wipers, which kept distracting her, since she had to use them that morning. She couldn't even see the front hood. When she was a kid, she loved the school buses with flat faces as opposed to those with noses, as her first-grade self used to call them. When she rode her bicycle, she used to pretend she was driving a bus.

When she grew up, she'd wanted to own a bus, not a car. Just like the Partridge family on TV. That would be cool.

Putting the car in gear, she tentatively placed her foot on the gas pedal, and the FJ barely moved. When she sank her foot even further and with more force, it jerked forward, and she yelped. Harvey, not yet in the house, turned around and winced before shaking his head with a laugh. He must have been regretting letting Skye drive his car. She hoped it was well insured.

Using a GPS app on her phone, Skye nervously navigated through the Billings grid of numbered streets and named avenues, driving at least five miles under the speed limit, until she found the store and arrived mere minutes before her scheduled interview.

The moment she entered the massive showroom, three associates convening around a teak-hued sofa greeted her with more enthusiasm than she thought furniture-buying warranted, but she knew the drill: the perkier, the better. They were following the script, and they saw her in dollar signs rather than human ones. She understood and didn't judge.

Skye informed them of her purpose, and one of them fetched their boss, a man she guessed to be in his late twenties. He swaggered onto the showroom floor dressed in black slacks, a blue shirt, and a maroon tie with soccer balls all over it. He greeted her, shook her hand, and introduced himself as Patrick Brody, and led her through the showroom and into the back of the store, pointing out various sales along the way. She remembered her first tour through Top Drawer, full of anticipation and excitement, going behind the scenes, ready to embrace the experience. A month ago, she would have balked at the prospect of another retail job. But a month ago she had taken being gainfully employed for granted. Besides, furniture sales, coupled with painting, would not only supplement her income but also move her further along this new path she was traveling, though the destination was still uncertain.

"You new to Billings?" asked Patrick.

"Very," she replied. "How did you know?"

"You have an East Coast look about you. And I suspect when we get talking, I'll be able to further deduce where."

She smiled, uncertain of how to respond. What did East Coasters look like? Lobsters?

The two entered the office—cramped, windowless, a desktop computer hidden in a swamp of papers and Post-it notes on a mammoth metal desk. A cheap swivel chair. A photo of him with his wife and two boys, all of them dressed up. A file cabinet in one corner, a closet in the other. A rickety tray table with a dirty coffeepot against the wall. A whiteboard on the wall filled with names and numbers and a lopsided drawn calendar. In other words, a typical retail-store manager's office. She'd seen it many times. Hell, she'd called one her own for nearly fifteen years.

Patrick pulled a second chair around to the front of the desk and invited her to sit. He then offered her coffee from the break room, which she politely refused. Patrick sat and swiveled and brought up her résumé on the PC monitor.

"OK, so let's get started. I see you've had a long and lustrous career with Top Drawer." She nodded. "What's that like?" he asked.

She froze. There she was, back in college, exam booklet and pen in front of her, following the instructor's prompt of "Begin." *What was the question? What does he mean? Where am I? What am I doing? WHAT IS THIS???*

Breathe, she silently said. She took a deep breath and returned to herself.

"Working for Top Drawer?" she asked. He nodded. "It was good, I guess. Challenging at times. I managed a staff, I had a sales quota—no commissions, but they were still vigilant about you keeping up your POSes." She figured he already knew *P-O-S* stood for *point of sale*. "I had one of the top-grossing stores in the district, not counting Providence."

"Ahhh, Rhode Island—that's where you're from. I was going to say Massachusetts."

"It says so right there on my résumé."

Patrick twitched, straightened up, and sheepishly peered at the monitor, as if the detail had been in fine print. "Oh. Yeah. You're right. I see you got Manager of the Month several times in a row too. Good for you. So what made you leave?"

She went blank again, fervently wishing she had accepted that district manager position and told Vance Sandler that if he really loved her, he'd move to Warwick. Then she remembered that Harvey had asked this question during their rehearsal last night. "I was looking for a change," she began, but Patrick interrupted her.

"Billings, Montana, is quite a change from"—he paused and read the screen again—"Warwick, Rhode Island."

You're telling me.

"It is," she said.

"What made you move *here?*"

"Um . . ." There was no way she could tell young Patrick—who had short, soft chestnut hair parted to the side, blue eyes, and enviable straight white teeth; he was kind of cute, actually—what had brought her here, and what was keeping her here. "Like I said, I needed a change, and I, um, I heard about Billings from an online friend and decided to give it a try."

"Well, welcome," he said with a toothy smile. "We're glad you're here."

Everyone she'd met so far extended her a friendly and earnest welcome. When they did the bookstore job, one volunteer there, a woman, had even hugged her. Skye had lived in Rhode Island her entire life, except when she was in college. Then she spent four consecutive Septembers to Mays in neighboring New Hampshire. But she couldn't remember being welcomed there, except during orientation week. It's possible she hadn't paid attention enough to remember, or that she had been too young to care. But sitting in the dingy office, suddenly it did matter and she did care. She appreciated the welcome. Especially the "we're glad you're here." It made her feel special. Wanted. Appreciated. It made her feel a little bit less like the outsider she knew she was, what with her accent and her yen for open water and having never eaten elk meat.

"Thank you," she said. She liked Patrick, was curious to know how old he really was. She was a bad judge of age, always being off in the direction that was most unflattering.

"So what have you been doing since you arrived here?" he asked.

Feeling sorry for myself came to mind, and that answer both surprised and bothered her. "Job hunting, mostly," she said. "The, um . . . opportunity . . . I thought I was coming to when I moved here fell through unexpectedly, so I've been scrambling. Right now I'm working as a painter's assistant."

"Well, that must suck."

Skye took offense, but answered as politely as possible. "Not at all. In fact, it's been great. He's really come through for me." The gratitude she felt for Harvey at that moment crested over her like an ocean wave and submerged her, enough that her eyes became glassy with brimming tears. Had it not been for Harvey, where would she have ended up? What if he had minded his own business at the airport that first night, never given her his phone number, just completely left her to fend for herself? What if he'd never talked to her on the plane, or she had been seated next to someone who didn't give a damn and didn't want to get involved? That most certainly would have been *her* reaction were she in Harvey's seat, and she was filled with shame.

"I meant that it sucks that your original opportunity fell through," said Patrick.

"Oh," she said, and silently chided herself: *Idiot.* She continued. "Well, it's only part-time, though, and it's an entry-level position."

"This is an entry-level and part-time position too," he said. "I want to make that clear."

"Oh, I know that. It's fine. I just need something steadier. I'd be happy to work here and supplement with the painting. Or eventually switch to full-time. What I mean is, this job would be my priority."

Patrick smiled again. "Well, good." He caught her inspecting his tie and lifted the end to get a better look at it himself.

"I coach my son's team," he said.

"Oh," she said. *Again with "Oh"? What kind of a dumbass response was that?*

"You have kids?" he asked.

She shook her head. "I have a cat."

"Nice," he said in a don't-upset-the-crazy-cat-lady way. Should she mention Bucky Barnes too?

The interview continued, although it was more of a chat. He explained the job responsibilities and the pay rate and the commission (it was lower than she thought: three percent for the first six months as a probationary rate, five percent after six months, and the salary would increase after one year or if she was promoted to a supervisory level). He also explained the staff hierarchy and the inventory, and she offered comparisons to Top Drawer, demonstrating her own knowledge.

"So we'd like to see what you're like on the sales floor. I know we're kind of ambushing you here, but would you be OK helping out a customer or two?"

Why did managers always say we *instead of* I?

"Sure," she said, although she didn't see any when she'd entered the store, evidenced by the way the sales staff congregated around the sample living room, or when she and Patrick walked through the showroom to the office.

The two reentered the showroom, and they found the staff still huddled in the front, one of them sitting in a recliner. He immediately rose when he saw Patrick and Skye. Patrick introduced her to everyone—Barbara, John, and Gary—and told them she was new to Billings. "Welcome!" they all said, and again Skye felt appreciated.

She wanted this job. Badly.

They made similar small talk with her—where are you from; how do you like Billings; do you miss Rhode Island; have you been downtown—until a man and woman entered the store together ten or fifteen minutes later. They were all ready to pounce on the couple, but Patrick ordered them to hang back and let Skye take over.

Early in her career, Skye had attended a sales seminar in which the speaker shared their sales acronym, ACME:

Acknowledge the customer.

Converse with them.

Meet their needs.

End the sale.

It was so basic and brilliant that on her first day back at the store, she doubled her day's quota and exceeded them for the rest of the month—far more effective than the stock greeting of "May I help you" and then leaving customers alone when they retorted "Just looking," sometimes even before she made eye contact with them. She'd since passed on the information during employee trainings.

The couple had been acknowledged by the sales associates and, judging by their blasé response and immediately walking in the direction away from their path, they didn't want to be hassled. Skye allowed them their space but lingered behind. At one point she circumvented them by cutting through a bedroom display and meeting them on the other side. The woman pointed to a sofa and the man lifted the price tag. "No," he said, before she could speak another word.

"I see you're interested in couches," said Skye. She knew words made a difference. For example, she loathed the word *panties* and always tried to refer to them by style—*thong, bikini, boyshort. Sofa* sounded more sophisticated than *couch*, and based on what they were pointing to, they seemed to be favoring function over sophistication.

They both responded curtly.

"I think I practically lived on my couch in Rhode Island, it was so comfy," Skye said. Might as well use her foreigner status to her advantage.

It did the trick, because they both perked up.

"You new here?" asked the woman.

Skye smiled. "Yep. Happy to be here too." She hated salespeople who so blatantly said whatever they could to get their customers to buy, but she hoped this little white lie would be forgiven.

"Did your couch come with you?" the woman amiably asked.

Skye silently mourned the loss of the cream-colored, microfiber Cardi's sofa that she and Julie had bought, on clearance, straight off the showroom floor shortly after she graduated college and moved into her first apartment. She even got an extra ten percent off when she found a stain the size of a pencil eraser head. The delivery guys had had a hell of a time getting it up the narrow New England staircase to her apartment on the top floor, so she rewarded them with Papa Gino's pizza and Sam Adams lager, although they took cans of Coke instead. Two days after they left, she'd called Julie and said, *The couch wants to be somewhere else.* She had cajoled Julie into coming over to help her move it away from the wall and, after two repositionings, settled on a placement diagonal from the bay window and so that one's back wouldn't be to the living room entranceway. *Yes, this is right,* she'd told Julie. *This is what it wants.*

As a result, the living room had earned its name and designation. Even though she had a square pub table in the nook next to the kitchen, framed by counters, she ate most of her meals on the couch—it had become a *couch* rather than a *sofa*—while she watched TV. When her friends Cam or Rory or a date came over, they convened there for glasses of wine, and a book-club meeting even took place when she'd still had time for book clubs, before she took over the Warwick store. When she'd adopted Chip, he'd claimed just about every space of the couch, in phases: The top for a few months. Then the armrest for another few, then the left end cushion, followed by the right. When she was home and not eating, he nestled in her lap. If a piece of furniture could serve as a metaphor for home, that one did.

In the course of those dozen years or so, it had acquired drink stains and cat hair (no matter how many times she vacuumed it) and slumped a little in the middle. Thus, she'd offered it up on Craigslist for free to anyone who could take it away within twenty-four hours, first come, first served. Just as well, it would have disappeared with her stuff that did make it out of Rhode Island.

"Sadly, no," said Skye. "I'm looking forward to buying a new one as soon as I'm more settled, though." She scanned the showroom for a sofa that matched her personal taste, and spotted one several feet away, a sectional adorned with giant, bold-printed pillows. "Like that one, for instance," she said as she pointed to it. "I could get lost in that." They migrated toward it, but the couple seemed unimpressed. Skye followed up with, "Is there a particular style you're looking for?"

"One that's easy to clean after the dog repeatedly craps on it," the man said, clearly irked.

The woman looked mortified.

"Ahhh, pets. Thank goodness you don't have to pay their tuition, right?" The woman half smiled. The man was not amused. Skye continued without pressing. In ACME sales terms, *conversing* wasn't about talking as much as *listening*. "OK, so you need a couch that's easy to clean and affordable," she said, looking directly at the man. "Yet attractive," she said to the woman. "This is for your den, yes?" The woman smiled. Skye had guessed correctly.

"Scruffy's not allowed in the living room," she said.

Skye thought of Chip, who used to sit on the kitchen counters when she wasn't home, although since moving into the condo, when he wasn't nestled in Bucky's bed with Bucky, he mostly stayed on her bed.

"Got it," said Skye. "What's your maximum budget?"

"Anything more than five fifty is a deal breaker," said the husband. She'd snuck a peek at both of their hands for wedding rings, and found a diamond setting for her, and a thick titanium band for him.

"OK," said Skye. So far most of the sofas she'd glanced at in the front were at least six hundred fifty dollars, but she knew there were a few sales going on based on the red tags she'd glimpsed as she'd passed through when Patrick took her back to the office. The showroom was akin to a maze. She knew Patrick was lurking nearby, observing her. She also knew she couldn't go it alone anymore; she wasn't familiar enough with the merchandise, and rather than fudge her way through, she would exude more competence—and confidence—by passing them on to someone who could genuinely help them. So she escorted them to Patrick, introduced him to them, and after he shook their hands, she armed him with everything he needed to know. "This couple needs a new couch for their den that contains a pet-friendly fabric and human-friendly comfort. They also have a strict budget of five hundred and fifty dollars to spend and don't want to see anything that is even a penny over. Can you help them find something that meets their needs?"

This. This was what Skye was good at. She could barely get out two sentences on a dinner date without sounding and looking like a complete schlub; but here, on a furniture showroom floor, she carried herself as if she owned the store.

But she'd had no problem talking to Harvey, or even Vance during all their long-distance dates and finally when they'd met up in Boston. What else had she underestimated about herself?

Everything her parents and Summer had underestimated.

She was good at managing and planning and organizing. She was good at anticipating what people wanted or needed—one thing Harvey had complimented her on early in their working together was the way she always got a room ready for him.

She still didn't love retail. It didn't bring her joy. But interaction did. Color did. Seeing a before-and-after on an HGTV show like *Flipped* or *Fixer Upper* did.

By eliminating what she didn't want, she was discovering what she did.

Everything about Patrick's demeanor conveyed that he was impressed with Skye's performance, and she couldn't help but grin as if she'd just won Manager of the Month again. He led all three of them to a sofa with both sales and Scotchgard tags on them as a start, extracting a little more information from them about their personal tastes. Skye paid attention while Patrick showed them more pieces. And even though the customers left without a receipt, and Devlin's without a sale, she was willing to bet the money in her wallet that they'd be back. If not for the couch, then something else the next time the need arose.

Patrick turned to Skye after the couple left. "You were fantastic."

She grinned again. "Thank you."

He extended his hand. "We'll be in touch," he said.

And just as quickly, Skye's power drained. *That's it? You're not going to say more? Tell me what I did well and what I need to work on? Ask more questions? Tell me that you need to interview more candidates, talk to upper management, something, anything?*

"Oh," she said. "Yes, OK. Thank you."

She was almost at the door when Patrick called out, "Hang on," and jogged up to her. "Screw that. When can you start?"

CHAPTER

SEVENTEEN

When Skye was back in the FJ Cruiser after working out a schedule with Patrick, she sat with both hands atop the steering wheel, trying to control the trembling that had taken over her body.

Yes, she was back in retail sales again. Back to nights and weekends. Back to crappy pay. Yes, it was only part-time, and she was starting at the bottom, still making less than what she deserved at thirty-six years old. Yes, she was still in Billings, Montana, single and alone.

Except instead of a dead end, the job was a stepping stone. A springboard. She wasn't settling, but choosing.

And wasn't alone. She could hardly wait to share her news with Harvey. She started to text him, but then deleted it and put her phone away because she also realized she wanted to tell him in person.

She wanted to tell Harvey first. Not Vance. Not Julie. Not Summer. *Harvey.*

The cognizance of it practically brought her to tears. She felt as if she were about to jump off Sacrifice Cliff, which Harvey had pointed out to her on the way back from one of their jobs. She had a parachute, but it didn't promise a smooth landing.

Skye put the FJ in gear, jerked the car out of the parking space more than backed up, and tried to handle the beast back to the condo, where she texted to let Harvey know that she would pick him up when he was ready.

How did it go? he texted back.

I'll tell you when I see you, she replied. It was a bit of a tease, but she didn't want to ruin the moment later.

An hour later, she met him at the job site, helped him load all his paint paraphernalia, and eagerly convened to the passenger's seat where she belonged, making a mental note to start searching for a lease agreement with no money down at a Honda dealership, given that she wasn't planning to stay for more than a year. After all, she could neither drive this big boxy monster again nor expect Harvey to chauffeur her; what's more, she hadn't mentioned to Patrick that she didn't have a car. He didn't ask. Should she have disclosed that? Would Patrick have changed his mind about hiring her if she did?

Harvey settled into the driver's seat after pushing it back and readjusting the mirrors—she'd forgotten to do that—and turned to her before putting the car in gear. He looked nervous, like he'd been living in suspense all day and couldn't take another second of waiting.

"Well?" he asked as he steeled himself, his tone indicating that he was hoping for the best but expecting the worst.

She grinned ear-to-ear.

"All right!" he cheered. "Congratulations!" He high-fived her. And then, without warning, he crossed over to pull her to him in a lopsided hug.

His gesture sent her heartbeat into a drumroll. She wanted more—God, she'd gone from never wanting even a glance in her direction from another man to wanting Harvey to know every part of her, from the crevices of her body to the crevices of her heart.

She let go quickly. "Thank you," she said.

"I'm proud of you."

She thought her face might freeze like the Joker, she was smiling so hard—not just from Harvey's validation, but from her own.

CHAPTER

EIGHTEEN

May

Patrick put Skye on Devlin's personnel schedule for the first week in May. Tuesday and Thursday evening, from 5:00 p.m. to 9:00 p.m., and Saturday from 8:00 a.m. to 5:00 p.m. with a paid one-hour lunch break. She couldn't help but groan at the thought of an all-day Saturday, but quickly admonished herself, because, one, she was gainfully employed again, and, two, her Saturdays hadn't been much more than watching too much HGTV or poring through career-counseling websites or doing a painting job with Harvey since she didn't have a car, although she'd Googled "Honda dealership in Billings," found one, and set a date to lease a Civic following her first paycheck, so she'd have an idea of what she could afford every month.

Only six people came into Devlin's Furniture the night of her first shift. On her second, however, a newlywed couple left with a dining room set, thanks to Skye, and you'd think she'd just sold the Hope Diamond. Patrick high-fived her and treated her to a Starbucks coffee. Her coworkers congratulated her as well. "It took me two weeks before

I got my first sale," lamented Barbara, a mom who'd been working at Devlin's part-time for three years and who had gradually decreased her hours. Skye appreciated her new coworkers' validation. Here she was, in the largest city of this humongous state, and she finally felt like a big fish in a little pond. She had felt that way for years at Top Drawer too. Thing is, she wanted to be the big fish in the big ocean.

After the store closed, Harvey picked her up, and she told him all about her good night. He held up his hand for a high five, just like Patrick had done. She wanted to clasp it and not let go.

After one week of Harvey rearranging his schedule so that he could drop off and pick up Skye, she thanked him by taking over every aspect of housecleaning. Better that than subject him to her cooking. Cleaning was therapeutic, although she'd never seen it as such before. It was always one of those it-is-what-it-is chores—just get it over with as soon as possible. Perhaps because she was no longer cleaning for herself, much like the way Harvey didn't like cooking for one. Was it better this time because she was doing it in service of someone else, a thank-you for his kindness? Was it because Harvey kept his condo relatively clean, the best that bachelors who aren't neat freaks can do?

She was also good at it. Skye had always tackled jobs like organizing closets or desk drawers or the stockroom at the store with a vengeance. She used to go into a Zen-like trance when she straightened the tables of lingerie, especially during the semiannual mega sales. Her friends always enlisted her to help them sort through their clutter. Skye had even considered going into business as a professional organizer.

Get paid to clean other people's messes? Julie had asked.

Why not? said Skye.

Skye couldn't remember her reasons for shooting down the idea other than that she was overwhelmed by the thought of starting a business from scratch. Who, other than her friends (who were used to paying her in wine and pizza), would hire her?

Maybe she hadn't believed in herself. Her parents had conveyed, either in words or deeds, that she wasn't good enough, couldn't match Summer in terms of grades or aptitude or success.

She'd never considered the possibility that her parents were wrong—not only to compare her to her sister, but that Skye couldn't measure up.

It finally struck her that all she needed to do was choose a different belief. All she had to do was choose to love herself. Because if she didn't believe in herself—didn't *love* herself—then why should Vance . . . or any man whom she wanted to love her?

In addition to sweeping floors and scrubbing the bathtub in the condo, Skye was refolding towels in the linen closet to look fluffier and neater, reorganizing the kitchen pantry and cabinets, and sorting through junk drawers. She especially had fun when she and Harvey dumped the contents of one drawer on the rug in the living room and began rummaging through.

"No, you can't throw out those screws—those are good screws!" Harvey protested.

"Then put them in your toolbox!" Skye replied in mock exasperation.

Harvey held them in his open hand, about a dozen in all, and gave them one last consideration before tossing them into the garbage bag next to him. "Ahhh, screw it," he said, prompting laughs from both of them.

Aside from not being able to find anything in the kitchen for the first few days and grumbling good-naturedly about it, Harvey liked the changes. And in an interesting coincidence, the more junk they cleared out, the more work came in. He had multiple painting jobs, many of them day-long gigs, lined up for the next two weeks. Not only that, but Skye finished her first week making her sales quota, as well as earning the highest commission.

"Beginner's luck," she said when Patrick shared the good news with her.

"Somehow I think it's more than that," he said.

◆ ◆ ◆

Skye had come to cherish Sundays off. With the weather so nice, she often accompanied Harvey and Bucky for a walk in the park or a jaunt to Big Dipper (she was determined to try every flavor they made), or they would spend time apart and she would catch up with Julie (she hadn't spoken to Summer since telling her to get bent) or go to the new co-op bookstore—the one she'd helped paint—and browse through the home-improvement section. She loved that regardless of whether she stayed in Billings or moved back to Rhode Island, she'd left her mark. She'd never felt that way about Top Drawer. Had always felt expendable. But the work she did with Harvey lingered. She didn't know if it was the work itself that made her feel that way, or the fact that it was work with Harvey.

Billings was becoming less of a place and more of a residence. And Vance Sandler was becoming less of a memory and more of a mirage. Moreover, Harvey's condo had become a sanctuary, a space that sheltered and nurtured her.

One day, Skye was in the living room, arms crossed, staring at the space, engrossed in it as if she were in a museum studying a painting.

Harvey, in the kitchen, seasoning a chicken for roasting, noticed how zoned in she was. "What are you looking at?" he asked.

"I finally figured out what's wrong with this room," she said. "What's wrong with this entire condo."

"Oh?"

She caught herself. "I'm sorry, *wrong* is a bad word choice. It's just that I've been feeling . . . the room wants to be balanced. Every room is missing it."

"What do you mean?"

"There's only one end table in each bedroom. There should be one on each side of the bed. And here in the living room too. There should be an end table on each side. Or a floor lamp, or no tables or lamps and just the coffee table in the middle. As long as it's even."

She'd made the same mistake in her apartment in Rhode Island. Only one table next to her bed, on the side she slept. Only one table next to the couch in the living room, in addition to the coffee table. She almost always sat on the opposite end. Maybe she was subconsciously trying to balance it out.

Two weeks on Devlin's Furniture showroom floor had revealed it to her. Those sample rooms worked for a reason. It wasn't to sell the room just as a package, but rather in pieces. It was about showing how the pieces worked together, like a band or an orchestra. The instruments sounded different together than solo. The whole was greater than the sum of its parts. Symmetry.

"Well, maybe we should do something about it," said Harvey.

"We?"

"It needs balance, doesn't it?"

He grinned. His grins made her all tingly inside. Like a breeze blowing under her skin. Different from the way Vance used to make her feel. Vance was more like a hurricane.

"Yes," she said softly.

"OK." And with that, he placed the chicken into the oven. They said nothing more about it.

When she lay in bed later that night, she wondered about Vance's home. Wondered if he would have been as allowing as Harvey had been in terms of her reorganizing cabinets and painting rooms and giving unsolicited commentary. She wondered if she would have been as at home in his house as she was in the condo. She wondered what lying in Vance's bed would have been like.

She moved into the warmth of Chip's body curled into her tummy to stave off the loneliness that had crept into bed with her.

Ten minutes later, Skye heard a knock on her door. "Skye?" called Harvey.

"Yes?"

She expected him to come in, but he spoke through the door. "I'm really proud of you. Keep doing what you're doing."

"Thank you," she said, the blanket of his words tucking her in and snuggling close.

"Good night," he said.

"Good night," she replied. His footsteps diminished in the dark.

CHAPTER
NINETEEN

The following weekend, Harvey went to Devlin's Furniture store and purchased everything in pairs—matching bedside tables for both bedrooms and a round coffee table for the living room. Of course, he went on a day Skye was working so she could not only help him pick out the pieces but also get the commission.

"You OK with making such a big purchase?" she asked.

"I invested well and saved a lot when I worked for Birch-McHale," he said. "Don't worry, I can afford it."

She smiled. "I think these are going to be such great additions to the condo."

He nodded in agreement. "It's high time I treated myself."

Something about the way he said *myself* echoed an assertiveness, as if he'd been lost or neglected and was admonishing himself for it.

After Harvey left, Patrick approached her.

"Nice job," he said.

"Thanks," she replied.

"So who's the lucky guy?"

"Huh?"

"You clearly knew him."

Skye's face heated up like a hot plate and turned as red. "Oh. He's, um . . . he's not my boyfriend, if that's what you're asking. He's . . . he's just a friend," she said. God, those had to be among the worst four words in the English language, right up there with *I don't love you; your credit card bounced*; and *we're out of chocolate*. The reality that they seemingly were every other kind of partner—roommates, painter-assistant, to name two—fell on her like a practical joke.

Patrick didn't respond. But she could have sworn that he smirked.

"I followed the protocol," she said, afraid he was about to reprimand her. She remembered the employee-training handbook—which she'd read cover to cover—in particular the rule about selling to family and friends. They were allowed to sell to that person (and thus receive a commission), but they were not allowed to ring the customer up or buy the merchandise themselves as a means of exploiting their discount.

"I know you did," he said. After all, he was the one who handled Harvey's payment after Skye handed Harvey off to him.

Feeling like the walls were closing in, Skye averted her eyes and said, "Well, OK. I need a bathroom break. Excuse me." She practically broke into a sprint off the showroom floor and into the back, locked herself in the restroom, and gripped the sink, taking deep breaths. Why in the world had Patrick's questions rattled her? When she picked her head up and faced the mirror, she knew the answer: *I am in love with Harvey.* And it showed.

She hadn't expected to fall in love, with him or anyone else. Hadn't wanted it. Of course, she hadn't expected Vance to come into her life when he did, but she was craving romance that time. No—she was in dire need of an escape hatch from her life. Admitting to herself that she was in love with Harvey was like cleaning out a closet and finding a precious work of art that had been previously hidden. And it was valuable. Whereas previous crushes had introduced themselves with a bang, falling in love with Harvey was a knock at the door. But what to do about it?

And if it showed, if someone like Patrick could see through her facade, then could Harvey see it? Because she saw no sign from Harvey that the feeling was mutual. And why should it be? She'd been a fool and had been duped by the same man who'd duped Harvey's wife. She was a reminder. He was just too nice a guy to punish her for it.

And she didn't want to risk her heart being shattered again.

Skye used the bathroom, washed her hands, and stopped at the watercooler in the break room for a few swallows before returning to the floor. *Get back to work,* she ordered herself repeatedly. The store had been busy all morning—Saturdays in retail were typically like that—but had died down since. When she reemerged, the store was empty save for its employees. They gathered in the living room display near the entrance, doing their best not to succumb to sitting on the sofa or leaning against the armrest of the love seat. While her coworkers Barbara and Gary—both in their fifties—talked about their spouses and children, Skye remembered Vance insisting that he didn't see the need to "produce progeny," as he called it, or "spawn," and Skye wondering out loud if she'd missed out on something when motherhood passed her by.

You could adopt, Vance had offered.

How had she not noticed the red flag, waving so close to her face it was practically smacking her? *You* could adopt. Not *we*. Not *us, together,* happily ever after. How had she not picked up the inconsistencies in his rhetoric, beckoning her to be with him but giving her no indication that he intended to follow through for the long haul?

More baffling, she had so easily denied it all. Excused his behavior. The depth of her desperation and willful blindness made her ill. She left for another cup of water in the break room and put Vance Sandler out of her mind. When she returned, a woman entered the store holding a stack of brochures. Skye greeted her.

"I work at the metaphysical bookstore downtown," said the woman.

"Yes," said Skye, smiling. "I know where it is." Harvey had pointed it out to her when they did the paint job for the new co-op bookstore on the next block. That something in Billings rang familiar pleased her, even though she'd never been to the store.

"Excellent!" said the woman. "Well, we're having a very special guest next week. She's a renowned feng shui teacher and expert. We thought your store would be the perfect place to leave some brochures in case your customers would like to get some free tips and consultations for their home. There's even a drawing for a free space clearing."

Skye had heard of feng shui (she had always pronounced it *fen shwee*, but this woman pronounced it *fun sway*) and had always wanted to learn about it, but dismissed it after Summer called it "new age nonsense." Sure, she'd used Yankee Candles around Top Drawer and incense in her own apartment, but that was her own kooky superstition, right?

"Oh," said Skye, "I don't think we're allowed to, but I'll ask my manager."

Skye fetched Patrick, who told the woman that accepting community brochures and advertisements of any kind had to be approved by corporate first, and gave her a toll-free number to call. She thanked both of them and headed back toward the parking lot.

Something filled Skye at that moment, ignited in her gut, and threatened to burst out of her chest. "Wait!" she called out, catching up to the woman just as she had pushed the door open. "Can I have one of those?"

"Sure," she said, and handed two over. "One for you, and one for a friend," she winked.

Skye smiled. "Thank you," she said.

"You're welcome. Hope to see you there."

"Me too."

Skye folded the brochures and tucked them into the pocket of her blazer. For the remainder of the day, she kept placing her hand in that pocket, making sure the brochures didn't slip out. She'd had ample opportunities to move them into her purse stored in a locker in the break room, but for some reason she wanted to keep the brochures close to her. She didn't even read it, choosing instead to wait until she got home from work, like a special treat or reward at the end of a long day. She could hardly wait.

CHAPTER TWENTY

That same Saturday, thirty minutes before the end of her shift, Patrick sidled up to her.

"How's it going?" he asked.

"Fine," she said, figuring he was just killing time.

"Doing anything after work?"

Reading a feng shui brochure . . .

"Not really. Finding something to watch on TV, I guess," she said.

"Wanna grab something for dinner with me?"

Holy moly, is married Patrick asking me out?

"Um . . . ," she started, searching for a clue in Patrick's face to correctly interpret the invitation. *It can't be a date.* They were just colleagues going for a drink after work. She'd occasionally done that with her Top Drawer staff. And it would be nice to hang out with someone besides Harvey.

"Sure," she said.

"Excellent. Need a ride too?"

Skye had signed a twelve-month lease for a Honda Civic with no money down two days ago; she could hardly wait to pick up the car on Monday.

"That would be great, thanks," she said. "I just need to text my roommate and let him know."

Dammit!!! She caught herself the minute it slipped out.

"*Him?* You live with a guy?"

"It's the twenty-first century, Patrick," she said a little too defensively. Maybe because she also caught herself wishing she was more than Harvey's roommate.

"No worries," said Patrick. "Tell him you just saved him a ride."

"OK." She went to the break room and texted Harvey, who wished her a good time. At five o'clock sharp, Patrick was again at Skye's side.

"Ready?" he asked.

"Let's go," said Skye.

Skye and Patrick sat opposite each other at a pub table in the crowded, noisy Jake's Bar and Grill on the west end. He ordered a mountain of nachos, while she opted for the coconut-battered shrimp. They drank beers (first round on her as thanks for the ride), clinking their glasses in an unspoken toast.

"So have you made many friends since moving here?" asked Patrick.

Skye shook her head. "Not really," she said. "Just haven't had time. Too busy looking for work and getting settled and stuff. I've only been here a little over a month."

He raised his eyebrows. "I didn't realize you were that new." Skye wanted to crawl under the table, as if she'd said or done something wrong. Not like she had to tell him about Vance. Patrick took another swig of beer before resuming the conversation. "What about your roommate? How did you two meet?"

"Would you believe on the plane to Billings? We just so happened to be on both flights out of Rhode Island."

She did a mental replay of that first day—those first conversations with Harvey, revelations about Vance, being stranded, lost luggage—and she could see why Patrick was surprised she'd been here for such a short time. In some ways that first day seemed like such a long time ago, considering all that had happened since—moving in with and working for Harvey, getting the job at Devlin's, signing the lease for a car. She realized how grateful she was, how much worse things could have been than humiliating herself on Vance's doorstep.

"Wow," he said. "That's what I call bonding." He messily broke a few nachos away from the sticky pile and stuffed them in his mouth, covering it with a napkin. Skye laughed. When he finally finished chewing, he asked, "So you never did tell me what fell through for you here."

Skye decided to play coy; perhaps the beer had gone to her head. "Maybe I don't want to tell you."

He seemed eager to play her game. "Was it a job?"

She took a sip of beer.

"A house?"

Another sip.

"Relationship?"

Yeah, playing coy was a stupid move.

Skye took a third sip and coughed and switched to water and said, "I'm not going to tell you what it was. It didn't work out, and I decided to make a go of it here rather than run back home with my tail between my legs."

"Fair enough," said Patrick. "But you should get out and make more friends, if you can. Billings is a great city with great people. Not all of them, of course, but I trust you to steer clear of the bad ones."

No need. Vance already steered clear of me.

"It'll be easier when I pick up my new car," she said.

"I'm surprised you didn't drive across country when you moved."

"I sold almost everything I owned—including my car—so I could come here with as much cash as possible. Turned out to be a stupid thing to do. I was living paycheck to paycheck in Rhode Island, but I cleared all my bills. Thank goodness for Har—for my roommate. Splitting the expenses has really helped me out and makes the payments on the car doable."

"I wish we could give you more hours at the store. Ditto for more money. You're such a dynamo."

Skye failed to suppress a smile and sipped from her beer in an attempt to hide it. Before he could pry further into her life, she asked him a question. "So what brought you to furniture sales?"

It was his turn to play coy. He leaned forward. "I'll let you in on a little secret, Skye." She leaned forward as well, ears open. "I'm a Devlin."

Because of the noisy bar, at first she thought he'd said he was a gremlin. Oh God, was Patrick one of those nutcases who somehow managed to fool society that he was normal? Was he like Kris Kringle in *Miracle on 34th Street*? Or was he drunk?

"Say that again, please?"

"I'm part of the Devlin family. You know, Devlin's Furniture? My mother is Anna Devlin, daughter of George and Carol Devlin, grand-daughter of Arthur and Ruth Devlin, the founders of Devlin's Furniture. My father is Richard Brody, vice president of merchandising."

Skye followed Patrick's lineage in her head, and finally connected the dots. "So . . . you, like, *own* the store."

"The *family* owns it," he clarified. "I'm only the store manager. I work for the same company as you."

"Why aren't you in corporate?"

"Our family believes that you work your way up to corporate. I started in furniture delivery and the warehouse. Then I worked on the floor in sales. Now I'm a store manager."

"Wow," said Skye. She decided to dive in with her next question. "Do you mind if I ask how old you are?"

"I'll be twenty-seven in two weeks."

Twenty-seven! Skye resisted gesturing a facepalm. "You're a baby," she said.

Patrick laughed. "Really? And how old are you?"

"Thirty-six," she said, and cringed, guessing he was about have the same sinking feeling she did.

"Wow, Grandma," he said. "And you're calling me a baby? There's only nine years between us."

"Think about it," said Skye. "When you were in the fourth grade, I was in college. Whereas you only knew Ronald Reagan from your social-studies textbook, I remember him being in office. You were only *eighteen* when I was the age you'll be in two weeks."

"So?"

"So . . ." *Come to think of it, what is my point?* That they couldn't be together romantically? That was obvious, considering he was married and she was in love with Harvey. "So you're my boss, and you're younger than me."

"So what? Does the fact that I'm younger make me less respectable or credible or good at my job?"

"Of course not."

"Does it mean we can't be friends or have common interests?"

"No," she said.

"Then who cares?" He leaned in again. "Look, Skye, I think you're great. You're an asset to our company, you're fun to be around, and you deserve better than what we can give you. In fact, I'm going to tell you something that you can't tell anyone else."

Anxiety began to swell in her gut. "I won't, I promise."

"We might not be around much longer."

Skye looked at him blankly. "What do you mean?"

"I mean our store location has experienced some losses, and we're not sure we're going to make it."

She was in shock. "Are you saying the store is going to close?"

"I'm saying it *might* close."

A flare of pain shot up her spine, as if a rug had literally been pulled out from under her.

"When?" she asked.

"That's the thing," said Patrick. "We don't know."

"Have you told anyone else?"

"No. And I'm not going to."

Skye shook her head in exasperation. Not to mention she was a little pissed off. "Then why are you telling *me*?"

"I don't know. I felt like you deserved to know."

"The others don't deserve to know? They have families."

"Of course they deserve to know. But they'll be OK. They have spouses and—" He cut himself off. "You . . . I don't know, I just felt the need to look out for you more than them. You're the newbie."

"Thank you for your pity," she said. She started to collect her coat and purse when she remembered she had no car. Too bad they weren't at the downtown location; she could have walked back to the condo.

"Skye, wait—I wasn't pitying you. I just wanted to be helpful."

"Why don't you just make it easier and fire me now? That way it's quick and easy. One bullet to the head."

"Because all this might have been for nothing. We just don't know yet. Look, it was stupid of me to tell you, OK? Forget I even said anything. It was completely unprofessional of me."

"I am not a computer, Patrick. You can't just delete a file or erase my memory. I have feelings about this."

It wasn't even six thirty yet, and she suddenly felt as if she hadn't slept in twenty-four hours. "Can we get out of here, please? I'm getting a splitting headache, and I need to process this. Plus, I'm going to have to get back on the job hunt."

Patrick, remorseful and defeated, far from the upbeat, perky demeanor she usually saw, stood from his chair and said, "Sure." He flagged the server and paid the bill while she used the restroom and buttoned her coat. She told him where she lived and he plugged it into his GPS, and they rode in that wormy, itchy silence all the way back downtown. When Skye pointed to the condo building, Patrick pulled the car over to the curb just outside the gate entrance. She extracted the keys from her purse and opened the door.

"Hang on just one more minute," said Patrick.

She closed the door. "What is it?" she said, still unable to look at him. Why did she feel like she'd just been through a breakup?

He took a hard breath and exhaled it. "I'm really, really sorry for telling you anything. Please, you can't tell the others."

"I already told you I'm not going to tell anyone anything," she said. Except maybe Harvey, who, as both her roommate and landlord, needed to know.

"Are we OK? Still friends?"

"We were never friends, Patrick. You're my boss. See you next week." And with that, she stepped out of the car, unlocked the gate, and entered the condo.

Harvey was in the living room watching an NBA basketball game. The Cleveland Cavaliers versus the Boston Celtics. Before moving in with Harvey, Skye had never cared much for basketball. Now, seeing the Boston home gym floor made her homesick yet again. The Celtics, Red Sox, and Patriots were "home" teams to all the New England states.

"Hey," said Harvey. "How was dinner?"

"Fine," she said as she headed straight to her room. *Her* room? *Ha.* This wasn't her room any more than Billings was her home. She closed the door and leaned against it and begged herself not to cry; she was sick of crying. Just when she thought she was making progress, just when she believed her life was on track and she was doing well and everything would work out . . .

Harvey knocked on the door, causing her to jump. "You OK?" he called.

"I'm fine," she replied, her voice quavering. "I'll talk to you tomorrow, OK? I'm just . . . *tired.*"

"OK," he said. "Sleep well."

Next thing she knew, she opened the door and went into Harvey's arms.

CHAPTER
TWENTY-ONE

The warmth of Harvey's hands on Skye's back appeased her as she cried. She couldn't remember Vance's arms feeling like that. Couldn't remember them soothing her, taking her in rather than pushing her away. She couldn't remember Vance's scent (Harvey's was a mixture of paint and aftershave and soap). She couldn't remember the sound of Vance's breath, never compared it to music, the way Harvey's breathing was downright rhythmic.

She wanted to stay in Harvey's arms forever. And yet she felt embarrassed about going there in the first place.

"I'm sorry," she said as she yanked herself away and sniffled, trying to control her tears. "I just . . . I needed a friend."

"You don't need to be sorry," said Harvey. "And I am your friend." He waited for her to finish calming herself, and then he asked, "Is there anything you want to talk about? No pressure. I just want you to know you can if you want to."

Yes, she wanted to talk. She wanted to collapse herself into him—his heart, his breath, his voice.

He went to the sofa and sat at one end. Skye followed him and sat at the other. "What happened at work today?"

"Not at work, after work. I found out that my job isn't as secure as I thought it was."

"You seemed to be doing really well," said Harvey.

"I was. I *am*," she corrected. "But the store isn't. It might not be around much longer."

Harvey raised his eyebrows. "Devlin's is closing?"

"They don't know for sure yet," she said. "I wasn't supposed to say anything, so please don't tell anyone. But you needed to know. This changes my standing here."

"I won't say a word," said Harvey. "As for your standing, I'm not going to put you out on the street or anything."

Harvey faced her, looking at her intently, to the point where she had to avert her own glance. Had any man ever looked at her with such focus and attention? Was that what male friends did? She'd never really had any— at least none with whom she was this close, both physically and emotionally. She averted her glance because she loved him. She loved when he looked at her, and she didn't want him to know.

"Skye, is going back to Rhode Island really not an option?" he asked. "You just don't seem to be happy here."

She darted her eyes at him. "What are you saying?"

"I'm saying maybe it's not worth showing Vance up."

She was on Vance's doorstep again. Another rejection.

"You think I'm not happy here?" she said. "You haven't been paying attention."

"Look, I'm not saying I want you gone. Are you afraid to face your family and friends? Because they're a pretty lousy bunch of people if they'd do anything other than welcome you back with open arms and love you through this crisis."

Skye leapt to her feet. "How dare you talk about my friends and family that way!"

"*You* talk about them that way—if you mention them at all. I haven't seen you call or reach out to them. And if they've not reached out to you, then what the hell kind of friends are they?"

She thought of how she'd shut down Summer, refused to call her parents, had been evasive with Sabrina and Cam and Rory and everyone except Julie. Harvey was right. She was the one who kept berating herself, kept repeating *I told you so.* And she could have had Patrick as a friend had she not shut him down too.

"Harvey, have you ever been so ashamed of yourself that you could barely look in the mirror, much less face your friends and family?"

He didn't respond, but his expression was one of empathy.

She continued. "I had become so unhappy in Rhode Island. So tired of the same old thing. I turned thirty-six and it was as if my life had flashed before my eyes, and all I saw was a life that had never really stacked up. Then this guy paid me a compliment, and we got to chatting, and when he told me he lived in Montana . . . it was so easy to build a fantasy. Day by day, he paid me another compliment, told me how welcome I would be here, how appreciated I would be. He played upon every vulnerability I had. I wanted to prove that I could be adventurous. That I could chase my dreams of being in love and being someplace larger than life."

Harvey's eyes became dark, as if he'd been transported someplace else.

"Skye, I do know what it's like. The same guy who screwed you also screwed me. But whereas you believed every word he said, ironically, my mistake was that I didn't believe a word he said. When Deb left me for Vance, I wanted to crawl into a hole and never come out. I was so damn *embarrassed.* Worse still, the kids blamed me for their mom leaving. Or rather, my son did. My daughter is just trying to please everyone by not talking about it, and I don't know what to do about that."

"So what did you do?" asked Skye.

"Got out of bed. Every day. Made a new plan. Decided to take control of my life by doing things that replenished my sense of self-worth if not my bank account. But it's not all there yet. I miss my kids. God, you have no idea how badly I miss my kids." He wiped a tear. "Skye, if you want to stay here, then great. If you want to prove to yourself what you're capable of, then do it for the right reasons. Not to prove something to Vance or me or anyone else in your life. Do it to prove to yourself that you're worthy of greatness. Do it for you and only you."

Do it for me. She had tried to convince Summer and Julie and others that she was moving to Montana for herself. But she wasn't. She was running away from herself.

Skye sat down and put her head on Harvey's shoulder and again felt the surge of current when he put his arm around her and gently squeezed. She inhaled the scent of his skin. She wanted to spend eternity in that moment.

"Therapy worked wonders for you."

He chuckled. "It's helped. I've got a long way to go."

As if her voice had a mind of its own, she blurted, "Have you dated anyone since your divorce?" She flushed with embarrassment the moment the words spilled out and Harvey abruptly let go. She covered her mouth. "Oh God, I didn't mean—"

"Not really," he said, seemingly unfazed by the intrusion and abrupt tangent. "I've not yet shaken the doubt that I'm good company."

"I think you are." He looked at her with curiosity. Her self-consciousness finally kicking in, Skye backpedaled. "I mean, you're a good roommate and I like working with you."

Harvey stifled a smile. "I appreciate that," he said. "And I'm sorry if I upset you. I just want you to know that if you want to go home, I'll fully support you in any way I can."

Home—the first image that came to her was trees: snow-lined in winter, green and fresh and new in spring, fluttery and carefree in summer, and lustrous gold and auburn and red in autumn. Montana had trees of course—the Billings neighborhoods were full of them, green and lush, although she had yet to see their ranges from season to season. But trees in New England seemed more like neighbors. Their branches would wave at you like arms, their leaves applauding as you passed under them. They hovered over backstreets like canopies. The closer you got to the open water in Newport and Narragansett, the more stunted the treetops became, and the air changed from suburban to salty.

She'd never been a tree hugger before. Barely took notice of or interest in any kind of tree other than the fake one she erected every Christmas season, when she had her first coveted day off following the insanity that the Black Friday weekend had been over the years. And yet, in that split second, she yearned to be surrounded by New England trees. Hugged by them. She wanted to know the different types specific to Rhode Island. She yearned to inhale that salty air as she dipped her toes in the water and let her hair go frizzy in the breeze. She yearned for people.

She could *go home.*

Or . . .

"Thank you, Harvey. That's incredibly generous of you. But I think I need to stay here for a little while."

WHAT IN THE WORLD AM I SAYING???

"You sure?"

No!

"There's going to be a thing at the metaphysical bookstore next week about feng shui. I thought I'd check it out."

Stay in Billings just to catch a bookstore event? Couldn't she learn about feng shui via Wikipedia?

No. It wasn't just about that. She wanted to decide for herself whether she wanted to stay.

And she wanted to be close to Harvey.

"Well, I'm glad," said Harvey. "I think if you give Billings a chance, you'd really like it. I know it's better having you around." Harvey didn't try to suppress the smile this time. Let it out completely, which made Skye smile, and she felt her face flush again, only not from embarrassment.

She kissed him on the cheek. "Good night, Harvey." She returned to her bedroom, tucked herself and Chip in, extra snug in the very thought of Harvey's arms around her.

CHAPTER
TWENTY-TWO

Skye entered the metaphysical bookstore at 5:35 p.m. and was bombarded with the scent of what she later found out was dried sage (the bundles of it were on display with a sign and a price tag) while flutey, ethereal music went to work on her ears. She didn't know where to look first. The walls were painted deep purple with silvery stars and lined with white twinkle lights. A mobile of crescent moons hung over the checkout counter. One bookcase stocked various kinds of card decks—tarot, angels, affirmations, Law of Attraction, and runes. Another stocked fantasy fiction books. An entire section of the store, near the window, was devoted to crystals and gemstones. Jewelry, talismans, music, books, even games adorned every part of the store, in what she referred to as "organized chaos." *This place could so use a planogram,* she thought as the woman who came to Devlin's the previous week with the pamphlets greeted her with such warmth and hospitality that Skye wasn't sure if it was because the woman recognized her from Devlin's or if that was her natural disposition. Skye got a better look at her this time: a shock of red hair, pixie style, oversprayed. Too much makeup. A magenta blouse paired with a multicolored skirt. Both pieces looked like they'd come from a sewing machine rather than a boutique. A talisman pendant around her neck, beaded bracelets adorning both wrists, and gemstone rings on almost every finger. In short, a woman who looked perfectly comfortable in her own skin.

Toward the back of the store, two rows of folding chairs were spread out in semicircle formation in front of a table containing various objects—a bell, a vial of sea salt, an array of stones, and more. Behind the table stood an easel with some kind of nine-box chart, like a tic-tac-toe board with borders, each box a different color with words like *Love and Relationships, Wealth and Prosperity, Creativity,* and *Well-Being* written on them.

Skye sat at the far end of the second row and rested her purse on her lap. Within ten minutes, the rest of the seats were filled with women who all seemed to know each other, and two store associates had to put out one more row of folding chairs, to the delight of the woman who greeted Skye, who Skye now surmised was the store manager. After another five minutes, the manager introduced herself as Mary Thompson, welcomed newcomers and regulars alike, and did a run-through of the events for the remainder of the month. From there she introduced the guest speaker, repeating most of the information from the flyer Skye had practically memorized: a feng shui practitioner for twenty-one years, author of three books known as the Make Room series, including the latest, *Make Room for Money: Using Feng Shui to Attract Wealth and Prosperity in Your Life.* Skye's ears perked up at that. The other two were *Make Room for Love* (also a must-read) and *Make Room for Wellness.* Finally, a name: Flora Davis.

Flora moved to the center as Mary stepped aside, and began with the basics of feng shui (it meant "wind and water") as more than just "the art of placement." As she described how everything—from tables and chairs to beaches and forests—was composed of matter (that is, "energy"), Skye felt equal parts validation and skepticism. Was this touchy-feely mumbo jumbo, as Summer had termed it, or were all the vibes she'd felt over the years—in Top Drawer, in her former apartment, in the authors' house with the coffee table, and even Harvey's condo—legit?

"Your personal space—be it in your home, work, or school—is a reflection of your life. If you live in a cluttered space, you have a cluttered life. If you're lacking something in your life—love, money, wellness—then look around and see what your space is lacking."

With that, Flora turned to the chart with the colors and boxes, referring to it as a *ba-gua* map. "Now, each one of you gets to take a postcard-sized one of these home with you, but here's how the map works. Each gua is an area of your life. Using this map, you can diagram any space, be it an entire house or just one room, even a coffee table or desk, for the purpose of identifying those areas that need balance or are lacking energy. For example,"—she pointed to the Love and Relationships box in the upper-right corner—"if you want love or more romance in your life, check where the relationship gua is, either in your bedroom or in your house. If the layout of your house is such that it's located in the bathroom, for example . . ."

The attendees chuckled.

". . . then you need to address that. Now, I'm guessing most of you can't afford to tear down a bathroom and move it to a different location of your house." More chuckles. "But with some paint and object placement—heart-shaped soaps, his-and-hers towels, red shower curtain—you can create an environment of love. And make sure everything in your home—especially your bedroom—is outfitted in twos. Two pillows on the bed. Two lamps, one on each side. Two end tables, also balanced. Even if you're single. Place objects and furniture as if you live with someone else, if that's what you want to bring into your life."

Now Skye was paying full attention. She flashed back to her apartment as well as Harvey's. *The imbalance.* Now that Harvey had paired everything up, would there be a change in his love life? In hers?

Flora continued to give examples for people who wanted to attract a new job or promotion or raise, lose weight, improve an existing relationship, and lower stress. Every example involved either color, an element (such as candles or a fountain or a plant), or an object, such as a good-luck charm or something of a certain shape.

"Touch everything in your home," said Flora. "*Everything.* Close your eyes and hold it and pay attention to how it makes you feel. If it makes you feel good, keep it. If it doesn't, get rid of it."

Skye struggled to focus her attention on the questions attendees were asking because her mind was racing so fast. What if the stuff in her home wasn't hers (especially considering it wasn't her home)? How could she afford candles and plants or a fountain? And what about color? Should she tell Harvey that it was imperative for him to paint the walls in the condo now? Had she chosen wisely when she chose lemon zest for the guest room?

She wanted to do everything all at once. She wanted to simply snap her fingers and come home to find the condo all feng-shuied up. She wanted to wake up tomorrow to a perfect life.

When the Q and A was finished, and the attendees applauded and took their books to Flora to sign, Skye picked up all three books, brought them to the checkout counter, and charged them to her credit card—her first true indulgence since she'd left Rhode Island. Afterward, she carried the books to the end of the line of attendees waiting for autographs and to snap selfies with Flora.

When it was finally her turn, Skye stepped up, placed the books on the table, and before Flora could open the first one to the title page for signing, she piped up: "I recently came to Billings under false pretenses, am renting a room in someone else's house with almost no belongings of my own, and need a complete life makeover. Where do you suggest I start?"

Oh wow. That was completely crazy.

Flora's eyes widened, yet sparkled. She looked at Skye the way a grandmother would look at her grandchild. "What do you need most?"

Tears came to Skye's eyes. She needed to be someplace that felt like home. She needed a career that brought her joy. She needed Harvey.

No, she'd needed Vance. She *wanted* Harvey.

Skye wiped her eyes and said, "I need you to teach me everything you know. I don't know where to start. I don't have money for throw pillows and curtains," said Skye. "I just don't understand—how does money come to you when you have no money to give?"

"What does that money represent to you?"

A way home.

"Freedom," said Skye.

"What does freedom feel like?"

Skye could feel a sensation like cogs in her brain turning. "I don't know . . . *free*," she stumbled. "Like you don't have to worry about anything anymore. Going wherever you want, in whatever car you want, wearing nice clothes, not worrying about bills or insurance or anything like that. Living wherever you want."

Flora placed her hands on Skye's arms as if to steady her. "Dear, you may not believe this, but everything you just described to me is entirely possible. Forget the actual dollars and cents right now. Focus on the *feeling*—that feeling of freedom."

"I *want* to believe you," said Skye. "More than anything. But my empty wallet and monthly bills keep distracting me."

Flora laughed, not in a mocking way but friendly. "You'll see," she said. "Thank you for purchasing the books. When you finish them, please call me. I think you would benefit from taking my course."

Skye smiled. "OK."

Flora signed each book, thanked Skye for coming, and Skye hugged her. "I'm sorry I made such a fool of myself," she said.

"Repeat after me: *I approve of myself.*"

Skye echoed, "I approve of myself." The statement felt inauthentic. Like a lie. She felt simultaneously awkward and surprised. She had never been cognizant of the fact that she'd not approved of herself.

"Say it whenever you doubt or criticize yourself," said Flora.

Skye flashed to when Harvey told her that the person she needed to love most was herself. She needed to start taking this advice like a prescription.

◆ ◆ ◆

When Skye left the bookstore and checked her phone, she was disappointed to find a text from Harvey saying he would be out having drinks with a buddy by the time she got home; she'd been looking forward to telling him all about the evening. Instead, she flopped onto the sofa with the books and opened each one. In the first one, *Make Room for Wellness*, Flora had inscribed: *To Skye, wishing you a life of serenity.* In the second, *Make Room for Love*, Skye read: *Dear Skye, the love you crave is already here.*

Skye's heartbeat quickened as she read the words. Did she mean Harvey?

No. No, no. Don't fall for it. The woman knows nothing.

Finally, she opened the third. *Dearest Skye, everything you desire is on its way in full abundance. Open your hands and receive!*

Was it really that easy?

By midnight, Skye had read over half of *Make Room for Money*, stopping only because she could no longer keep her eyes open and needed to be up early the following morning for the opening shift. She fell asleep that night repeating *I approve of myself* like a mantra.

CHAPTER
TWENTY-THREE

With Harvey's permission, Skye took the following week to transform the guest room into a personal space—*her* personal space. Just as Flora Davis had recommended, Skye began by touching every belonging she owned, and every item in the room that belonged to Harvey. After cradling the end table lamp in the guest room for a good thirty seconds (the conjured feeling was "an afterthought"), she swapped it out for two she found at Target for just ten dollars apiece. Additionally, she printed a photo of a New England fall landscape from the Internet and bought matting board to make a frame for it. The moment she handled the finished piece, she felt as if she'd just created some kind of portal—that at some precise moment she'd be able to jump through it and wind up back in Rhode Island whenever she was homesick, just in time for hot caramel cider and leaf-peeping.

In the Wealth and Prosperity corner of the condo's guest room (according to the ba-gua map), she converted twenty dollars (may as well have been one hundred dollars, money was so tight) from her most recent paycheck into quarters, poured them into a cut-crystal bowl from one of the kitchen cupboards (OK, so it wasn't real crystal, but she liked that it looked expensive), and vowed to keep adding to it.

She also typed and printed an affirmation on a card and left it next to the bowl: *I am a money magnet.* At first, she felt stupid every time she recited the words, especially when she said them out loud, as Flora's book suggested she do. Very much the same way she still felt awkward every time she recited *I approve of myself* when she looked in the mirror. However, by the end of the week, she'd stopped rolling her eyes and started saying the words with more authority, with declaration rather than corniness, and the voice in her head that usually retorted with things like, *Oh yeah? Well, where's the money, dumbass?* and *Say it again, fat girl* was quieting down, especially when she reprimanded it with *Stop being so mean.* It was the first time she could remember speaking up for herself and shutting down that inner voice, the one that picked up where her parents had left off, like when she came in third in the school spelling bee and her parents asked why she didn't come in first. Or when she tried out for the tennis team in junior high, was assigned a doubles match, and they reminded her that Summer had been placed in singles. And won every match.

Money didn't start pouring in like a slot machine, but Skye noticed little coincidences. She spotted loose change on the street almost every day and picked up every single coin, offering a silent thank-you. She exceeded her sales quota at Devlin's by the end of her shift, and a customer even took the time to tell Patrick how helpful and friendly she was. And at the most recent job she worked with Harvey, the client thanked them with an extra twenty dollars each—equivalent to the amount she'd exchanged for quarters. Had such things been happening all along and she was now keen to them, or had something really shifted because she literally moved matter in her bedroom?

In terms of redecorating the room (although she didn't think of it as redecorating so much as "realigning"), Skye kept the wall color but juxtaposed it with plum-purple velvet fabric that she found in a remnants bin at a fabric store, which she used for curtains she made herself, thanks to a YouTube how-to video and a sewing machine she borrowed from her coworker Barbara. She planned to make sheets and pillowcases when she could afford more fabric. She loved the contrast of the rich, royal plum hue against the sunny yellow. As for the pink dresser, Harvey helped her sand it down, and she painted it an eye-popping lime green. She also replaced the brass hardware with gold that Harvey had bought but never got around to replacing himself. All of these changes captured a sense of *wealth* and *luxury* to her. Green and purple were colors mentioned in *Make Room for Money*. And she liked the velvet and gold touches.

Harvey, upon seeing the results, seemed surprised by his satisfaction. "Any other room or house and I would have thought it was all too bright and color overloaded, but it somehow works in here. Like . . ." And then he smiled. "Like a comic book come to life."

Skye's smile felt as radiant as sunlight.

"I like what you've been doing here, Skye," he said. "You're making this place into a home."

"It's not too intrusive?" she asked.

He shook his head. "Maybe it needed a woman's touch all along."

Skye also noticed that she and Harvey were becoming more like partners than roommates. Each took the initiative to do something for the other without being asked. Harvey fed Chip and bought him catnip. Skye took Bucky for walks. Harvey restocked her shampoo and conditioner. Skye had his coveralls laundered. When they did a painting job together, they worked so in sync, knowing how long the other person took, who was better at cutting in and who was better at taping off, who preferred painting ceilings as opposed to cleaning the brushes and rollers, and so on. They conversed easily, took turns watching each other's favorite TV programs, bought each other coffee.

He was her best friend, she realized. She was still attracted to him, still got a flash of heat if he accidentally brushed up against her or smiled that delightful Harvey smile. But she was busy enjoying that friendship rather than fixating on the "more" she wanted.

◆ ◆ ◆

Skye had pored through Flora's other two books, and although she wanted to transform Harvey's entire condo, she knew she had to, one, be patient and, two, stick with a sole intention for now. She was beginning to understand. If your home was a reflection of the life you lived, then everything else around you was also a reflection. The people you were friends with. The books you read or programs you watched. The men you dated. In order to *be* prosperous, she had to *think* prosperously. She only ever thought in terms of lack—not getting enough for the time and effort she put in, not having enough money in her wallet or bank account, not enough time, not enough sleep, not enough confidence. Prior to feng shui, the only thing she'd felt she'd had in abundance was pounds of fat.

She was living a good life. Or rather, she was *creating* it, room by room, piece by piece, section by section.

◆ ◆ ◆

One week following the workshop at the bookstore, using the phone number Flora had written down in the corner of the title page of *Make Room for Money*, Skye called her and, as Flora had promised, she answered the phone and seemed to be delighted when Skye introduced herself and reminded the woman of their conversation.

"I am so glad you called," Flora said. "How are you?"

Skye filled her in on all she had done that week, and all that had followed.

"Wonderful. Oh, I just love hearing things like this! You're on your way, honey. You really are."

With the exception of Julie, Skye couldn't remember the last time anyone, especially a woman, called her *honey*, and she discovered that she missed it fervently. Like eating something scrumptious and thinking, *Where has this been all my life?*

"Well, that's another reason why I'm calling," said Skye. "So much of what I read in your books resonated with me. I can't tell you how many times I've moved a piece of furniture or painted a wall or something because it felt off to me. I thought it was just some weird quirk of mine, but now I think I might be on to something with this feng shui thing." She'd been practicing pronouncing it the right way and messed up again, reverting back to *fen shwee*, certain Flora was about to scold her and retract the term of endearment.

Instead, Flora responded with, "Isn't it lovely to be validated now?"

Skye became choked up with emotion. "It is," she managed to say without blubbering again. "But here's the thing. I want to learn—I really, *really* want to learn what you do. I think I could be good at it, and I think I would enjoy it. But I'm barely making ends meet right now." And without warning, Skye poured out her entire story to Flora—meeting Vance online, packing up her life in Warwick and flying to Billings, being ghosted by Vance, meeting Harvey on the plane, Harvey taking her in, and the uncertainty of her fate not only at Devlin's Furniture but in Billings, Montana. When she finished babbling, she became aware of what she'd just done. It was the first time anyone in Billings other than Harvey knew the truth.

"I . . . I'm so sorry for rambling and dumping all of that on you," said Skye.

"It's really OK," said Flora. She was so patient, so matronly, so nonjudgmental, just as she had been in the bookstore. "Sounds like you've had quite an adventure."

"I have," said Skye. "And I'm ready for more now."

"Well, let's make that happen. I too think you need to learn to be a practitioner. From what you've said, it sounds like you're a natural.

A financial solution will come. Don't worry about the form it comes in. Just trust that it will and say thank you, as if it's already been given to you."

Skye liked the idea of acting as if something she wanted had already been given to her. Almost like an advance on an allowance or a retroactive raise.

"OK," said Skye with a smile. "I can do that."

"Good," said Flora, and Skye could tell she was smiling as well. "It's all going to work out, honey. In fact, you'll be amazed by how perfect it all comes out."

Skye hadn't been this excited since she was a kid on her birthday. "Yay!" she heard herself say, and both she and Flora laughed. She felt light and bouncy, and that alone was cause for glee.

CHAPTER
TWENTY-FOUR

Since the end of her dinner with Patrick two weeks ago, even though Skye had apologized the first time she'd returned to work following the incident, things had been awkward between her and Patrick in that let's-try-to-pretend-something-that-happened-never-did way. Of course, it wasn't like they'd done anything inappropriate like share a kiss, but every time one of her coworkers mentioned how long they had worked at the store or long-term plans, Skye had to smile through the tension of knowing something they didn't, especially when Patrick was within hearing range and wore the same smile.

One night before closing, Patrick entered the break room as Skye was stealing a bite of a peppermint patty from her purse. As if she'd just been caught with her hand in the till, she reacted with a startle, and, to stave off the embarrassment, she offered him a piece, but he waved his hand away and thanked her.

"Listen, I'm truly sorry for having spoken out of turn," he said. "I can tell it's bothered you ever since."

Finally. The ice was broken. She should have done it herself the day after it happened, she realized, and chided herself for not taking the initiative.

"I don't like keeping something like this from my coworkers," she said.

"Well, I don't think the store is going to close. I just wanted to tell you that so you can rest a little easier."

"But there's still a possibility," she said.

Patrick didn't respond.

"Patrick, I appreciate that you had good intentions when you told me. But I can't just 'rest easy' when I don't know how much longer I'll be employed."

Patrick dejectedly looked at his shoes. "You're right," he said. He paused for a minute before adding, "I wish we could be friends."

Skye was touched by his sincerity, and felt guilty for having put up a wall. Perhaps it had nothing to do with Patrick's misstep and had been more an attempt to protect her heart from another rejection at the hands of a Billings resident. As if Billings had been the cause of her heartbreak.

"We are friends," she said. "I was wrong to say we weren't."

He picked up his head and smiled. "You're the best associate we have here. If I could promote you, believe me, I would. I'd put you in corporate as a buyer or a marketer or something."

Another realization struck her: she'd always attached an asterisk to every compliment. For every award or honor she'd received at Top Drawer, she shrugged it off with a thought like, *Well, this job isn't rocket science,* or *Summer would be running the damn company by now.* Exactly the types of things her parents had always said whenever she aced a test or won a tennis match. That was why she gave up the tennis team, why she didn't strive for a 4.0 grade point average in college. Why bother? No matter how well she did, Summer either already did it better or would do it better or could do it better. It was why she gave up any pursuit of a career other than retail manager; there was nothing to work for if you were going to be beaten down moments later. It was also the reason why she didn't tell anyone when she was named Manager of the Month or anything else. Why raise herself up only to be struck down?

Her parents were wrong. Beyond wrong. They'd treated her so unfairly. And maybe they'd treated Summer unfairly too. Maybe instead of settling for less the way Skye had always chosen to do, Summer constantly pushed herself harder.

Which led her to think that maybe her resentment of Summer was misplaced too.

Patrick was seeing the same things in her that her bosses at Top Drawer had seen. She wasn't going to dismiss them anymore. And she smiled not only in response to the compliment, but to the revelation.

"I appreciate your confidence," said Skye. And then, in her managerial voice, commanded, "Let's get back on the floor and get ready to close." Patrick dutifully and amiably followed. As they passed the office on the way out, Skye peeked in. "Hey, Patrick—that desk in the office needs to go."

"No kidding," he said. "It's a monster."

"Can't you purchase something new through the store and expense it?"

"I honestly don't know," he said as they reentered the showroom. "Which one do you think I should get?"

Skye looked at Patrick, and then scanned the panorama of the showroom. "What are your goals beyond the store? You told me that you believe in working from the ground up, but where in the company do you really want to be?"

Patrick looked at her contemplatively, and she wondered if she'd just crossed a boundary by asking her boss such a personal question. Maybe that's why she had originally rejected him as a friend.

"That's a good question." An expression of sadness took over. "You're going to think this is really stupid, but"—he paused to take a breath, as if he were about to make a leap—"I want to be in charge of social media marketing. I think the company is severely lacking in its social media outreach, and that's one of the reasons why this store is struggling." He said the last part softer, even though they were out of hearing range of John, the assistant manager, who was on the floor talking to a customer.

"What's so stupid about that? I think it's an important job."

"My family thinks it's an excuse for me to goof off. I want to work from home. They think that's code for laziness." He shook his head. "I used to write. They think that's for lazy people too."

"That's too bad."

Skye began to look for a desk that would somehow serve as a symbol of what he truly desired. As she walked around the showroom to survey the various pieces—traditional rolltop desks in walnut or cherry, glass-topped computer desks with built-in shelving and storage, faux granite tops, and durable Formica for kids—she stopped at one that she deemed suitable for Patrick. Contemporary in design, it was a painted piece, Facebook blue with white hardware, wide enough to hold either a desktop monitor or a sizable laptop, yet not so mammoth as to invite clutter. The desk was light, portable, and came with an aerodynamic chair in black or white.

"This is it," she said, pointing to it. "This is your desk." She lifted the tag and took a peek. "Good price too."

Patrick looked at the desk, and then Skye, in wonderment, as if to say, *How did you know?* He turned away as if someone were watching over his shoulder, and then faced Skye again.

"It's perfect," he said. "I don't know why I never noticed it before, but it is. Maybe I can buy it and use it in my home office."

"No, I think you need it here for now. It wants to be in the store office."

Patrick laughed. "The desks wants that? It told you?"

"As a matter of fact, it did," she said, uncertain of whether she was joking or completely serious.

"Well, I'll ask the regional manager about it tomorrow—who just so happens to be my uncle," he added.

"Sounds like a plan," she said.

"If he says no, then I'll just buy it for myself as a birthday present."

Skye gasped and covered her mouth. "Patrick! I completely forgot it was your birthday."

He laughed. "It's OK," he said. "I wouldn't expect you to remember something like that."

"But I should have. I'm so sorry."

"Really, it's OK."

"Is your wife throwing you a party or something?"

He visibly tensed. "We're not big on birthdays in my family."

Skye wasn't sure how to respond. "Well, happy birthday. I'll buy you a beer next week. Blew my paycheck for this week."

He laughed again. "I'd love that," said Patrick. "And thank you, Skye. That was an awfully nice thing you just did—taking the time to select something that was perfect for me, considering my needs, supporting my goals—not to mention more of your excellent salesmanship. You should get the commission for it."

"I didn't do it for the commission," she said. "I did it because we're friends."

"Well, you're a good friend," he said.

A friend. She had another friend in Billings. You'd think it was *her* birthday, she was so grateful.

CHAPTER
TWENTY-FIVE

June

Skye sat in City Brew with Flora Davis after her second-week follow-up phone call. She had called Flora to thank her for writing the books as well as for her generosity, and invited her for coffee to "pick her brain" on some things. Skye sipped a huckleberry-flavored Italian cream soda (huckleberry was officially her new favorite flavor) through a straw and picked at a slice of pound cake while Flora enjoyed an iced coffee. In contrast to other coffee chains, City Brew seemed friendlier and less pretentious. The round tables and chairs evoked the same hues as the coffee flavors—hazelnuts and vanillas and mochas—while natural light streamed through the picture windows. Soft-leather reading chairs in the corners with faux fireplaces were offset by the pub tables against the walls in the back, next to outlets. Skye wondered if she was taking more notice of the way spaces were set up as a result of the feng shui books or because of all she'd learned at Devlin's. She was delighted to learn that prior to learning feng shui, Flora had also begun in furniture sales.

"I kept rearranging the living room and bedroom sets on the show-room floor to get the right 'feel,'" she said with a laugh. "Drove management nuts!"

"I can imagine," said Skye. "I made Harvey—the guy who owns the condo where I'm renting a room—move a few pieces around last week. *His* furniture! Not even mine."

"Sounds like you found a real keeper," she said.

Skye jumped to correct her. "Oh, we're not, like, *living together*. We're just—he's just been a good friend."

Was she certain about that? Yes, they weren't sharing a bed, weren't cohabitating as lovers, but they were living together. In fact, she'd never shared a space so easily with anyone.

"Certainly," said Flora, neither confirming nor denying Skye's admission. She took another sip of iced coffee before continuing. "So let's talk about the course."

Skye opened a manila folder that she took from Patrick's office (with his permission) and removed two typed pages that she had printed out on Harvey's printer.

"I've written a proposal," said Skye. "I want to propose a payment plan. I take the course and pay you back in six monthly installments, the first payment being at the beginning of the course. I've already lined up a third job."

When she had decided that she wanted—no, *needed*—to take the feng shui course, Skye had walked down the street to Nellie's, a local breakfast nook, and begged for a waitressing job, promising to learn quickly. Nellie's daughter, the manager and proprietor, gave her the chance and started her off on three mornings per week, no weekends. So far, she'd been slow but determined, and her determination was paying off. She'd already taken home sixty dollars in tip money her first week—hardly a windfall, but Skye was so proud of herself for stepping outside her comfort zone, working toward a purpose, that you'd think she'd won the lottery. Between that, painting, and Devlin's Furniture store, she was back to forty hours per week and caught up on all her expenses.

Flora perused the proposal as Skye spoke. "And what if you default on your payments?"

"I am *not* going to default on my payments." She spoke with the utmost confidence and resolve. "If we put it in writing, it would be a legally binding agreement," said Skye. "You could take me to court were I to default."

"I wouldn't want to do that," said Flora.

"But you *could*. It's business, not personal. This holds me accountable."

Skye was speaking with so much authority she barely recognized her own voice. What was more, she believed every word she said. More than believed—she *knew*. She knew she would hold herself accountable and that she would deliver.

Flora smiled as if she was in the know. "OK," she said. "I'm going to hold you to your word and your contract. You're going to be a natural, an absolute dynamo. Don't let us down."

Skye finished the last of her cream soda and basked in Flora's words. She already felt like a dynamo. She was looking forward to telling Harvey about it when she got home.

Skye hugged Flora goodbye and walked out into the sunny parking lot, chin up, feeling the warmth on her face. She looked up and saw the rimrocks behind her. They were quite a sight.

Billings really isn't so bad, she told herself.

And then, as she was about to drive away from City Brew and onto Twenty-Seventh Street, she watched a man, who was completely oblivious to her, saunter from his car to the coffee shop, his arm around the waist of a waif of a woman.

Vance Sandler.

CHAPTER
TWENTY-SIX

The contents of her stomach churned. Her body turned to stone. Her hands shook and she gripped the steering wheel to steady them, her knuckles turning white from the pressure.

Skye couldn't be certain that the man who just strode into City Brew was Vance Sandler. For one thing, he never looked in her direction, so she didn't see his face in full. She caught the salt-and-pepper hair and the stark cheekbone and the rounded chin from a three-quarter view, but she was also distracted by the sturdy hand around his female companion's minuscule waist, and her long, silky dark hair, and the difference in height between them. Vance was six two, but judging from what she just saw, he didn't seem to be as towering as she'd remembered him to be.

Would he have recognized her even had he been looking? Would he have cared?

Nausea seized her, and she swallowed hard to keep it down.

She had wondered how long it would take before she ran into Vance. Wondered what she'd do or say or how she'd feel or act. And even if it wasn't Vance—she wasn't inclined to go back into the coffee shop and find out for certain—she had been completely unprepared. She was wearing clothes from Walmart. She wore no makeup on her days off from work. Her bottled burgundy hair was unstyled, and her gray roots were showing—she couldn't afford to get it professionally colored and hadn't yet gotten around to buying a home-coloring kit. All the lightness and hope she had felt only moments ago had been sucked out of her and into the black hole that was Vance Sandler and all that he'd represented.

She had to move. She had to leave Billings. This city of one hundred thousand people and forty-something square miles was too small for her, too crowded. She wanted to go back to the anonymity of Rhode Island. The vastness of Montana suffocated her, whereas the tight corners of the East Coast allowed her to breathe.

She didn't belong here.

But she liked it. The uniqueness of the rimrocks and Sacrifice Cliff, the sparse yet active downtown, and the sky—always the vast expanse of sky, even in tree-lined neighborhoods, with painted clouds and marvelous sunsets and blue that stretched as far as an ocean. Could she get such variety anywhere else? She still wanted such ubiquitous landmarks as a Target and a mall and a chain supermarket. But she also wanted the feeling of small-town friendliness and familiarity, like when the City Brew baristas already knew her order before she stepped up to the counter. How one of Nellie's customers was also Harvey's paint client and remembered her face, if not her name. She'd never felt anything but anonymity when she lived in Warwick. How much of that had been her doing? Had Warwick, or any Rhode Island town, possessed something unique and beautiful that she'd never before noticed?

Her enthusiasm completely deflated, Skye drove back to the condo. Upon entering, Harvey greeted her with, "How did your meeting with Flora go?"

"Fine," said Skye.

Harvey pressed. "You OK?"

She sucked in a breath and let it out. "I think I saw Vance today."

Harvey gasped. "Holy shit."

"I don't know for sure if it was him, but it's absolutely wrecked me, and I hate that I let it," she said, trembling, fighting off tears. Harvey rose from the couch, walked over to where she was standing, and put his arms around her. Every corpuscle in her body twittered with exhilaration as his touch traveled beneath her skin. What kind of hug was this? Was it a you're-my-pal hug? Was it a solidarity-against-Vance-the-fuckface hug? Or was it a we're-getting-closer-every-day hug?

As if he heard the voice, Harvey said, "Don't beat yourself up, Skye. You're doing so well. You're working and meeting people and you're making a life for yourself. Hell, you're making a *home* for yourself." He added, "Here, in this condo. It feels so much less like a bachelor pad and more like—" He stopped short.

Like it's ours, Skye wanted to say.

Home. In this condo. Of course, whenever she'd mentioned her Warwick apartment, she'd called it home. But thinking back, it had been a residence. A place to sleep and eat and hang out. But here in the condo, Skye felt safe. Cuddled. Nurtured.

"Thank you, Harvey," she said. She wanted to bury herself in the strength and warmth of his arms. She wanted to move even closer into him. She wanted to kiss him and run her fingers through his unruly hair and . . .

She pulled herself away from him, flushed and sweaty.

"Fuck Vance Sandler," said Harvey.

"You can," said Skye. "I'm done."

Harvey laughed, causing Skye to laugh as well. She was laughing more and more since she'd arrived in Billings, and it felt good. In fact, laughing with Harvey was one of her favorite Billings pastimes.

"You're so much more than he'll ever be," Harvey said, his eyes brimming with warmth. "Just remember that."

I am so much more. Perhaps she would use that as her new mantra and replace *I approve of myself.* Harvey could see it. Patrick could see it. Flora could see it.

It was time for Skye to see it—to *know* it—as well.

CHAPTER
TWENTY-SEVEN

July–August

Summer in Billings wasn't much different from summer in Rhode Island, with the exception of the humidity. Not living so close to the water made a difference. Skye didn't feel like she was trying to wade through pea soup in ninety degrees. Her hair didn't frizz as much. That said, there also wasn't much of a breeze. Or rain. Still, she liked the way the downtown restaurants were packed with outdoor seating, and the line spilling onto the sidewalk outside Big Dipper, yet she wondered why no one complained about not having a beach to go to for sunbathing or swimming.

In addition to herself, there were five other students in the feng shui course, including Jack, an interior designer who wanted to expand his business, and Errin, a schoolteacher who was hoping she could apply the techniques to her classroom to the benefit of her students. Skye envied them for their careers—she was embarrassed to tell them she was a part-time retail employee, down from a retail manager. Even with her bachelor's degree, she felt like such an underachiever. But both her classmates and Flora repeatedly insisted that she was the one who was naturally gifted. The other students were either interested in improving their own homes and life situations or practicing for friends and family as a hobby.

The course met six hours per week—two nights and on Saturdays—for six weeks. Skye had worked it out with Devlin's and Nellie's to work around the course schedule, meaning she worked morning shifts during the week and late-night shifts on Saturdays, alternating between the store and the restaurant. Even though she went to bed exhausted every night, Skye enjoyed being a full-timer again and loved every minute of the course. She loved the sense of purpose she now had and how her paychecks were helping her achieve that purpose. She had to temporarily give up working for Harvey, who said he missed her not just for the extra set of hands but for the companionship; and even though she missed him as well, she liked the idea that she was earning on her own without his assistance, although she'd been grateful for every moment of it. As a way of paying his kindness forward, she recommended him to all of her furniture store clients and her feng shui classmates.

Week one consisted of the basics of the ba-gua method of feng shui (there was also something called the compass method, which Flora said was more complicated and a matter of preference for most practitioners). Almost all the material was in Flora's books, so Skye breezed right through it but loved the practical-application component of the course, like mapping out a room or moving furniture or simple objects into or out of gua spaces. Week two was all about color. Week three, the elements (water, fire, metal, wood, and earth). Weeks four and five were about space and energy clearing, and week six was all practice, in which they went to each other's homes and took turns "consulting" the student as if he or she were a client.

Each week, Skye reported back to Julie, even told her about her possible run-in with Vance. She also decided to renew her efforts with Summer and called her one weekend.

The conversation began chilly. "Hi," said Summer, sounding wary, the wound from their last call still open.

"I'm sorry for the way I acted during our last call," Skye began. "It was rude and childish of me."

After a beat, Summer's tone softened. "I should have been more supportive of you," she said. "If you want to know the truth, I'm kind of jealous."

Summer?! Jealous?! Of me?!

"Jealous of what?" asked Skye.

"That you got to just pick up your life and move and try something new."

Skye couldn't believe what she was hearing. "But you have a great life, Summer. You've got a mega-successful career, a dream husband, a supersmart and likable kid. Why would you want to give any of that up?"

"Do you know how much work it takes to keep it all? How much pressure I'm under to write another book, apply for dean, keep my husband happy, make sure my kid keeps up her grades . . . because if he fails or she fails, it's not on them, it's on me?"

Skye had never considered this. "You chose all that, though," she said. "I didn't have the luxury. No matter what I achieved, Mom and Dad drilled it into me that I would never be as good as you."

"Exactly. They expected me to be perfect at everything. Did you know they didn't speak to me for a week when I came home one semester with two B-minuses? Never mind that they were two of the hardest courses in the program. Never mind that I caught the flu along with half the student body and faculty that semester. They literally didn't speak to me. All they said was 'You let us down.'"

Summer's voice quavered as she spoke. Now Skye understood. While Skye resented Summer for besting her and getting all the attention, Summer resented Skye for having the freedom to fail. Now Skye realized that whereas she couldn't possibly reach perfection, Summer wasn't permitted to settle for anything else. She wasn't allowed to have a bad day or a bad marriage. She wasn't even allowed to have a B-minus.

And now she felt nothing but empathy.

"Summer, I'm so sorry they did that to you. I'm sorry they pitted us against each other like that. They were wrong to do it. And neither of us has to take that shit anymore."

"Easy for you to say."

"Well, of course it's easy to say. But what do you truly have to lose by doing it? Their love? Not speaking to you for a week because of a fucking grade isn't love, Summer. It's cruel. You may give up a lot, but you'll get something really big back—*you*. Your life. The life you really want. That's what I'm doing here in Montana."

"But you're working multiple jobs and your relationship went sour. Is that really the life you want?"

Had Summer said that at any other time, Skye would have accepted it as more judgment and criticism. But now she saw that Summer was genuinely trying to understand.

"Yes," said Skye. "Because by eliminating what you don't want, you figure out what you do want. By losing Vance the way I did, I discovered it wasn't the relationship I really wanted. And these jobs have led me to find what I really enjoy, and I even took a third job to help me pay for it. I'm taking a feng shui course."

"Really?" said Summer.

"Yes, and it's just the coolest thing ever. I've been doing it most of my life and never knew it. I know you think it's a bunch of mumbo jumbo, but—"

"When did I say that?"

Her sister couldn't even remember? Another revelation for Skye: perhaps Summer's criticism had been a projection of jealousy, something she was expected to say rather than what she really believed.

"It doesn't matter. The point is that I'm finally on a certain path, and it doesn't matter what anyone else thinks or feels about it. It matters how *I* feel. And I finally feel good."

Summer didn't respond right away, as if she were absorbing the entire conversation.

"Maybe you're right, Skye," she said. After another pause, she followed with, "I'm glad you reached out to me."

Skye had never felt closer to her sister than she did at that moment. It was as if the tug-of-war rope they'd spent their entire lives pulling on had frayed to nothing, allowing them to simply let go. "Me too," said Skye. "Maybe you can visit for a weekend before the new semester starts in. You have to see the sky out here. It's pretty amazing."

"I'd like that," she replied, a new lightness to her words. "Have you gotten a chance to see any more of Montana?"

"No," she said. "I'm going to have to fix that."

When Skye and Summer ended their call, both promising to call again soon, Skye looked at the part of her room represented by the Family and Creativity section of the ba-gua map, which happened to be where the bedroom window was. All her photos were still in storage, so she had printed out some photos of Summer, Brent, and Kayla online, and taped them to the edges of the window. She smiled when she saw them, completely in love with feng shui.

◆ ◆ ◆

When Skye graduated from the course and received her certificate, she, Flora, and her classmates held a formal ceremony in Rose Park, one of the first places she'd ever been to with Harvey. In addition to taking Bucky Barnes there, she and Harvey had attended the outdoor concert and Fourth of July fireworks show.

All the students brought spouses and significant others and children to the ceremony, but Harvey had a painting job scheduled at the same time, so she knew not to expect him even though she was disappointed.

She nearly fell over with surprise when she saw him amble across the field to their circle, a bouquet of flowers from Albertsons supermarket in hand. His face—smiling, supportive, even a little mischievous—made her tingle all over. She loved everything about it—its olive tone, its crow's-feet, its squared-off chin and pockmarked skin. Eyes the color of mocha. She wanted to cup his face as she would an oversized mug of hot cocoa to warm her hands. Even in the middle of August.

When Flora presented her with a certificate, Skye erupted with emotion. "I graduated from a university with a bachelor's degree in marketing and management," she said, choking back tears. "And this means even more."

Harvey applauded louder than anyone.

"You're going to do big things," said Flora following the ceremony. "I know it like I know the sky is blue."

"Big Skye," said Jack, the interior designer. He laughed heartily, as did the others. It didn't hurt this time. Maybe because Jack said it with such affection. Maybe because she was taking things less personally. Maybe because she was loving herself a lot more. Or maybe all three. "How appropriate," he said with a smile, and pointed up to the postcard view above them. Breathtaking. "See?" he said. "You were meant to be here."

Imagine that.

Skye framed and hung the certificate in the Career part of her room rather than the Wealth and Prosperity corner. But what to do with it now? She knew what she was good at: organizing, decluttering, and transforming a room to meet the needs of the client. Thanks to her ACME sales training, she knew how to listen to the client, and she trusted her instincts when the room "spoke" to her. Now she had to figure out how to turn that into a business.

She could use the condo as her model. It had turned out spectacular. She had escorted Harvey room by room, making him touch everything he owned and getting rid of anything he didn't like—he'd wound up packing two large U-Haul boxes with stuff to donate to a thrift store, the kitchen being one of the only rooms spared. She bought plants and gemstones and placed them in various corners. Together they chose new colors for the walls—a nautical navy blue for the living room accent wall and a striking pewter for the other walls in the living room, and a terra cotta for his bedroom that was warm and masculine and earthy. Harvey reported better nights of sleep ever since.

He was working almost full-time now. He was going out with friends more after work. His kids came back from Seattle for a visit, and he picked them up at Deb's house on a Friday afternoon, took them to Bozeman for the weekend, and dropped them off on Sunday night. Skye, meanwhile, worked and kept the place clean and welcomed him back. He looked happy. Lighter. Recharged.

Together they'd made a home. Did he see it as such? Did he see it as their home? Or did he still see her as a roommate, or maybe even a tenant?

Would he ever see her as more than his friend? And if he did, how would that affect her plans to leave Billings when the year was up?

Because even though she was growing to like Billings more every day, was becoming more a part of it, Rhode Island was still within her sights. And she couldn't see herself giving that up.

CHAPTER
TWENTY-EIGHT

On the last Saturday in August, as she and Patrick prepared to open the store together, Skye asked him how the desk was working out.

"Amazing how one little piece of furniture can change not only the outlook of a room but also a person," said Patrick. He chortled. "Even though that's what we tell our customers every day, isn't it."

"What's changed?" she asked.

"Well, I made up a proposal, for starters," he said. "In fact, I pitched it to my uncle last week. I want to devote a portion of my workdays to consistent online social networking."

"That's great!" said Skye. "Do you think it will help?"

"It can't hurt."

Skye looked around at the empty store as if business hours had already started. "I hope it does. And speaking of social networking, I'm starting a new venture, and I wanted you to help me with that part of it. Set up Facebook and Twitter pages, Instagram, Pinterest, maybe even a website . . ."

"Sure!" he said. "I'd love to. What's the venture?"

"I'm starting a feng shui business."

"Fun what?"

She laughed. "Feng shui. The ancient art of object placement."

"Didn't someone come here a couple of months ago with a pamphlet about that?"

"Yep. I took the course."

"Cool," he said.

There was a time when Skye would have braced herself for criticism. Would have waited for him to say something like, *Why are you wasting your time on something like that?* Trusting the support of her friends felt so good, a worry let loose. And it finally clicked what Flora had told her that night about attaining *freedom*—getting it had nothing to do with dollars and cents. Skye had always put the cart before the horse. Like with her weight—she'd always believed she would love and appreciate herself, and others would love and appreciate her, when she shed the pounds and rocked a pair of skinny jeans. Now she knew that as long as she loved and appreciated herself, others would too, regardless of her body size. That was true freedom.

"So what do you want to do?" Patrick asked.

"I want to try to get some clients and start my own business, including organizing closets and stuff like that." She spoke with authority; saying it out loud felt empowering.

"How about this," started Patrick. "How about in exchange for my social media services, you do some feng shui on a room in my house. Then we can refer each other. Deal?"

"Deal," said Skye.

◆ ◆ ◆

In addition to bringing her laptop to Patrick's house, Skye brought her feng shui tool kit, which consisted of a jar of sea salt; a "smudge stick" made up of dried sage; a compass; paint swatches; laminated cards of the ba-gua map, like the ones Flora had handed out that night at the bookstore; and a notepad for her personal use. She hadn't yet made business cards.

Patrick lived in a yellow house on Clark Street in what was known as Central Billings, near downtown. The first time Skye had been through this neighborhood with Harvey, she thought the houses were small, clearly built in the earlier part of the previous century. Some had been maintained or upgraded, while others showed signs of dilapidation via chipping paint or broken shutters or hail-damaged roofs. Harvey had explained that the exterior appearances were deceiving and that most houses were rather spacious on the inside, with full basements and multiple bedrooms. This was later confirmed when they had a painting job in one of those houses in which the basement was being renovated.

Skye had always dreamed of living somewhere more modern, like the home of the authors in the Heights, or a historical-but-affluent home like those in Bristol, Rhode Island. She didn't like what were known as "McMansions," but her sister had a home in Wakefield, Rhode Island, that Skye downright salivated over every time she entered it—cathedral ceilings and skylights; an open-concept kitchen-living-dining area, the kitchen complete with six-burner stove, two-door oven, monstrous island, and quartz countertops; endless bedrooms and full baths; and a recreation room with a viewing screen and movie-theater sound system, pool and ping-pong tables, and a full bar. Given the low retail salaries, she'd previously doubted she would ever own a house, much less a reasonable condo like Harvey's, but at the beginning of her feng shui course she'd created a vision board on which she pasted pictures of houses she'd like to live in.

Only problem was she didn't know *where* they were. East Coast? West Coast? The beach? The mountains? Billings? Bristol?

She had no idea. But for the first time, she liked that the possibilities were as vast as the Montana sky.

Patrick opened the door of the screened-in porch as she approached. She liked screened-in porches. A soccer ball sat on one of the wicker chairs. "Come on in," he said with a smile. "Welcome to Casa Brody."

"Thanks," she said. Patrick opened the second door, and the moment she stepped in, she smelled fresh-brewed coffee. She surveyed the living room—hardwood floors, cream-colored walls, and one of Devlin's leather living room packages complete with sofa, loveseat, and chair crammed in with a dark cherry coffee table, end tables, and floor lamps.

"One of the discontinued floor models," he explained.

"Nice," said Skye, although her vibe kicked in and noticed immediately that something was off. *This room wants to be more feminine.*

"The furniture is a little big for the room," he remarked, stating the obvious, "but I didn't want to break up the set."

"I understand."

He continued the tour, taking her through the small kitchen ("Upgraded appliances," Patrick said—she was beginning to feel like a prospective buyer) before showing her the three bedrooms and full bath on the main floor, followed by the den, office, and second full bath in the basement.

Cream walls everywhere except in the bedrooms, where the kids' walls were what Skye now knew to be "Superman blue," thanks to Harvey, and cranberry for the master. The rooms were neat, but dusty. She felt like something was missing—not an object or piece of furniture, but an energy, like that of a person.

"It's nice," said Skye when they retreated to the dining room and sat at the table, each with a mug of coffee in hand and a plate of store-bought cookies between them.

"It's OK," he said. "Good starter house."

"I almost forgot that you're originally from Bozeman. Which city do you like better, Billings or Bozeman? Just curious." Ever since Summer had asked if Skye had seen more of Montana, she'd had a desire to visit more cities. Bozeman was on the short list, partly because it was only about two hours away from Billings (a doable drive), and partly because it would be nice to see where her friend grew up.

"Hard to say. They both have their pluses and minuses. Bozeman has so many great cultural outlets and just about everything else you need in terms of shopping and stuff, but sometimes it feels way more crowded than Billings. Billings is a little grittier. But it's also got some really good things happening downtown, like the new bookstore and all the restaurants and brew pubs. It's got culture, but you have to actively look for it. And once you find it, you wonder how you missed it. I think Bozeman is a little more cliquey, whereas Billings will try anything once."

"I've never been to Bozeman," said Skye. "In fact, I haven't been anywhere outside of Billings yet, as far as the rest of Montana goes."

Patrick's eyes widened. "Well, what are you waiting for?"

Skye laughed. "A reason to go, I guess. And someone to go with." Maybe she should ask Harvey to take a day trip with her. Or one of her new friends from the feng shui class. Jack, the interior designer, once mentioned a client and some stores in Bozeman to pick up good accessory pieces for around the house.

"It's *Montana*," said Patrick. "That should be reason enough. Seriously, Skye, you've got to see this state. It's incredible. There's just so much beauty and quiet, so much history and wildlife. There's no other place like it."

Vance had advertised Montana pretty much the same way, beckoning her to give him the chance to show it to her, to add her to its beauty. She'd found the notion romantic. But since she'd arrived in Billings, she'd had no desire to leave the city limits, to go exploring, to experience the wonders of Montana. Her Devlin's coworker Barbara had grown up in the southeastern part of the country and settled in Billings. She said, "I didn't choose Montana. Montana chose me." Skye wished she could have that connection to a place. She'd always taken Rhode Island for granted; it wasn't until she left it that she developed an appreciation for all it had to offer. So far, Montana hadn't seeped into her soul the way it did for others, and she wondered if that made her defective, or revealed her as the outsider she knew she was. She wondered if she'd ever be an insider.

"I'd really like to see it," she said.

"Do it while the weather is still good," said Patrick. "Maybe next time we have a corporate meeting in Bozeman."

Skye's muscles tightened. She was about to say, "Maybe you should check with your wife first," when Patrick seemed to pick up on the tension and quickly segued back to their business. "So which do you want to do first, the social networking or the feng shui consultation?"

Skye sipped from a faded SpongeBob coffee mug. "Let's do the social networking first." She pulled her laptop from its case and powered it on. Her PC was fast becoming a dinosaur. Earlier in the year, she'd had plans to take advantage of Rhode Island's tax-free weekend—happening as they spoke—and buy a MacBook Pro at the Apple Store in Providence Place Mall. One thing she'd learned about Billings—they had no sales tax at all. If only she could capitalize on it with a new Mac.

Patrick opened an orange folder and pulled out mock-ups of various social media and website pages, logos, and a calendar plan. Skye looked at the header: *Skye Littleton: Home Consultant* in smaller type underneath.

She loved it. It echoed professionalism. Importance. Someone with a career and a purpose.

"And then, underneath, you can specify all your services. You can post videos and client testimonials as you accumulate them. You can even do some cross-promotion, like for a paint store or, say, furniture sales." He nudged her with his elbow. She chuckled. "These days marketing is about *content*. You're using video and audio and flyers and social media not just to get your name out there, but more important, to give customers an experience rather than making a sale."

Content marketing. She should have known that. She should have kept up with the times and kept her finger on the pulse of the trends when she got her degree, like Summer had done. Skye had always been discouraged, but that didn't mean she had to play the victim. She could have kept up with the trends the entire time she was at Top Drawer. She could have taken initiative that went beyond the confines of the store.

"I love it," said Skye. "It's perfect."

Together they set up social networking accounts, although Skye wasn't yet ready to upload any personal photos—Patrick recommended she have one professionally taken, and she agreed with him; it would have to wait until she had the budget for it, however. Ditto for a logo. In the meantime, she uploaded a generic yin-yang symbol as a profile photo. Next, they went to work on setting up her website domain name and construction. Skye was impressed with how much effort Patrick put into everything. Social media marketing, whether for Devlin's Furniture, Skye Littleton, or any other business, was definitely his forte and his passion. Maybe she should recommend him to Harvey to promote his painting business. The more Patrick shared his ideas, the more they woke Skye's long-dormant education and sparked her own ideas. When she'd gone to college, the Internet barely existed. Heck, maybe she could take some refresher courses at MSU-Billings.

Almost two hours later—two hours that had passed like ten minutes—Skye had posted her first tweet, shared the links to her new Facebook and Twitter pages on her personal Facebook page, and was in a position where she could continue to build the website on her own as she went along. Never had she felt so invigorated or empowered. *I am a business owner,* she said to herself. No capital, no office space, no clientele, but still. She had a certificate and a bachelor's degree and a desire. Sometimes that was enough capital to start with.

When they finished, Patrick looked at his watch.

"Do you need to pick up your kids or something?" she asked.

"They're with my wife," he said in the same tone Harvey used when he mentioned his kids or ex-wife: sadness, regret. "It's OK, we can start with your consulting."

"Oh," she said. "OK." She shut down her laptop and put it away, and pulled her tool kit out of a knapsack along with a folder like the one Patrick used. "Did you do your homework?" she said in a mock teacher voice, as if speaking to a younger student, before losing out to a giggle.

Patrick chuckled. "I did. It's here." He pulled a sheet of paper from the same folder and slid it in front of her. Skye read it. "I hope you don't mind, I just did a bullet-pointed list. That's where I like to start rather than write everything out. But I did handwrite it, as you can see."

Skye had asked him to write about any major life changes he wanted to make—career goals, relationships, home improvements, et cetera. Patrick nervously tapped his fingers on the table as her eyes scrolled down the list, seeing some of the more familiar points—redirect his career toward social media marketing, help keep the Billings store from closing. However, she involuntarily dropped her jaw and quietly gasped when she saw the last item: *Reconcile with my wife.* The tapping grew louder.

She looked up at him. His eyes were filled with shame and sadness.

"Patrick. I don't know what to say. Why didn't you tell me?"

That explained the missing energy she felt when he showed her the house earlier. *She* was missing. His wife. Their love.

"I don't know," he said. "I haven't really told anyone outside of the family. I wanted to tell you because I look up to you—you seem so wise about these things. But . . ." He trailed off.

She was struck by his admission: he looked up to her. She'd never been told that before. She wanted him to finish his thought, though. Wanted to see where it went. "But what?"

He redirected. "We married young. Sandra was pregnant, and I loved her and wanted a family, but I don't think either of us were ready for the responsibility. I mean, we just didn't want it yet." He dropped his gaze to the tabletop. "And I might dislike my job more than I let on."

His story sounded a lot like Harvey's. Skye remembered Patrick lamenting about how he wished they could be friends. She felt guilty for not realizing how badly he'd needed a friend the night he'd said it. Especially his saying he looked up to her . . . maybe that was why he'd invited her out that night. Maybe his other friends hadn't been as supportive. Maybe they'd all been his wife's friends. Or maybe he just needed a new lens through which to see.

"I'm so sorry," she said. "I really am." At that moment, she wanted to tell him all about what had brought her to Billings. She also knew that this was the kind of thing she was going to have to expect from her clients. Some of them were going to want big things—to overcome an addiction or a past trauma, reconcile with a parent or child or spouse or lover, get out of poverty, accept their cancer diagnosis. Was she in a position to say, *Sure, just move your couch across the room and light a candle in that corner,* as if that would solve everything?

She suddenly had major doubts about what she was doing, whether it was a bunch of nonsense or whether it could make a difference in someone's life, however small. She doubted that one six-week course had fully prepared or even qualified her to do so.

But didn't buying that desk make a difference in Patrick's life? Didn't it light a fire under him? Didn't the new wall color and curtains make a difference in the room Skye now called *her* room, by opening her up, helping her to change her feelings not only about the room, but about being in Billings?

She took a breath and began. "So here's the thing: feng shui isn't some kind of magic trick, where if you do it, everything in your life suddenly goes right. Your home is a reflection of you and the life you're living. So what you want to do is get a clear picture of what you want your life to be, and let your home reflect that. It's really about tapping into the *feelings* you want, and then adjusting your home to attract that."

"Well, that sounds doable," said Patrick. "So where do we start?"

Skye looked around the dining room and the adjoining living room. "Do you *like* this furniture?" she asked. "I'm not asking that in a judgmental way. I'm asking why you bought it."

"It's OK," he said. "It was the floor model, and we were clearing it out. I got it for a fraction of the retail price." He stared at it as if seeing it for the first time. "It's very . . . brown."

She laughed. "It is," she said.

"Sandra only liked the price." He paused. "Come to think of it, the entire house is outfitted with showroom leftovers."

"What are some of Sandra's favorite colors?"

"Lemon and lime. She loves that combination. Both in color and flavor."

Skye looked around. "I see so little of it."

"We bought this house in a whirlwind. It was like, pregnant, married, house—boom, boom, boom. We had to save every penny for the baby, and then once the first one came, followed by the second . . . well, there just wasn't any time for Sandra to decorate. Plus, she works too. She's a receptionist and trying to get into nursing school."

"Sounds like you've both had a lot on your plates for a long time."

He nodded. "We just started growing apart. I was all wrapped up in the family business and not having the guts to tell the family I wasn't happy, and she was frustrated because she couldn't do the things she wanted. She's taken on a lot of the child-rearing."

"What made her leave?" asked Skye, quickly adding, "Assuming she left."

Patrick's eyes became glassy as yet another revelation came to him. "She said she couldn't be in this house another minute. Obviously, there was more to it than that—it wasn't literally about the house, although it certainly didn't help. She needed time to think, to figure out what she wanted for herself. She moved into an apartment. The kids stay with me. It's just easier with their school and stuff. But she's with them every chance she gets."

Skye became misty-eyed as well. She couldn't fix his marriage; that wasn't her job. Her job was to help make any living space—be it a room, apartment, or house—a reflection of one's life, and vice versa.

"OK, Patrick. Here's the deal. You tell me the picture of what you want this house, and every room in it, to be. For example, 'I want the kitchen to be the place where everyone convenes. I want the bedroom to be a sanctuary. I want the house to be a magnet for productivity.' And so on. But tack on 'for Sandra' at the end of every statement. Then I'll help you bring that picture to life."

Patrick wiped a tear from his eye and smiled. "That is very doable."

"Also, let me know how much money, if any, you are willing or able to spend. Not for paying me, but for the rooms." Flora had discussed how much to charge clients during one of their class sessions. Skye was going to have to determine what she was worth, although she liked bartering for services too. If only bartering could pay her bills . . .

"How much do you think I need?"

"Depends on what you want to do. Just repainting the walls in every room would make a world of difference. But if that's not an option, we can get creative in other ways."

His smile widened, his face brightened, and he looked even younger than usual. "This is going to be fun. Thank you, Skye." He pulled her in for a hug. It was warm and tight and gratifying. Skye was beginning to realize just how important hugs were, and how many she'd taken for granted.

"You're welcome," she said. "And thank you too."

"My pleasure."

The two talked about the Devlin's schedule as Skye gathered her things and they walked outside. He hugged her one more time, and she drove down Clark Street in the direction of the condo with the windows down. She felt as if she could coast the entire way. The sun shone on her face, and the wind blew her hair back. *This is what freedom feels like.*

She had a purpose in life now. A calling. The beginning of a career for which she was truly suited.

CHAPTER TWENTY-NINE

When Skye returned from Patrick's house, she found Harvey dressed up in khakis, a button-down shirt, a jacket, and Oxfords, a far cry from his usual blue jeans and Henley shirts or paint coveralls and work boots. She hoped the quickening of her pulse and the flame up her spine upon seeing him wasn't noticeable.

"You clean up good," she said. "What's the occasion?"

"Get dressed," he said. "I'm taking you out."

Her heart was beating so fast she thought it would explode. "How come?"

"We never celebrated your graduating your course."

"You came to my graduation and brought me flowers."

"You deserve more," he said.

She wanted to cry. To throw her arms around him and kiss him. To inhale and breathe in his scent for eternity.

"That's very sweet of you," she said, choked up. She frowned seconds later. "I don't have anything nicer than work clothes, though."

"Wear what makes you feel good."

Skye went to her room and opened dresser drawers and closet doors. Just like Patrick's startling realization that the only thing about the furniture that appealed to his wife, Sandra, was the price, Skye's realization regarding her wardrobe was the same. Thrift stores, Walmart, clearance racks at Kohl's—these were the dominant factors in her selection. Fit was second, although sometimes even that took a seat further back. She liked the clothes OK. But she couldn't remember the last time she wore an outfit—one that wasn't work-related—that made her feel anything other than cheap or frumpy.

That needed to change.

She still had the sewing machine from making the curtains. Perhaps she could teach herself to make some clothes too.

In the meantime, Skye didn't want to wear work clothes. At least, not slacks or pantsuits or anything like that. Instead, she chose a pair of boot-cut dark-blue jeans, paired them with a floral-print blouse and red clogs, and untangled a necklace that Julie had given her for high school graduation.

She went into the bathroom to put on some makeup and attempt to style her hair—she really, *really* needed to color and cut it; it was past her shoulders and the gray had grown out yet again. When she finished, she checked herself out in the full-length mirror and for the first time took notice: the shape of her body had changed. It was leaner. Her jeans didn't feel quite so snug at the waistline. Her legs looked more streamlined. Her arms had definition.

I approve of myself. She mouthed the words to the mirror. "I approve of *you*," she said to the reflection, and smiled.

When she emerged from the bathroom, Harvey turned around and grinned. "Hey! You look nice!"

She beamed and blushed and bashfully averted her eyes.

"Is it OK to wear jeans? Where are we going?"

"I thought I'd take you to Ciao Mambo. Good Italian place. And zeppole with a huckleberry dipping sauce that will knock your socks off."

"You had me at huckleberry," said Skye. "Let's go."

◆ ◆ ◆

Skye couldn't help but feel the date vibe as she and Harvey entered Ciao Mambo, casually dressed but still *date-ish*, and he requested a table for two. The vibe only increased in volume when the server led them to a corner table, not secluded but certainly cozy, and Harvey held a chair for her and seated her himself. *Do guys even do this on dates anymore? Was it a date? Should she ask if it was a date?*

Harvey was fidgety at first as he fumbled with the wine menu and changed his drink order twice. They talked mostly about Skye's day over drinks before splitting a pizza, as the place jostled with servers scribbling their names on the paper-lined tables with crayons (although it was far from a typical family chain like Applebee's or Olive Garden), and crooners like Dean Martin and Frank Sinatra serenaded them. The walls were lined with artwork of wine bottles and loaves of bread. It was . . . *romantic*.

"Providence has some great Italian restaurants," said Skye. "Funny, I lived, like, ten minutes from Providence—literally—and so rarely went there. Even when I was working at the Providence Place Mall. I don't know why. It's a neat little city. Got its warts like any other place. But now I miss it, you know?"

She'd been thinking a lot about Rhode Island lately. Thought about the decision she'd made when she'd first arrived, that she'd give Billings a year and then move back to Rhode Island. Sometimes she wondered if she would leave sooner. Or later, even. She still wanted to see more of Montana. But she was craving something. She was craving a sense of place. She had it in the condo, but once she was outside the condo, it faded.

"I get it," said Harvey. "You never know what you'll really miss until you leave it."

What would I miss in Billings? she wondered.

Big Dipper.

The rimrocks.

The bookstore.

The sunsets.

Patrick.

Flora.

Her new feng shui friends.

And Harvey, of course. She would miss Harvey like crazy.

"Would you miss Billings if you left it?" she asked.

"Of course," he said.

"What would you miss?"

He gestured to the air above them. "This place, for starters. The people. The neighborhoods. The nooks and crannies that make Billings so great."

She took a breath. "Would you miss me?" Her voice quavered on the last word.

He looked at her with equal parts conviction and tenderness. "I'd miss you most of all."

Her heart throbbed. She had to take it slow, lest she blurt out right there, over the bread basket, that she was in love with him.

"Do you think you'd ever leave? Like, a full-out move?" She held her breath in anticipation of his answer.

"I guess if there were a certain opportunity or person or experience that was too good to pass on, then I'd consider it."

A person? Now her heart beat double-time. She couldn't help but feel the rush of excitement over this. What if she could get Harvey to move back to Rhode Island with her?

As if he heard her thought, he added, "Probably not until both my kids are fully grown, settled in college, and on their own, however."

And as quickly as it inflated, her heart deflated.

She'd gotten carried away. Thought there was something more than friendship. Thought he was on the same page.

She grew quiet, distant.

Before dessert arrived, Skye asked a question. "Harvey, I've been living with you for almost four months. Why haven't your kids been to the condo?"

"You know they've been in Seattle." He wasn't defensive so much as matter-of-fact. "They came home just a couple of weeks ago."

"I'm asking why they haven't been there since I've been living there."

She was treading in dangerous territory. And yet she couldn't stop herself.

"Skye, please don't take this the wrong way, but you're not a parent. You don't understand how difficult it can be to navigate relationships. My kids are still dealing with the divorce. How do I explain who you are to them?"

She took a pull from her drink, feeling the sting from his words, trying not to "take it the wrong way." She'd been dipping her toes in so far. It was time for her to dive in headfirst.

"Who am I to *you*?" she asked.

Bam. It was on the table now.

Harvey was taken aback, as if he'd just been splashed with ice water. "You're . . . you're my friend and my roommate and my colleague."

Every word sounded pulled, as if they were lies. And every one, albeit factually true, was a dagger that stabbed her.

"That's all?" she asked. He didn't answer. Just stared at her, frightened. A deer in the headlights. "Because you're way more than that to me. And judging by the way you've been acting—the hugs, the support, heck, just tonight, your opening doors and holding chairs—it seems that I'm more than that to you." Her courage surprised her. Rather than her needing to muster the gumption, it found her on its own.

He stared at her for several seconds, long enough to make her uncomfortable. "Put yourself in my daughter's shoes," he started. "Or my teenage son's. How would you interpret us living together, working together?"

"I'd interpret it as us being a couple."

She held a breath in anticipation of his response.

"Exactly. I can't do that to them, Skye. They're still reeling from their mother leaving me for fuckface. They're mad because I didn't fight for her. How can I tell them that I don't want to anymore?"

She had her answer, and the truth of it stung. But was this even about her? She had more to say.

"So you're withholding your own happiness for them?"

"That's what parents do."

She didn't buy it. "Sounds to me like you're punishing yourself."

She struck a nerve with him. The dessert arrived, and neither of them touched it. He looked ready to overturn the table and stomp out.

"Sounds to me like *you're* punishing me," he said.

Maybe she was. Maybe she wanted him to fight for *her*. Then again, maybe she was punishing him. Maybe she was being selfish. She'd never been with a man who had kids. They would always come first. She couldn't resent that. But at that moment, she did, and she hated herself for it.

Skye removed her napkin from her lap and placed it over the plate.

"You told me you rebuilt your life. But that's not what I saw. I saw a condo that was neglected, with bare white walls. A comic and card collection that's boxed up in storage. That's *your life* that's boxed up. You said you didn't fight for Deb. And you fought for your kids and lost. But did you fight for *you*? Because maybe if you do that, all that other stuff will fall into place."

His eyes went fiery, then dark.

"Skye, you don't get to paint a few walls in my house and think that solves everything. You don't get to bully me into buying matching end tables and think that fixes my love life. You especially don't get to psychoanalyze me. I've already paid for those services, thank you. You get to stay at my house and pay rent and decorate it, but you don't get a say in how my life is run."

Tears came to her eyes. He'd just negated her passion. Her work. He'd just negated her.

"I didn't bully you into doing anything," she said under her breath, her lips clamped shut. She stared at her plate.

Gobsmacked, he lifted the napkin from his lap and covered his plate with it. "I'm done eating," he said. "And celebrating, for that matter." He signaled the server and asked for the bill. After hastily paying it, he headed for the door without waiting for Skye, although she was ten steps behind him, shaking, bewildered by how quickly a delightful evening spun out of control.

Outside on the sidewalk of Montana Avenue, the sunset cast a purple glow, the beauty of it in sharp contrast to the darkness between them. He stopped and waited for her without meeting her eye, and they headed down the street side by side yet miles apart, in silence, back to the condo.

CHAPTER THIRTY

When they reached the condo building, Harvey headed for the garage rather than the main entrance.

"Where are you going?" she asked.

When he reached the FJ Cruiser, he pointed the key fob at it and unlocked it.

"Get in," he said, quickly adding, "please."

She looked at him, nervous. "Where are we going?"

"You'll see."

She remained in place. She didn't even want to be in the condo with him right now, much less a car.

"Please?" he repeated, this time with more sincerity, even remorse.

"OK," she said quietly, and pulled on the door handle.

Once in the FJ, Harvey cranked the air-conditioning, pulled out of the garage, and turned onto Twenty-Seventh Street, cruising all the way up to the roundabout that led to the airport.

"Where are we going?" she asked again, having a fleeting thought that he was going to let her out in front of the terminal and speed away, yelling *Go home* out the window as he did.

"Not there," he said of the airport, and took the exit just before the roundabout, the one with a sign pointing to Main Street. Not more than a few feet down Airport Road, he turned into a gravel lot on the right, pulled up alongside a line of cars, put the car in park, and killed the ignition.

They were on top of the rimrocks. And in front of them, stretched far and wide, was the bowl of Billings that the rimrocks and Sacrifice Cliff enclosed. A vast sea of twinkle lights underneath a midnight-blue sky with painted clouds silhouetted in the moonlight. The Heights were behind them. In front, to the far left, the refinery—even that looked lovely from above, like its own little white diamond city—and the south side on the other side of the railroad tracks. The south side had a reputation for being less desirable. Its people were ignored by the rest of the city. Many of its buildings neglected. Its property undervalued. It seemed easily overlooked even from above. Somewhere in the middle of the view, near downtown where they had just been (they never did eat the zeppole), was Clark Street, where Patrick was living in a house full of furniture but empty in every other way. And far off to the west—too far for her to see—was Devlin's Furniture, getting ready to close, perhaps one day for good. But you couldn't see any of that from the top of the rims. You couldn't see flailing retail or homeless people or boarded buildings. All you could see were the sparkles, dappled and dainty and . . . *magical*. It transformed Billings from a place to a possibility. A sea of wonders.

Billings, Montana. The Magic City.

Warwick, Rhode Island, didn't have a view like this. Skye tried to picture what Providence looked like from an airplane. Would she see the same splendor?

Skye placed her hand on her chest. "It's beautiful," she said softly.

"I know," said Harvey. "I love coming here at night. You should see it in the fall in daylight. All the trees . . . and on a clear day you can see the Beartooth Mountains too. That, and the sky"—he seemed momentarily breathless—"well, it's not even the best part of Montana."

"What is the best part?" she asked.

"God, if we could just go right now. Just get on I-90 and drive west. I'd show you the Crazy Mountains, Paradise Valley—that one lives up to its name, believe me—downtown Livingston . . . heck, you haven't even been to Yellowstone National Park, have you."

Skye ached with longing. She wasn't even sure for what.

"Thank you for taking me here," she said.

"I almost didn't."

"So why did you?"

"Because I didn't want what was supposed to be a special night to be ruined. Because this view has a way of putting things into perspective." He fixed his gaze on it again, as if to take another drink of it. Every intake seemed to ground him.

Skye added one more reason. "Because I fucked everything up."

He turned to her. "You didn't fuck anything up. You pushed some buttons that needed to be pushed. You were right about what you said. Doesn't mean it wasn't hard to hear."

He was so forgiving. She wasn't sure she deserved it. "I didn't mean to hamper the evening, though. Especially since it was supposed to be a celebration."

"Neither did I," he said.

The two gazed at the view. Their silence was soft rather than awkward. The dappled vista filled her, like sitting in front of a Christmas tree on December 24. The gift wasn't under the tree, but was the tree itself. *Billings is a gift.* And then, without warning, Harvey took Skye's hand and held it; his fingers slipped and locked into hers, his thumb caressing her wrist. Her body tingled. Her heart raced. A surge of current shot through her. She closed her eyes and panicked. What if this was a dream? What if she was misreading the signs? What if . . .

Harvey pulled her hand to his lips and kissed it. Like touching silk.

She opened her eyes and could hear herself breathily say, "Harvey," and the next thing she knew, their lips were joined. Had she kissed him? Had he kissed her? She couldn't even remember who had moved first.

Consumed with desire, she opened her mouth and let his tongue in, moving her hand to the nape of his neck, feeling his coarse hair, allowing herself to be submerged in sensory overload. He, in turn, tried to maneuver them closer together, took hold of her thigh with his free hand, and uttered a sound of pleasure, as if he'd just tasted the huckleberry sauce he'd tempted her with earlier.

They remained in the car together for a long time, absorbing every moment of this new addition between them. This spark of heat. This beauty. This newfound warmth from holding hands and kissing and breath on breath.

"Let's go home," whispered Harvey directly in Skye's ear as they both breathed hard and loud, steaming up the window beside her.

Home. She wasn't sure what the word meant anymore, but hearing it gave her goose bumps.

He started the car, pulled away from the vista, and coasted down Twenty-Seventh Street, back into downtown and into the parking garage and the condo building.

CHAPTER
THIRTY-ONE

Skye was never what you would call skinny. At least not since she hit puberty. By age fifteen, she'd developed breasts and hips and a belly. Junior high and high school girls wanted curves, but not the kind that required you to wear anything above a size zero or a 36C. And in gym class, both the boys and girls let her know that Skye's curves were the unwelcome kind. They called her "fatty." They told her to sit at home and bake on Friday nights. They told her to dress up as Miss Piggy for Halloween.

Didn't matter that she was on the tennis team. Didn't matter that she hated Doritos and soda. Didn't matter that she was, relative to the rest of the country, the median size for her height and weight and age.

She couldn't remember a time when she didn't hate her body. Even as a child, an aunt had called her "thick" and Summer "stick."

Vance Sandler's backhanded compliments had made her feel uneasy, no matter how hard she'd convinced herself that he didn't mean to be hurtful, that he was the only one who loved her body as it was. *You won't need to eat so much when you're with me,* he'd said.

Fuck that shit.

Skye lay in bed with Harvey, her back to him as he spooned her, his arms pulling her into his cocoon. It didn't seem to matter to him that the last person she'd had sex with was his archnemesis (although of course she didn't know that at the time). It didn't seem to matter to him that her breasts flopped wildly as she bounced on top of him, or that she was on top of him in the first place when she figured her weight would crush him. He'd kissed so many parts of her, from the curve of her neck to the edge of her shoulder, on the back of her wrist and each fingertip, down her back as he ran his hand along her torso and hip and waist and thigh. Her naked body, with all its folds and flab and wrinkles, didn't turn him off. How was that possible? She wondered this as she lay there, still and silent, while Harvey slept, breathing calm and even and content.

When she was sixteen, almost immediately after the first time she'd ever had sex (with her mixed-doubles partner, Kyle Corbin), she'd engrossed herself in fantasies about weddings and honeymoons and where she and Kyle would live and how many kids and pets they would have. She'd begin making lists about whether to have a beach wedding or a church wedding, whether she should buy a strapless gown and starve herself or a classic A-line gown like Princess Diana had worn, perhaps without as many puffs and ruffles and tulle. She'd believed in fairy tales back then. And she was let down with a crashing thud when Kyle made a pass at Brittany Lester in her gym class the very next week, one of the girls who'd taunted her.

By the time she got to college, she was less dreamy and more realistic. Sex didn't always lead to love. Love didn't always lead to sex. But she still wanted it to.

By the time Vance Sandler came to Boston for their weekend, she was so happy to finally have sex after such a drought that she overlooked his lackluster performance.

She enjoyed sex with Harvey, though. It was intimate. Meaningful. Complete. And yet, she still worried: Was the sex good for Harvey?

Would he regret that they'd had sex? Whose bed was she going to sleep in the following night?

But then she gave herself gentle instructions: *Breathe, Skye.*

I approve of myself. She almost had the affirmation down to a conditioned behavioral response anytime her thoughts became too negative or self-defeating.

She took deep breaths, closed her eyes, and fell asleep blanketed in Harvey's warm body. Chip and Bucky Barnes were each left to find accommodations elsewhere.

◆ ◆ ◆

Skye awoke to the buzzing and beeping of the alarm on Harvey's phone. She stirred and turned over, accidentally smacking Harvey upside the head. He moaned and stirred as the jolt woke her completely. "I'm so sorry," she croaked, and he opened his eyes. And smiled.

"Hey," he said. He turned over and leaned on his elbow, facing her.

"Hey, yourself," she said, returning the ear-to-ear grin.

He reached over to pull a strand of her hair away from her face. "Sleep OK?"

"I guess."

He squinted and peered at her. "You all right?"

She decided to come out and say it. "This is weird, Harvey. I'm naked in your bed. Because we had sex last night."

"That's usually the order of how these things go, yes."

"We had *sex*," she said, as if he didn't hear her the first time. "You and me."

"I know . . . ," he said in an extended, exaggerated voice. "And . . . ?"

"And . . . it changes things."

Harvey rested on his side, propped up by his elbow. "In what way?"

She opened her mouth as if she were about to utter an answer, when she realized she had none.

Harvey pointed at her in a teasing way. "That's what I thought." He rose from the bed, and Skye took in an eyeful of his naked body, sculpted, thanks to hours of wielding paint rollers and brushes and moving ladders and hauling gallon cans.

And then she knew.

"It's just that I'm afraid you're not getting the best of me. I want to be better," she said. She'd never been so honest with anyone before, especially herself. She couldn't remember having such insight. That she did and was able to voice it comforted her.

"I disagree," said Harvey. "Based on what I know about you, I think this is the best you've ever been."

"It is. But I can be better."

"How so?" he asked.

"I want to love myself more. And even though I've lived on my own for a long time, I haven't really taken care of myself."

Harvey sat on the end of the bed and took hold of a pillow and pulled it to his chest, as if shielding his heart. His eyes projected worry. "You can work on being better and still be with me, can't you?" he asked.

"I don't know," she said. "I've never been at this place in a relationship before. This state of mind."

He squeezed the pillow. "I want *you*, Skye," he said. "Just as you are." He rose and came to her side of the bed, pulled the covers away from her, and caressed her tenderly. His very presence radiated warmth. "You can be afraid, or whatever you're feeling, but walk through it and hold my hand."

Skye trembled and her chest tightened and her stomach turned as if her world was falling apart yet again. She had no fantasy to cling to this time. No false hope. No snap reaction to a number on a calendar or a scale. Harvey was the real thing.

She had survived losing Vance and losing herself, hadn't she? In the four months that she'd been in Billings, she put her life back together, piece by piece, and found which pieces worked. By eliminating what she no longer wanted, she found what she did want: Freedom. Security. Acceptance. Respect.

She learned how to give those things to herself rather than get them from someone or something else. She learned how to be those things rather than demand those things. She learned to see through a lens of abundance rather than scarcity.

She saw her sister through a more accurate lens now. She saw her as a *sister* rather than an opponent.

When she first arrived, she had believed that Vance had lured her away from the only home she'd ever known, and then left her out in the cold. That he'd taken her dignity.

Maybe he had. But only because she'd given it to him.

But what he couldn't take, what no one could ever take, was her response to it. She could accept it all and wither away or she could rise up like the phoenix from the ashes, or like the guy from the TV show: Better. Stronger. Faster.

That was freedom. That was acceptance. That was respect.

She closed her eyes and took a breath. *Be still. Listen.*

She opened her eyes and looked at Harvey. He was so handsome with his eyes round and dark and sad like a dachshund's, and his hair tousled and his biceps twitching and his big feet glued to the ground.

She stood up, took a step forward, and leaned into him. He slowly, tentatively put his arms around her. And when she felt herself folded into him, when his warmth and envelopment took over, she released a long, deep breath and nuzzled into his neck, and he inhaled the scent of her, and kissed her temple and cheek and ear and neck before meeting her lips.

Morning breath, she thought. Both of them.

She didn't care.

"I'm not going anywhere, Harvey," she spoke into his ear.

"Promise?" he whispered, nuzzling her neck.

"Promise," she said.

CHAPTER

THIRTY-TWO

Mid-September

With Harvey's help, Skye completely revised Patrick's kitchen by painting the walls lemon yellow and outfitting the chairs with lime-green cushions she'd made herself. She also replaced the dusty white curtains with a friendly printed fabric of lemons and limes that she'd found on clearance at the fabric store, hung canvas artwork of a bowl of green pears she'd found at Target, and painted the chairs and tables white with green piping. All within Patrick's allotted budget. Furthermore, she scrubbed the countertops and appliances, cleaned the floor with the heavy-duty steamer Patrick had borrowed from Devlin's Furniture store for a day, and cleared all the clutter from the countertops.

When Patrick saw the finished room, he and Skye stood in the entrance, both overcome with emotion.

"It's beautiful, Skye. It's light and cheery and . . . it's *her*," he said, wiping a tear.

"Don't just send her a photo over the phone," beckoned Skye. "Ask her to come over. Show her. Tell her this is only the beginning. Make a new vision *with* her, not *for* her."

"I will," he said. He hugged her. "Thank you," he said when he let go. An expression overcame him that Skye couldn't detect.

"You OK?" she asked.

"Seeing this kitchen . . .well, I know what I want now. It's all so clear. I just have to make it happen step-by-step."

This. This moment. She wanted to create this over and over and over again for her clients. It wasn't about the transformation of the room. It was about the transformation of the person.

Before she left, Skye agreed to make new throw pillows for the living room furniture and all the bedrooms. In return, Patrick completed her website for her and agreed to post before-and-after photos of the kitchen on all her social media sites after he showed Sandra. He also came up with ideas for themed posts: Feng Shui Color of the Day, Gua of the Week (from the ba-gua map), Tip Tuesdays, and so on. Skye loved them all and couldn't wait to apply them.

Between her work with Devlin's Furniture, Nellie's, assisting Harvey, and building her business, Skye was feeling the exhaustion of putting in so many hours. And loving it. She was energized, alive, focused. She was driven.

And, of course, sex with Harvey almost every night was a delightful cherry on top.

Despite having spent so much time converting the guest bedroom into her own sanctuary, Skye all but moved into Harvey's bedroom. She was surprised by how quickly she adjusted to sleeping next to someone who wasn't a cat, yet purred when he snuggled up to her. She was equally surprised by how *plain* it all felt—none of the crazy, frenetic treadmill of thoughts that had always burned out her brain when she was in love with Vance. No daily calls to Julie to report every text, analyze every action, keep track of every compliment. (Of course, she did tell Julie about this latest development with Harvey; but it was more like secret sharing than making an announcement via a megaphone.) Being with Harvey felt calm. An ebb and flow. Their daily routines were mostly the same. Harvey cooked; she cleaned; they did laundry together. He drove her to work. She put gas in his car.

Not plain—*normal.* Grounded. *Real.*

"I don't want this place to be where you're staying anymore," said Harvey one night following their lovemaking. "I want it to be where you *live.* I want it to be *our* place. That goes for Billings too."

Skye froze. It was the first time he'd said the words, asked for more. The tug-of-war was instant and fierce—stick to her goal of making enough to go back to Rhode Island, or stay in Billings with Harvey for good? Rhode Island was still and always would be her home. But she was just as at home with Harvey. Did it have to be an either-or?

She didn't respond to Harvey's question. Instead, she asked, "What about your kids?"

"I'm going to tell them about you. Things have been better lately. I think the time in Seattle did them a lot of good. Come to think of it, it's time to look for a bigger place. Like a three-bedroom house. Maybe we could start with a rental."

"We? All of us? You and your kids?"

He nodded. "Sure. Maybe they would be receptive to the idea."

There was a time she would have jumped up and called the real estate agent herself. But her head was spinning, her insides churning with worry. "Harvey, slow down. I don't have the finances for a house. I'm making ends meet here, but that's because the rent is cheap and we split expenses."

"I told you, I have savings. I've invested well."

"But then it would be *your* house, wouldn't it? And you don't know if your kids will want me in their lives," she added. "You can't jump too far ahead. Baby steps."

His head drooped and his smile sank for a moment, but he picked them up again. "You're right. I'm getting way too ahead of myself. I'm just . . . I'm happy, Skye. I haven't been happy for a long time."

She snuggled close to him. "I'm happy too."

CHAPTER
THIRTY-THREE

Skye had become a fan of the farmers' market when she'd started walking to it almost every Saturday morning in Billings during the summer months, if she wasn't scheduled to work. Several blocks of downtown streets would be closed off to traffic, replaced by vendors putting up tents and carts and trucks, selling everything from sugar-cinnamon-coated donuts to eggrolls to Nutella crepes. Hutterites selling freshly baked breads and ears of corn by the dozen and other hearty produce. Small businesses offering samples of pepper jelly and tea and hot sauce. Plants for sale. Artwork. Sidewalk sales of books and clothing and antiques. Friendly clowns on street corners made balloon animals while accordion players nearby kept things festive. Parents pulled their tots along in wagons; others used wagons to tow their purchases. The market would be ending very soon, in just a couple of weeks, until next year.

Skye and Harvey had begun going together since August when neither had to work. On this particular Saturday, they were celebrating a successful first meeting with Harvey's kids. Harvey had called them the day after he and Skye discussed it, speaking first to Scott, whom he'd surmised would be the more resistant of the two. Scott, it seemed, had done a bit of growing up while in Seattle. He'd had a part-time job at a coffee shop and, like Harvey, reserved some of his pay every week for comics—graphic novels, to be exact. He'd been crazy about The Dark Knight ever since he was a kid. He was less angry at Harvey. He'd missed his dad, it turned out. Kelly, on the other hand, was more reserved at first. She'd agreed to the meeting, but only if her brother was with her; Harvey guessed that if he approved, then she would approve. Though he didn't want Kelly to try too hard just to please her father.

They'd come to the condo for dinner. Skye had spent days cleaning, got her hair done, even bought a new outfit. She hadn't been this nervous since she tried out for the school play in the fifth grade. Even anticipating her first meeting with Vance, accompanied by all her what-if-he-doesn't-like-me-in-person worries, diminished in comparison. There was more at stake here. If Harvey's kids hated her, how would that affect their relationship? She didn't want him to be put in a position where he'd have to choose her or them. It was no contest—his kids were the clear choice.

She shook hands with each of them upon being introduced. Scott was a tall, gangly version of his father. Kelly, more petite, had fair skin, luscious dark hair, and blue eyes that were probably from her mother's gene pool. She was beautiful, and Skye told her so.

The kids loved the changes to the condo.

"Skye did most of it," said Harvey. "We're going to convert the guest room into a memorabilia room."

Skye winced when he said *we*, afraid it was too much too soon for the kids to handle.

"Then where will we sleep?" asked Kelly. Skye watched Harvey's eyes become glassy over the validation that his daughter still considered herself a part of his life, very much wanted to be.

"Don't worry, Kel-Kel." She rolled her eyes upon hearing the nickname, at the bridge between wanting to still be Daddy's little girl and all grown up. "You'll always have a space here to call yours. I'll make sure of it."

"Why don't you just get a bigger place?" said Scott.

Both Harvey and Skye, unable to conceal their grins, exchanged knowing glances out of eyeshot from Scott. "That's a great idea," said Harvey.

◆ ◆ ◆

As they turned the corner from the condo, each with an empty tote bag (two hours later they would return with full bags and full stomachs, if today was like the other Saturdays), Skye and Harvey strolled hand in hand. She waved to Dottie, one of the women who met with her knitting club every Tuesday at Nellie's (they always left Skye a generous tip and promised to make her a pair of wool mittens and matching scarf for her birthday), and Sammy, Harvey's buddy from the brew pub who watched the baseball playoffs with him over beers. They even ran into Jack, her friend from the feng shui class.

"We need to talk, honey," he said to Skye. "I've got an idea for a business and want to run it by you."

"Sounds great!" she said. "Come to Nellie's when my shift is over on Tuesday and we'll chat."

She loved running into people she knew. She loved that she knew people, that she had friends. She loved running into them with Harvey, being seen with Harvey, and their exchanges of telling grins.

As she watched Harvey buy a bag of eggrolls from one of the vendors, she realized she was living every fantasy she'd ever had about being in a relationship, despite still being the same height and weight with the same fine hair and the same no-name brand clothing. The closeness, the intimacy, even in a crowd of people, the togetherness.

This is what home is all about.

Right there, on the street, in the swell of the crowds, it hit her: *I love Billings.* She certainly loved it on summer Saturday mornings. She loved it during the week too. Now that it was fall, she looked forward to the leaves turning. She looked forward to spending her first birthday in Billings. Maybe she'd throw a party. She had enough friends to invite now.

She wanted Billings. And she wanted to see more of Montana—Bozeman and Livingston and the Beartooth Mountains and Yellowstone National Park. She wanted to live here with Harvey.

She could barely wait to tell Harvey this, when someone's pull wagon accidentally overturned, causing a domino effect of people bumping into each other, causing someone to stomp on Skye's foot, causing her to yelp, causing the unintended stomper to turn around and apologize, causing Skye to turn into a statue when she saw his face. Funny, she'd thought he was handsome. Thought his eyes were piercing rather than plain. That the lines around his face were "distinguished" rather than frowny.

Vance Sandler. She was certain this time.

"I'm so sorry," he said before he got a good look at Skye. The woman beside him said to him, "You OK, sweetie?" Skye immediately recognized the lustrous hair and the blue eyes. She'd just complimented Deb's daughter on them.

Skye blurted, "It's me, Vance."

Vance wore a face of terror for only a split second when he registered recognition, and then his expression turned cold, and then he grinned.

"Skye . . . ," he started, with the voice of a used-car salesman. As if he was about to ooze with charm.

The woman instantly became annoyed and accusing as she shot daggers from her eyes at Vance and cut him off. "You *know* her?"

"He knows me," said Skye, staring him down. She flashed back to that morning she showed up on his doorstep, desperate for answers, foolishly hoping he'd see the error of his ways and take her back. Longing for his arms, craving him. And here, now, she felt nothing for him—not a spark of affection, not a trace of trust, not a prickle of friendship. Nothing. She saw him for the coward and the liar he was.

Vance said nothing. Just stared back at Skye as if they were in a game of chicken. No way was he going to intimidate or manipulate her. The longer she stared him down, the more empowered she became.

Deb started interrogating both of them at once: "How do you know him? How does she know you?" Neither Vance nor Skye said a word.

Seconds later, Harvey, with one eggroll halfway in his mouth and another in his hands, returned from the vendor, sidled up, and said, "You have got to try one of these," through his teeth. When he took in the full view, the eggroll dropped to the ground as he went slack-jawed.

"Oh my God," said Deb. "I cannot believe this."

Harvey looked at Deb, then at Vance. Unlike Vance, who still remained calm and zeroed in on Skye, Harvey went from friendly to fiery in a nanosecond. And then he went eerily calm, even more so than Vance, and smiled.

"How do you like me now, jackhole?" said Harvey. And with that, Harvey Wright took his second eggroll and attempted to shove it up Vance Sandler's nose.

CHAPTER THIRTY-FOUR

It took both Skye and Deb to pull Harvey off Vance, who had a face full of eggroll and soy sauce dripping down his chin, coughing and blowing out eggroll innards. Meanwhile, Harvey kept yelling, "I've got her now, you fucker! What do you think of that? You didn't wreck her after all, you incredible piece of shit!"

"I'll sue you!" yelled Vance, his eyes watery and face sticky.

"Go ahead and try."

"Witnesses," said Vance, looking around at the crowd of people pretending not to see anything.

Skye was mortified.

"What are you doing?" she yelled at Harvey.

"What do you think I'm doing? I'm giving that fuckface everything he deserves."

"No, you're putting yourself in a position to be arrested for attacking someone without being provoked."

"Listen to your girlfriend, Harvey," said Vance. "Apparently, she's not altogether with you if she's defending me."

Skye whipped around in a fury. "And *you*," she said, pointing a finger at Vance so forcefully that he jerked backward, "can go fuck yourself. I am *not* defending you. You're lucky I don't clock you with an ear of corn, the way you treated me. You ghosted me. You tossed me like a sack of garbage." Skye faced Harvey's ex-wife. "Did you know that? Did you know he courted me for months long-distance? Did you know we spent a weekend in Boston in February? Would you like to see the texts? Would you like to see the dick pic he sent?" She had deleted every communication the day after she and Harvey made love for the first time, but correctly guessed Deb wouldn't call her bluff.

"Oh my God," said Deb. She turned to Vance. "*That's* what Boston was about? You told me you stopped. You looked me straight in the eye and lied to me without a care in the world. Worse than that, you called me paranoid. You *gaslighted* me."

The next thing Skye knew, Deb proceeded to beat Vance with an ear of corn as he attempted to cover his face in defense rather than strike her back. "You press charges against Harvey, and I'll say you provoked him."

"All right, stop it!" he said. Skye was surprised that Vance had caved so easily. Perhaps he wasn't a sociopath as much as he was just a plain ol' coward.

Deb dropped the corn on the ground and ran down the street, zigzagging through the crowd in tears. Harvey watched her, and Skye deduced from the look on his face that he was contemplating whether to run after her. The mother of his children. Skye realized she could never reach that level of importance no matter how in love they were or how solid their relationship was. The same feeling of inferiority that had always submerged her where Summer was concerned bubbled up again: the inability to measure up, to be more.

Harvey grabbed a couple of napkins from his pocket and washed the gunky eggroll off his hands. Skye stood there, in a stupor, desperately wanting to run but not knowing where to go. Vance, humiliated, yelled at the onlookers. "Any of you post this to Facebook and I'll hunt every last one of you down and beat the shit out of you." By now, just about everyone seemed to have moved on.

Skye surveyed Vance head to toe—pieces of corn husk stuck in his hair and face, shirt disheveled, wiry body, scuffed loafers. He was so far from the hunky guy she'd once believed him to be, the man he'd told her he was. He stood there, pathetic, alone, stripped of dignity.

She wanted to be happy to see him taken down. She wanted to spout something about karma and how everything he was feeling at that moment was exactly how she felt that first night in Billings, and for days afterward. She wanted to applaud. But she knew two things: One, that Vance was incapable of empathy. If he was feeling humiliated or anything else, it was someone else's fault. And, two, if she raised herself at the expense of his being taken down, then she was no better as a human being, and she wanted to be.

What made her happy, she realized, was that she was no longer that person who'd been dumped on her ass in the middle of a strange, albeit magical, city, broke and humiliated and abandoned. She was no longer at the mercy of a lifetime of underachievement. She was no longer helpless or afraid. She was no longer alone.

Until she remembered what Harvey shouted at Vance.

"Let's go," said Harvey to Skye. "We've disrupted the peace enough, and I don't want to press my luck."

Skye glared at him. "*You* disrupted the peace, not 'we.' You're the one who caused this scene."

Harvey strode away from the crowd and onto the sidewalk, taking Skye by the arm. "Are you seriously taking that assclown's side?"

"I'm telling you that I've worked very hard to build some credibility with my clients and my job, and I want to build a business. Now, thanks to you, I'm entangled in a punch line."

They stood at the street corner, waiting for the light to change. One more block and they would be back at the condo.

They crossed the street.

"What did you mean when you said, 'I've got her now'?" asked Skye.

"What?" said Harvey.

"When you were attempting to make Vance eat an eggroll with his nostrils. You said, 'I've got her now,' and 'You didn't wreck her after all.' What did you mean?"

Harvey stared at her in bewilderment. "I . . . I don't know what I s—"

Skye interrupted him. "You wanted revenge."

"Well . . . of course," he said slowly, unconvincingly, as if he were still trying to piece the situation in front of him together. As if he was trying to recognize Skye. "He stole my wife. He wrecked my life. He wrecked *your* life."

Skye shook her head. "No. I wrecked my life a long time ago. All Vance did was take advantage of it."

"What are you saying, Skye?"

"You told Vance 'I've got her now.' Meaning you've got *me* now."

"So?"

"So . . . that's all I was to you—a plot for revenge? A rescue mission? Your comic books come to life? 'Let me save poor Skye Littleton. Let me build her up so that when the day finally comes, I can throw her in Vance's face.' Which is what you did in addition to that eggroll. You used me as a weapon."

"Skye, no—"

"No? You're going to stand here and tell me that all these weeks and months weren't about you finally having your comeuppance? That it wasn't to play Superman or whoever and defeat your archenemy? You're going to tell me that you would have taken in any random woman you met on an airplane?" She didn't want to believe her own words. Could hardly believe she was even saying them. Couldn't believe everything was falling apart so quickly.

"If you think that's why I slept with you—"

But Skye put up her hand in protest and brushed past him into the condo building and up to the apartment. She attempted to slam the door behind her, but Harvey caught it and pushed himself in, calling her name and trying to explain himself to her.

"Skye, that's not what happened, OK? Anything I said to Vance was just in the heat of the moment. It was seeing him standing there and thinking he hurt you again. It was—"

She was hearing none of it. Instead, she closed both doors leading to her room—the guest room—where all her things still were, and retrieved her empty suitcases from the top shelf. She packed everything she could, leaving behind the old paint clothes and anything she touched that didn't spark even a hint of joy at that moment.

Slow down, Skye. Make a plan.

Harvey knocked on the door and pleaded for her to let him in, but she refused.

You did it again. You trusted. You put your faith in something that turned out not to be real.

No. She couldn't go through it again. She couldn't let the disappointment crush her. She couldn't give it power. She had choices now. She was still short on cash, still didn't have a place to live.

But she had a Facebook page and a website and a business she could activate wherever she lived. She had tools and skills that didn't limit her to a store in a mall. She had a solid reference in Patrick.

She packed all her feng shui books and materials and tool kit into a second suitcase. Whatever didn't fit wasn't coming with her. She'd started with nothing before. She could do it again.

She turned and looked at the royal purple curtains, the ones she had made by herself, and burst into tears.

Before the night was over, Skye booked a one-way flight to Providence at the end of two weeks—after all, she had to give Patrick and her boss at the restaurant the proper notice. She also called Julie.

"I'm coming home," said Skye.

"Ohmigod, for good?"

Her heart pounded as she spoke. "I'm really not sure. Could Chip and I crash on your couch for a few days, though?"

"Skyebaby, what happened?"

She fought back tears. "I tried to make a go of it, but it's just not working out here."

"What about Harvey? Last time you filled me in, you said it was wonderful. In fact, you never sounded so certain in all your life."

"I'll fill you in when I see you. I have to finish up my two weeks at work."

After hanging up with Julie, she called a cab to take her to the Best Western she'd stayed in when she first arrived in Billings. Funny how things came full circle.

When she opened the door and emerged with Chip's carrier and juggling her suitcase and carry on, Harvey practically jumped from the couch and looked in bewilderment at her and the load she towed.

Before he could say a word, Skye took in a breath and said, "Harvey, I have something to say, and I want to say it in its entirety, so please don't interrupt me."

Harvey stood, motionless, powerless, vulnerable. Like a superhero without his shield or cape or utility belt or magic lasso. Knowing he was about to take the hit. And he was letting it happen. She took another breath and let it out.

"You gave me a place to live when I was homeless. You were a friend when I didn't know a single soul. You cooked delicious meals. You gave me a job and an opportunity to learn something new, and you made it possible for me to get back on my feet. You gave me countless rides and trusted me with your car. You gave me advice, and you gave me some wonderful nights with you." Her voice grew shakier by the second. "But after all that's happened, I don't think Billings will ever be home. There's just been too much deception. I'm going back to Rhode Island."

"That's not why you're leaving," he said, completely defeated. "You're running back to something familiar. You don't want to try anymore."

"That's not true," she said. *Or is it?* "It's high time I rescue myself."

He paused before speaking, as if to make sure she'd said everything, to digest it all, to not say the wrong thing.

"You're leaving tonight?" he asked. His voice almost sounded mousy.

"Back to the friendly Best Western for now. I'm giving notice to my other jobs."

"You have a job with me too. I don't deserve the same courtesy?"

Damn. He has a point.

"I'm sorry, Harvey," she said, her voice breaking into a sob on the last word. "I'll miss you. More than you know."

She wiped a tear and placed an envelope on one of the living room tables.

"What is that?" he asked.

"My key and a month's rent."

Harvey ignored it and took a step toward her, placing a hand on one of her suitcases. "Please don't go."

She couldn't even look at him. "I can't stay here another minute. I have to go." She turned and pulled her suitcases to the door to collect Chip, who, upon hearing the zipper on the cat carrier, ran to the opposite side of the room and backed himself into a corner, meowing in protest. Bucky Barnes trotted to the corner and stood in front of Chip, blocking Skye from picking him up. Harvey called him, but Bucky whined. When Skye attempted to reach over him and place a hand on Chip, Bucky actually growled. He'd never been anything but a teddy bear to her.

"Bucky!" Harvey said sternly, walking to the dog and taking him by the collar. "Let it go, man." Bucky cried as Skye scooped Chip up and placed him into the carrier, his bowls and food already packed away. She was at the door when Harvey stopped her again. His eyes were dark, glassy. "Skye, please. You need to give me another chance. You need to give Billings another chance. This city needs you. *I* need you."

"I need to go home," said Skye. "I've been needing to go home for months. Even before I came here." It seemed an odd thing to say, especially since only hours ago she was convinced she'd officially made Billings her home. What did that word mean, anyway? What was it? Was it four walls, a floor, and ceiling? Was it Oz, or was it Kansas, as Dorothy wrestled with in the movie?

She was heartbroken and confused, yet she'd made up her mind.

"Will you at least let me know when you get back?" he asked. She nodded, unable to ignore the desperation in his eyes.

Without a hug or even so much as a handshake, Harvey turned around and pushed open the door in a whoosh, pounding down the hallway, hands jammed in his pockets.

When Skye drove to the hotel, checked in, and closed the room door behind her, the dam finally broke, and the deluge of tears gushed out.

CHAPTER
THIRTY-FIVE

Two weeks later

So as not to break her lease agreement with Honda, Skye sublet her Civic to Barbara. She said her goodbyes to Patrick and the rest of her colleagues, her feng shui classmates (she never did find out what Jack had wanted to pitch to her), and her customers and coworkers at Nellie's. She also prepared for the boxes in her storage unit to be shipped to Summer's house, an arrangement made after she called Summer to tell her what happened and that she was coming home.

"I'm really sorry things didn't work out for you there," said Summer.

"Me too," said Skye.

"Where will you stay when you get back?"

"I'm going to crash on Julie's couch for a couple of days. After that, I'm not sure."

"Why don't you stay here? The guesthouse out back is finally finished. That way you can have privacy, come and go as you please. It's got everything you would need. You could live there until you get back on your feet. Just pay for utilities."

Months ago, Skye would have felt as if Summer were making the offer just to lord her failure over her. As if relegating her to the guesthouse was a punishment. But today, Skye saw the generosity in the offer. It would be an opportunity to get to know her sister in ways she never had before. It would be a gentler transition with less pressure. Skye teared up when she realized it was exactly where she would want to be.

"Thank you," said Skye, "You have no idea how much your offer means to me."

◆ ◆ ◆

A cab picked up Skye at the Best Western at 6:45 a.m. She sobbed all the way to Billings Logan Airport. The rimrocks looked impossibly beautiful against the sunrise, the sky a canvas of pink clouds so magnificent her breath caught in her throat.

CHAPTER
THIRTY-SIX

Skye spent the entire trip unsuccessfully trying to put Harvey out of her mind. She felt guilty for leaving him. Kept second-guessing herself, even though Flora and Patrick—yes, she'd told Patrick everything—both told her she'd done the right thing and was very brave to return home and clean the slate one more time. Harvey had texted her several times since she'd left the condo, making sure she was OK, asking her to reconsider, apologizing profusely. Remembering how she felt when Vance had left her hanging, Skye promised not to do that to Harvey. So she answered his texts and accepted his apologies, but was still wounded by what he'd said to Vance, what the words meant. She didn't know how to get beyond feeling as if their relationship had been nothing but a rescue, a coup against Vance Sandler, and she didn't want Vance Sandler to have that kind of power, didn't want him to be the common denominator between Harvey and her. What was more, she was afraid that if she stayed with Harvey, he'd either keep trying to rescue her, or the relationship would no longer work because she didn't want to be rescued. She'd learned a valuable lesson the last six months: people treated you the way you let them. They also tended to treat you the way you treat yourself.

Maybe she just needed time.

She texted him when the plane landed at TF Green because he'd asked her to; he wanted to know she was safe.

Welcome home, Harvey texted in reply. The words didn't have the same meaning as they did six months ago.

She missed every wrinkle, every eyelash, every fingerprint of Harvey's. She missed his cooking. She missed his laugh. She missed the smell of the condo. She missed Bucky Barnes.

Skye arrived in Rhode Island around five thirty—the two-hour time difference worked against her—and she would have burst into tears the moment she saw Julie had she not been so dog-tired. Julie squealed with delight upon seeing her friend and practically jumped into Skye's arms. Thankfully, Skye's luggage made the trip with her this time.

"Wow," she said as she took in a view of Skye head to toe. "You look . . . *different*."

"How so?" asked Skye.

"You're so . . . *fit*. Like, the shape of your body has changed."

Skye didn't think the change had been enough for anyone to notice. Was anything else noticeable? That she'd become more confident and self-respecting, despite this most recent upset?

"Tell me *everything*," Julie demanded the moment they got to the car. Skye had been holding off until they were physically together rather than tell her everything on the phone from her hotel room.

"Coffee milk first. Talk second," said Skye.

"Happy to oblige." She drove straight to the Dunkin' Donuts, and was shocked when Skye told her Billings didn't have a single Dunkin' Donuts or Panera Bread in the entire city. "God, Skye," said Julie. "How did you manage to live there this long?"

As they drove through Warwick, past all the side streets and neighborhoods and shopping outlets that she could get to with her eyes closed, Skye couldn't help but notice: Rhode Island was wicked small.

Not small. Just . . . dense. Crowded. Even from the airplane window. She remembered thinking how claustrophobic it made her feel before she left. Like living in a shoebox. Granted, outside of Billings, she'd only seen Montana from the 250-mile stretch of I-90 between Billings and Bozeman—she'd driven herself the day after her final days of work—but the vastness of land and mountain and sky that surrounded the interstate was nothing short of heart-in-throat magnificent. It wasn't even that Rhode Island wasn't pretty or didn't have its own sights. It was just . . . well, *not Montana*. She kept looking up at the sky—no, she was looking *for* the sky—and instead found small patches of blue obscured by trees and buildings and streetlamps.

But still. She was home. And for the first time in all the months she'd been away, she felt a part of herself that had been missing return to her. The sight of the trees, their height stunted by the coastal waters, their colors already peaking. The voices and conversations she'd not heard in six months. The place where her family was. Was that what *home* meant—feeling like you knew who you were and where you belonged? Had she ever felt belonging? Did she feel it now?

Skye drank her coffee milk (divine) and threw away a chocolate-glazed donut after two bites (because it tasted fake) as Julie drove them to her apartment. At Julie's, they sat on the couch so that they were facing each other, ready to dish. (Skye figured she'd wait a few days before telling Julie her couch wanted to be on the other side of the room, catty-corner.) Even Chip wandered around the room, scoping it out, relieved to be off the plane. Skye was almost certain he was looking for Bucky, had been ever since she carried him out of the condo. His heart got broken too.

"OK, spill it," said Julie.

"Well, for starters, I finally ran into Vance, that fuckface."

"No sir," said Julie.

"And Harvey was with me."

"No sir!" said Julie.

"And . . . well, let's just say he tried to measure whether an eggroll can fit into Vance's nostril. Newsflash: it can't. But Harvey made a valiant effort."

"No suhhh!" exclaimed Julie. Skye had never noticed how thick Julie's New England accent was, or how harsh it was on the ears.

"And then, well . . ." Skye took in a breath. "That's when it all fell apart. Harvey got all macho and bragged that he was with me now, as if the only reason he'd slept with me was to somehow get revenge on Vance, with whom he has his own baggage."

"Oh shit, Skye. That is so not what you want to hear from a guy. That's almost as bad as one saying he just wants to be friends."

"Well, yeah. So we got into a fight, and I finally decided that it was never really going to work in Billings. So here I am. I still don't know if I'm going to stay in Rhode Island, but at least here I'll be able to recover and make a plan."

"Sweetie, when you first left to be with Vance, I thought you were behaving so rashly. It wasn't like you. I mean, you were always a bit of a dreamer, but you never did anything about it. Oh my, that came out terrible! I'm so sorry."

"It's OK," said Skye, despite the words stinging. "I freaked the fuck out. I admit it."

"But here's the weird thing: I think it was the best thing that ever happened to you."

"I do too," said Skye. "Had I not picked up and gone to Montana, I'd probably have taken the district manager job at Top Drawer and drudged through that for another fifteen years, hoping and waiting for yet another break but not doing a damn thing to make life any better." Tears slipped down her face. "It's just that . . ." She sobbed and let it out. "I miss Harvey. I shouldn't have left him the way I did."

"Fuck him!" said Julie. "After what he did to you? He used you, Skye. You were nothing but a weapon for him to use against Vance the Cancer. OK—not the best rhyme in the world, but still."

"It was awful."

"He's a scumbag, and you should just forget him and stay here with your friends and family who love you."

She cringed at the word, and Julie's rage. "He's not a scumbag, Jules. Vance was a scumbag. Harvey made a mistake."

If that was all it was, then why couldn't she forgive him?

"Fine. I'll take your word for it. But I am so happy you're home! And oh my God, you should see my closets since you left—they're a disaster! I must be some kind of clutter magnet. It's like I wake up and it's all there."

"Well, let's get on it," said Skye. "Consider it payment for letting me crash on your couch until I get everything settled at Summer's house. After dinner—I'm starving."

As sad as she was about what she'd left behind, she could hardly wait to get started. Not only on Julie's closets, but the rest of her life. She was starting over yet again. But this time, she was ready. Willing. Able.

◆　◆　◆

After Skye and Julie went out for dinner and a movie at Providence Place (she felt like she was being suffocated by wall-to-wall people, even more than the droves who showed up to the farmers' market in downtown Billings every Saturday), they came home and dressed up the couch with linens, and Skye changed and washed up and crawled under the sheet. She was beyond exhausted, mentally, emotionally, and physically. But two hours later, she still couldn't sleep.

It would be close to ten o'clock in Billings.

She was missing her friend. She was also missing her lover.

It had felt right to buy the ticket, board the flight, walk through the jetway, and breathe New England air. As right as being with Harvey had felt. How could those two things be polar opposites? She fervently wished she could have both.

She picked up her phone and began to type out a text to Harvey, but promptly deleted it, opting instead to call him directly, despite not knowing what she wanted to say, or if calling him was a good idea in the first place.

"Hello, Skye," said Harvey. Her body completely froze, including her vocal cords. She couldn't get a read on whether he was angry, sad, or indifferent.

"Hi, Harvey," she said, her voice quavering. *What am I doing?*

"Happy to be home?" he asked. Again, she couldn't get a read on his tone.

"I am," she started. "But I miss . . . I am just so sorry."

He was silent for what seemed like ten minutes but couldn't have been more than a couple of seconds. "You have nothing to be sorry about. You were taking care of yourself. I'm the one who ruined everything."

If only she could tell him he didn't. If only she could open her heart one more time. If only Montana wasn't so damn far away. If only they'd never gone to the farmers' market that day. She probably would have stayed in Billings for as long as she and Harvey wanted to, together.

"It was bad circumstances from the beginning," she said.

He paused yet again. "Would you come back to Billings because I asked you to?" he asked.

She wanted to emphatically say yes. But the word was stuck, lost, missing.

"There's nothing in Billings for me," she said through her tears. She didn't believe it, but it didn't change the fact that she didn't think she wanted to be there anymore.

"I thought you had a home here. I thought *we* had a home."

"I need to be here. I need to regroup. Get back in touch with my roots. It's long overdue."

Every pause seemed as if he were trying to see her through the phone. She was glad they weren't using FaceTime. "You don't sound at all like the Skye who sat next to me on the plane how many months ago," he said.

"I'm not her. She wasn't me."

"That's a good thing," he said. And then, softer, he added, "I miss you, Skye. Not her. You."

Her heart turned somersaults.

"Can I call you again?" he asked. "Maybe in a couple of days?"

"Maybe." And then, without warning, she said, "Or we could write to each other."

Her offer surprised her as much as it did him. Having grown up in the texting and chatting generation, she'd never been one to write letters or e-mail, but she remembered a chapter in one of Flora's books that talked about the energy of letter writing, and how you could write them to your past, present, or future self, to someone who was no longer alive, even to the house you wanted to create for yourself. Writing letters could be cathartic, give people a chance to really think about what they wanted to say. Writing letters was a form of honesty one would never find on Facebook.

She could almost hear him smile. "That would be nice," he said.

And for the first time since leaving him, she felt hope. For what, she wasn't sure. But she decided not to question it.

They each said good night, and Skye put her phone on the floor next to the couch. She stared up at the ceiling. She missed the sounds Billings made at night. She missed the sound of paint rollers on walls. She missed the sound of Harvey's breath.

But she was going to be OK. She'd never been so certain of that, and she clung to that certainty like a rope.

CHAPTER THIRTY-SEVEN

October–November

Skye Littleton turned thirty-seven in October, also acknowledging it as the anniversary of her freaking the fuck out. She'd ordered a custom cake from an Italian bakery in Providence, and celebrated with Julie as well as Cam and Rory, whom she hadn't seen in almost a year. It was nice to have a girls' night out.

"So what was it like in Montana?" asked Rory.

"It's *huge*," said Skye. "Billings itself wasn't much different in terms of day-to-day living. They've got just about everything we have."

"Except a Dunkin' Donuts," Julie chimed in. "That's just so weird."

"Well yeah, no DD and no Panera Bread. But there were some really cool shops and stuff downtown, and it wasn't as hurried. You have to see the sunsets there too. A-MA-ZING."

She felt a pang for another view, wished she had taken photographs, although no camera phone could capture the magnificence of that big sky. She also fought the disappointment that she wasn't celebrating her birthday with Harvey.

One year—it had been one year since everything had been set in motion. She was still single and childless and without a mortgage or a marriage or any of the other things she'd once believed were so crucial to a meaningful existence. But now she had purpose. She had self-worth. She had a business and a plan. She had gratitude and appreciation. She still had Chip.

She had everything she needed.

Since returning to Rhode Island, she had already booked two closet cleanings, a basement decluttering, and a feng shui consultation for a new local business, thanks to a combination of her social media marketing, hanging flyers in paint stores and coffee shops, and a talk at the public library. Julie offered word-of-mouth as well. Taking a suggestion from Patrick, she'd also started a weekly podcast with monthly subscribers and was already up to twenty. She had a side business of furniture painting, and even began shopping at flea markets looking for small old pieces to paint, refinish, and resell. She also started working part-time at Cardi's Furniture store.

In the second week of November, Skye was about to follow up on a lead about a rental in Newport, Rhode Island, when she received a text from Patrick with a photo of his wife and kids sitting at the table in their kitchen, the one Skye had helped redecorate, followed by photos of each child in their newly painted rooms. Our bedroom is next, the message read. Skye smiled and texted smiley faces in reply. She and Patrick had talked or messaged almost every day since she'd left Billings. She was grateful to have made a difference in his life, as much as he had made one in hers.

"You were always too good for Devlin's," he said. "Besides, we just got confirmation: the store is closing right after the holidays. Your employee file is still active, which means you can still buy furniture if you need it. I'll make arrangements to get it shipped to you. Take advantage of layaway before it's too late."

Summer's guesthouse came furnished; however, Skye let her former feng shui classmates know so they could either take advantage of the sales or tell their clients.

She loved the water view from Summer's cozy guesthouse, loved the nautical colors and decorations of each room. She hadn't planned to stay this long, but she was enjoying the time with Summer and Kayla, and she paid Summer for more than just utilities. Still, she looked forward to finding a new place, also as close to the water as possible. She'd never realized how soothing the beach was to her until all those months in Montana away from it.

And yet, she missed the sight of the rimrocks every day. Ditto for that big, beautiful sky. And the taste of huckleberry.

She also missed Harvey. And Patrick. And Flora Davis and her classmates and Devlin's Furniture coworkers.

One day, as Skye was sitting outside on the lanai of the guesthouse, updating her social media sites, she received a text message from Harvey. She'd not heard from him since their phone conversation. Her heart leapt into her throat when she saw a photo of the memorabilia room, formerly the guest room and her bedroom. On one side of the room sat the sofa bed Skye had picked out before she left—Harvey got an excellent deal on it, thanks to the store's closing sale—and a coffee table displaying comic books. On the other side sat the chest of drawers with action figures posing on top. She guessed the drawers now stored trading cards and more comic books. Posters adorned the walls, their bold colors popping against the yellow backdrop, and the purple curtains remained intact.

She was overcome with emotion. It looked beautiful. But it was no longer *her* room. And she was equal parts happy for Harvey and sad for herself.

Skye replied: You did a fantastic job.

He responded with a smiley emoji, followed by a message: Kids love it too. They alternate staying over on weekends. Working on getting them a space of their own.

Her heart filled with joy. I'm so happy to hear that.

Five minutes later, he sent a follow-up text. How are you?

She replied with a thumbs-up emoji. A cooler response in comparison to her previous texts, but she felt the need to protect her heart. Harvey didn't reply. Had the boundary been too blunt?

The next day, Skye received a letter—an actual letter in real penmanship, delivered in an envelope via the post office—from Harvey. The first since she'd suggested they write.

> Dear Skye—
> I wanted to fill you in on some things that have been happening since you left. For starters, I went back to counseling. Figured I needed the tune-up. It's been helpful. Second, I called Deb and apologized for what I did at the farmers' market. Not that I'm sorry for fuck-nose's sake, only hers and yours. Deb apologized as well, said she'd been terrible to leave me. It was the first time she admitted that. She also admitted that she played a role in my estrangement from our kids. She agreed to do some joint counseling sessions—not so we can get back together, that is *never* going to happen—but for the sake of the kids. I even asked them to join me. Kelly said yes, definitely. Scott said he'd think about it, which is as good as a yes.
>
> I also needed to tell you something. It occurred to me that I never told you who my favorite superhero

was. You'd asked once, and I said something stupid like "they all are" so I wouldn't have to be honest.

All superheroes are flawed in some way—not only physically, but more so humanly. Even the ones who aren't human. For example, Batman could save just about everyone in Gotham City but his parents, who were murdered when he was a child. He's haunted by that every day. That's just one example. Batman was never my favorite, though. No, my favorite is Captain America. He was one of the first comics I read as a kid. Him and Spider-Man and Superman—I was into all the big-name guys, although I also admit to having massive crushes on Wonder Woman, Supergirl, and Emma Frost, but that might not be appropriate confessions right now. (Damn, I can't delete all this. So much for handwriting letters.) Anyway, I won't bore you with Captain America's history (that's what Wikipedia is for), but he was created in the 1940s and fought the Nazis. So did Wonder Woman, by the way. I loved the idea of fighting an enemy who was capable of taking away your heart and soul. Not that I'd lost either growing up. I had your average childhood and average adolescence, if you don't count the bullying I got in high school for loving comic books, which you were supposed to give up when you were a kid, according to those losers. Little did they know the nerds were going to run the world and beat their asses at everything, the fuckers.

I'm off track again. Sorry.

Captain America is a bit of an idealist and always wants to do the right thing. I think he's got initiative too, something I've never had. When I try to take initiative, like the time I tried to stop that guy who took your overhead bin on the plane, and going after Vance on that regretful day, I fuck up royally.

There might be a metaphor regarding Captain America's shield too, but I won't go there without my counselor present. And the movies have been under-whelming too. Just saying.

This is a very long way of me wanting to share something with you and maybe explain why I went after Vance that day. I was wrong to do so, even though you know the asshole deserves it. But he took my heart and soul when he took my wife. I know that sounds hypocritical based on what I've told you about my mar-riage, but he did. He took my security, the same way he took yours. I just wanted to let him know he didn't completely break either of us apart. And maybe, just maybe, I wanted the satisfaction of taking something away from him. Even though Vance walked away from you, I believed he still had power. I wanted to take his power and restore some of mine. It was ego all the way.

And it was absolutely, completely, undoubtedly unfair to do that to you, because it took *your* power away too. I stole your thunder. I stole your chance to show Vance that you didn't need him or me or anyone else to rescue you. I stole your chance to be your own superhero. Because you are, Skye. You're powerful. You're strong. You're super.

And I love you.

Always, Harvey

The paper bobbed in her hand as she reread the letter again and again, shaking, her throat tight, her eyes wet.

Especially when she came to the last paragraph.

And the last line.

Skye wrote back:

Dear Harvey—

Thank you for your letter. It was certainly a surprise. Thank you also for sharing so much. I was never into superheroes or comics, but your passion motivates me to learn more. I always loved when you showed that side of yourself.

I am slowly but steadily building my business while I work at Cardi's. I've also built new bridges with my sister since moving into her guesthouse. I used to wake up almost every morning in Billings in disbelief that I was there. Now I'm waking up in Wakefield every day and feeling something similar, but it's more like wonder than disbelief. I feel like something inside me has woken up right along with me. That's not to say that I don't miss Billings. In fact, I'm surprised by how much I've missed it, and you. I miss you every day, Harvey.

I still love you, Harvey. It frightens me to tell you that. I feel vulnerable. I feel like if I tell you that, then I'll wait for the fairy-tale ending, and I no longer want the fairy tale. I want something way more real and imperfect. I don't know if that could be us ever again, especially given where we each live. But if there's a chance, then I want us to work for that. If you still want to, that is. Can we keep writing to each other? I would really love that. And talking on the phone, maybe. Old school!

Love, Skye

One week later, Skye received a postcard with Captain America on the front.

> Dear Skye—
> I'm in.
>> Always, Harvey

CHAPTER
THIRTY-EIGHT

December

Christmas was coming.

When she'd worked at Top Drawer, Christmastime meant longer hours, more time on her feet, swarms of customers on endless lines, and incessant loops of bad Christmas-song remakes by pop stars she wasn't even familiar with. When she got home every night, the last thing she wanted to do was make merry. She just wanted to sleep.

Not this year.

This year, she bought a real tree and placed it right in the picture window of her new apartment, not in Newport or Narragansett (she couldn't yet afford those rents) but in Barrington, right on the Rhode Island–Massachusetts border, closer to work and still within decent driving distance to water. She bought ornaments and garland and a star, and invited her niece Kayla to help her decorate it. She even hung some plastic ornaments on the bottom for Chip to bat with his paw.

Skye also sent out Christmas cards this year, something she'd never had time to do before. Some of it was capitalistic in nature—she sent cards to all her clients with After-Christmas Clutter-Clearing specials, as well as to Sabrina, her college roommate, and her Billings friends. One day, she stumbled across a comic-book store and couldn't resist going in. She could almost smell Harvey in the store. There she found an action figure of Bucky Barnes, Captain America's sidekick, and sent it to Harvey, along with a bag of Christmas stocking–shaped treats for Bucky Barnes the dog.

Two days later, she received a package in the mail, postmarked Billings.

A jar of huckleberry jam, with a letter enclosed.

> Dear Skye—
> Big news. I displayed my collection at one of the galleries downtown, near Ciao Mambo, during Art Walk. (I wish we'd gone to an Art Walk. They can be a lot of fun, especially with the right amount of wine.) It just so happened that a guy with connections to the comic-con in Seattle was visiting a friend, popped in, and was impressed. We went out for beers the next night, and he's interested in hiring someone to help him coordinate lower-key events around the Seattle area—collection showings, panel discussions, movie screenings, and vendor tables.
>
> There's a lot to consider, mainly the kids. They really did like living with their grandparents in Seattle, so were I to move and take them with me, I don't think it would be too big an adjustment for them. Of course, that would leave Deb in Billings, although she might be up for a move too—did I tell you she and fuckface split up? Day after the farmers' market. Maybe we could all make the move—not as a family, per se, but where we could both be close to the kids.

That said, this job would mean a lot of hours and travel, and I'm not sure it's where I want to be in terms of the scene. I'd rather be one of the vendors than the guy who books the vendors. I'm also torn about leaving Billings. There's already a comics store in Billings; I don't think it needs two. Owning a store had been my dream once, but now I'm not sure that's right for me either.

I need a change, though. The paint jobs are starting to wear on my back and shoulder muscles. It's not as relaxing as it used to be. And since you've left, working alone is no longer enjoyable.

Another thing, Skye. Were I to take the job, I'd want you to come with me. I know it's a lot to ask you, especially with all the uprooting you've been doing lately. But consider this: it's a fresh start for both of us. A new place with no reminders of Vance Sandler. I think you would also find plenty of opportunities for yourself concerning your business ventures. Please think about it. It would start in February, so there's plenty of time and no rush.

No matter what, I see good things ahead for both of us, regardless of whether we're together. I can't remember the last time I felt so full of hope.

Love, Harvey

Skye read the entire letter with her hand on her heart, taking quick breaths. Put it down and said, "Holy shit." Read it again.

Skye texted Julie: Love SOS.

Julie replied, I'll be over tonight, and showed up a few hours later with wine and cheese and crackers. Skye read the letter to her, and Julie's mouth dropped closer to the floor with every paragraph.

"No way!" she shouted when Skye finished.

"I know, right?" said Skye. "What am I supposed to do with this?"

"Throw it out, of course."

This was not the answer Skye had expected.

"What, does he think you're going to fall for that again—dropping your entire life and running across the country to some guy who promises you the moon?"

Odd, she hadn't seen it that way at all.

"Whoa—Harvey is *not* Vance," said Skye. "And I'm not that woman who freaked the fuck out on her birthday. I'm in a really good place now."

"Exactly. So why leave?"

"I meant emotionally."

"Look, Skyebaby. First you up and leave Rhode Island. Then you up and leave Billings. Now you're going to up and leave Rhode Island again?"

When she put it like that, it did sound impulsive. And not in a good way.

"I miss him, Jules. A lot. Every time we've corresponded, he's shown remorse and that he learned from his mistake. Vance never even blinked an eye." The realization that she'd forgiven Harvey hit her right in the chest. But she wasn't sure if forgiveness was enough. She wasn't sure if she had another move in her, especially so soon. Not to mention packing yet again, dragging Chip across the country again, starting over one more time, pounding the pavement for work while she built her business, scraping together enough money for a monthly car payment.

"Fine. He's *sorry,*" Julie said, the word dripping with disingenuousness. "Doesn't mean you should go crawling back to him."

"Who's crawling back to him? He sent me an invitation. I'm free to say no. He knows that. He won't think less of me if I do, and he won't pressure me to say yes."

Julie's eyes glassed over. "I've missed you too, you know. I just don't want to lose you again."

Skye became misty as well. "Jules, you could never lose me. You were the only person who knew in the beginning what happened with Vance. The only person I trusted. You were also the first person I came to when things fell apart with Harvey. I know I've bounced around this last year, but I'll always be there for you, no matter where I live." She pulled Julie into a hug, and the two cried it out.

By the time Julie left, Skye was more confused than ever. Her insides swirling with anticipation, she called Harvey. She wasn't even sure what to say. She only knew she wanted to talk to him. To hear his voice. To be in the moment with him.

"Hi," said Harvey. The lilt in his voice made her heart smile. "You get my letter?"

"I did," said Skye. "And I think it's great news. I'm super excited for you, regardless of what you decide."

"And . . . ?" he asked, a tinge of hope lingering.

"And I need more time to think about it."

The lilt in his voice disappeared. "Of course. Take as much time as you need."

"I can't afford to be whimsical this time. Or uninformed. If I were to do this, I would want to see Seattle. I'd want to spend time there. Look at houses. Meet people. Find out if I could make a living there."

"I would love to help you do that."

The thought of being with Harvey again, of beginning a new adventure, was so appealing, so tempting. But the thought of sticking around and rebuilding her life on her own was equally appealing. For the first time in her life, she enjoyed being on her own. She enjoyed her life. Her big, beautiful life.

"What about Billings?" she asked.

"What about it?"

"Do you really want to leave it?"

"I would if it meant we would be together."

Her heart did a backflip. "What are you saying, exactly?"

"I'm saying I want to find a way for us to be together. One that's a win-win for everyone—you, me, my kids . . ."

Now her heart moved on to cartwheels. Her head began to spin. If only she could just say yes.

"I just don't know," she said, and began to sob.

"Skye, it's OK. I sprung a lot on you. Just think about it, please. That's all I ask. I'll be OK with whatever your answer is. No matter what happens, we're both going to be happy, together or separate. That's what matters."

"I wish I felt as certain about that as you do right now."

"You will. In fact, you're the one who inspired me."

She was taken aback. "How?"

"By taking a chance. By being brave. By being bold and big and taking charge."

Every word was a lever, lifting her, holding her, carrying her wherever she needed to go.

Big Skye Littleton. Superhero. She could even fly.

CHAPTER
THIRTY-NINE

On Christmas morning, Skye sat in the living room with Summer, Brent, and Kayla, exchanging presents. Summer loved the vanity table Skye had found at a yard sale and refinished to look like a contemporary classic piece.

"It looks like something off a showroom floor—I had no idea you were this talented!" said Summer. Skye beamed not only with pride, but also from the compliment her sister gave her, one that wasn't backhanded or laced with passive-aggression or anything other than genuine love and appreciation.

For Brent, she had special-ordered a huckleberry pancake mix and syrup from a Montana company. "The only problem is that you'll be hooked," said Skye.

And Kayla loved her Top Drawer gift card, as she'd confided that she was ready for something more grown-up. Skye had checked with Summer to make sure it was appropriate, and Summer feigned surprise when Kayla opened it, yet nodded at Skye.

Skye was also pleased to find that Summer and Brent had signed her up for a three-week marketing course at the university, something to help her business. And she adored the heart keychain that Kayla gave her, complete with Skye's name engraved.

She'd had her sister and brother-in-law and niece for so long, but for the first time, she felt like she had *family*.

Her parents, on the other hand, were another story. Even before she'd moved to Billings, she'd not kept in touch with them on a regular basis. Restricted visits mostly to family occasions, and phone calls to once every other month. When she'd arrived in Billings, she'd let them know she arrived safely and left it to Summer to fill them in on the subsequent twists and turns. Instead, she sent postcards once a month with majestic sunsets captioned *Greetings from Big Sky Country* or a panorama of the rimrocks that she purchased from a gift shop in downtown Billings. She inscribed them with little more than messages like *It's true what they say about the big sky!* or *You should see the rims in person,* knowing they'd never take her up on the offer. (She liked using the local lingo of "the rims.")

Not much had changed since she'd come home. She found herself angry when she spoke to or saw her parents—years of delayed response to the way they'd pitted her and Summer against each other. She'd been able to peacefully confront her sister and patch things up. So why couldn't she do the same with them?

Her New Year's resolution would be to change that.

In the meantime, she'd stopped by their house the night before, dropped off a platter of assorted homemade cookies wrapped in green and red cellophane and tied off with a white bow, and listened to them ramble on about the neighbor's tacky lawn display, the diminished quality of the church's nativity pageant, and who got the best grab-bag gift at her father's office party.

The negativity.

It lived in the walls, it seemed. She noticed other things about the house as well: Too much wood element in one room, not enough fire element in another. Poor lighting. Artwork that was stoic. Linear. Impersonal.

"Hey, Mom," Skye had said as she was buttoning her coat. "I'm going to give you guys a room makeover for Christmas. Any room you want. I'll paint, rearrange, decorate, everything. Nothing gets thrown out without your approval, and if you don't like what I do, I'll change it back, no hard feelings. What do you say?"

Her mom had said little about Skye's new career other than it seemed a waste of her college education. But she had said that about Top Drawer too. Here, she seemed taken aback.

"Sure," she'd said. "Why not?"

A feng shui miracle. Skye had smiled at the thought. "OK," she said.

While Brent was in the kitchen making the pancakes, and Kayla was preoccupied with her gifts, Skye sat with Summer on the couch and filled her in on Harvey's letter.

"I just don't know what to do," said Skye. "I love him and I forgive him and I want to be with him. But I've fallen in love with Rhode Island too. I'm not sure I want to pick up and leave it again. Or you guys."

"Seattle is a wonderful city," said Summer. "I've attended academic conferences there."

"I'm sure it is," said Skye. "I want to see it for myself."

"What about Billings? Would it really be so bad to go back?"

Skye thought about her adopted city, and a warmth, like one that comes from a crackling fire, coated her, inside and out. "It's not a question of good or bad. You know how I get these vibes about a room or a space?" Summer nodded. "I sort of have this vibe, like Billings served its purpose. Kind of like having a starter home or an entry-level job. Does that make sense?"

"I think so," said Summer. "But I guess what you really need to decide is what home is to you. For me, it's Brent and Kayla. The rest of this is just wood and drywall and carpeting and furniture," she said, gesturing to the four walls of the room and beyond. "I'd live on Mars if that's where they were."

Skye considered this. She had once believed home was wherever Harvey was. But sitting with her sister, surrounded by the scents of pine and cinnamon, those homey scents, another thought struck her: *You have to be at home inside yourself first. Then you can live anywhere.*

And then she knew the answer.

CHAPTER FORTY

April

Vashon Island. That was where she had decided she wanted to live. She had fallen in love with it almost instantly.

She and Harvey had spent two glorious weeks in late January combing every part of Seattle and its suburbs, from Olympia to Tacoma to Bellevue to Everett to Bainbridge, Mercer, and Vashon Islands. She loved the city proper. She loved Pike Place Market and the Space Needle and the Museum of Pop Culture. Seattle was Providence on steroids, but without the New England accent.

But when she and Harvey toured Vashon, she was hooked. The beaches. The mountain views. The friendly residents, year-rounders and summer-goers.

Then she found out the cost of living.

"We'll make it work," Harvey said. "There are some houses that are in need of heavy-duty work. We'll get them cheaper, but we'll have to put more into it. Between the two of us and some reliable contractors, I think we could pull it off." After a beat, he added, "Reliable contractors—is that an oxymoron?"

Skye laughed. Her very own fixer-upper. And her very own Chip Gaines.

Harvey had taken the job a week after their trip. And Skye, after calling Jack and asking if he had any referrals, contacted a friend of his who worked in home staging, who Jack thought would welcome her on their team.

They did.

And so once again, as winter came to an end, Skye packed up her belongings—she touched every item to make sure it still sparked joy—had them shipped to the condo, and returned to Billings, Montana, with Chip, giving Summer and Julie and all her friends, even her parents, a proper goodbye and no expectations. And as she descended the stairs to the baggage claim in the Billings airport, there was Harvey, at the bottom, in a ski jacket and jeans and work boots, a single rose in hand.

She'd never been so happy to be there.

She spent the week catching up with Patrick and her other friends, bingeing on all things huckleberry, and visiting her other favorite places: The bookstore. Big Dipper. City Brew. She and Harvey went back to Ciao Mambo and finally ate the zeppole—*worth the wait.* They also took Bucky to Rose Park and drove to the top of the rimrocks at night.

She loved Billings. She would always cherish its people and places and lessons.

From Billings, they drove to Seattle, Bucky and Chip in tow (Kelly and Scott were already back with their grandparents), equally happy to be reunited. Skye had never seen such beauty as they crossed Montana—the magnificence of the Crazy Mountains, the overwhelming expanse of land, without a human being or skyscraper or the noise pollution of traffic. And small town after small town, where downtown was a mile-long main street full of mom-and-pop shops and bars and boutiques, a storefront post office, a clapboard-facade bank, as if she'd stepped back in time. Each town was separated by miles and miles of ranch land, fenced off with barbed wire to keep cattle in and trespassers out. The contrast to the East Coast was so palpable, where one town blended into the other and "small" meant you had to drive an extra fifteen minutes to find a Target.

She came close to not wanting to take one step further when they stopped in Coeur d'Alene, Idaho, for a bite to eat and a gas refill. *Just send for our things,* she thought. The best of all worlds—pine trees and mountains and lakes and little beaches and more shops and Starbucks and just about anything else you might want. Harvey persuaded her to press on. "Seattle. Remember?" he'd said. She was grateful he did.

She and Harvey held hands almost the entire trip. And every day since.

When they reached Vashon, they moved into a temporary apartment until the house they'd purchased was fully renovated. Skye oversaw many of the renovations herself, foreseeing yet another twist in her career.

As she sat in a chair on the beach in the solitude of morning, a cup of hot chocolate nestled in her mittened hands (it was chilly for spring), she looked out at the horizon, at an endless painted sky as the sun rose, and smiled at the splendor.

What a grand life, she thought.

ACKNOWLEDGMENTS

I have the following people to thank for making this book possible:

Miriam Juskowicz and Danielle Marshall, for overseeing this project and believing in it all the way, and especially for their patience with my deadline-extension requests.

Nalini Akolekar, for all her support and guidance, and for getting the ball rolling.

Tiffany Yates Martin, the personal trainer of developmental editors. She always makes my books better. She makes me better. (Thanks for the five bucks! I'll take it in chocolate.)

Gabe Dumpit and everyone at Lake Union, who have continued to believe in me as well as the books I write.

The Billings community, who have adopted and embraced me like no other. I'm honored to be one of its residents.

This House of Books in Billings, Elk River Books in Livingston, and The Country Bookshelf in Bozeman, because they are awesome.

The Undeletables, because they too are awesome.

My readers, who continue to bless me with their patience, kind words, sharing, and unending support.

Zula and Bodie, for giving me the space to work in exchange for peanut-butter treats, and Spatzy, the newest member of the furbaby family.

My Lorello family and my Lancaster and Clines families, for all their love always.

And Craig. My love. My light. My darling. Always.

CONNECT WITH ELISA

On Facebook: Elisa Lorello, Author

On Twitter: @elisalorello

On Instagram: @elisalorello

Sign up for the latest updates and special offers at: elisalorello.com

ABOUT THE AUTHOR

Elisa Lorello is a Long Island native, the youngest of seven children. She earned her bachelor's and master's degrees at the University of Massachusetts Dartmouth and taught rhetoric and writing at the college level for more than ten years. In 2012, she became a full-time novelist.

Elisa is the author of seven novels, including the bestselling *Faking It*, and one memoir. She has been featured in the *Charlotte Observer* and, more recently, *Last Best News* and was a guest speaker at the Triangle Association of Freelancers 2012 and 2014 Write Now! conferences. In May 2016, she presented a lesson for the Women's Fiction Writers Association spring workshop. She continues to speak and write about her publishing experience and teach the craft of writing and revision.

Elisa enjoys reading, walking, hanging out in coffee shops, Nutella, and all things Duran Duran. She plays guitar badly and occasionally bakes. She moved to Montana in 2016 and is newly married.